CW01433105

Back from the Shadowlands

The Golden Wolf Series Book 2, Volume 2

Tori Lennox

Published by Shadowlands Publishing, 2024.

BACK FROM THE SHADOWLANDS

First edition. October 24, 2024.

Written by Tori Lennox.

To my readers with heartfelt gratitude. Without you, Tori Lennox wouldn't exist.

PROLOGUE

Northumberland, England 1139 AD

"Wolf."..."I am the Wolf."...The golden-haired giant dragged filthy fingers through blood-matted hair..."I am the Golden Wolf."..."Sheriff of Lothian and David's sworn man..."

Croaked words forced through cracked lips, he felt human again. More than human. Alive. Powerful. Like the warrior he was. All it had taken was a single memory piercing the mental haze for others to break through.

In a matter of hours, the game had changed. He was Thor, son of Sweyn Sword-Cleaver, the most feared warrior in the lands. The fools who left a dying man to rot in this cesspit were clueless to the danger in their midst.

Wolf...The Golden Wolf...He was the Golden Wolf. The most feared warrior in the land. His captors sealed their fate by hiding the only man their king would give half his kingdom to claim. Laughing harshly, he admitted what they wished they knew. It would have been wiser to kill him while they could.

Relieved the shards of his splintered memory were piecing together, Thorauld Sweynsson prayed to a God he barely knew to remain forgotten long enough to escape this hole. If he didn't, he was a dead man. The Golden Wolf was much too dangerous to ransom. He would eventually fall to the executioner if neglect and infection didn't claim him first.

While he would have quickly dispatched a threat like him, his captors chose vindictiveness over wisdom. To allow a warrior of his stature to remain alive invited attempts to free him. Or it would if anyone knew he was here. They didn't. None of his party escaped the ambush to share their tale.

Scratching another mark in the wall, Thor was fortunate he'd overheard the guards discussing a breach in the dungeon wall that would take several days to repair. One caused by an instability in the ground beneath the foundation which led to a section of stone collapsing from too much rain. While unfamiliar with the dungeon's layout, he recalled the general direction of that breach from his initial journey to his cell.

At that time, he'd clung to consciousness by a thread until he was dropped on a hard stone floor. Blacking out, he'd roused a few hours later to the clank of manacles and knew he would venture no farther than the chains allowed. He knew as well that his wounds would go untreated and his stomach unfilled as long as he clung to life. Ransom nor survival was part of the plans. Painful, drawn-out retribution was.

However, as he visibly wasted away, his manacles loosened bit by bit. Imperceptibly testing his bindings, Thor was satisfied he could easily wriggle free and spring like a rat from a trap at the appropriate time. Studying his surroundings, he was fortunate that while a place of darkest horrors, this oubliette possessed no walls or cell doors. Just iron shackles and short chains suspending lost souls in the pit of hell. Were he a lesser man, insanity would have claimed him long ago.

Looking to the left, his fate played out in the rotting corpses of three fellow Scots lacking his fortitude. Looking to the right, the dangling skeletons of three unfortunates drawing final breaths long ago testified to the hopelessness of his situation. As discouraging as their death grins were, he refused to accept that his life would end the same way. However, he wasn't above letting his captors believe he did. Beneath his powerless demeanor, a Wolf calmly plotted actions that played to his strengths and his captors' weaknesses.

After three long months of festering wounds and deprivation, he was les morts-vivants bound for the shadowland. Right. Leaning against the wall, Thor's laugh was manic. That sound issuing from the lips of another would signal his rapid descent into madness. He wasn't any other man. He was the Golden Wolf. He lived for victory. He lived for vengeance. He lived to spill crimson rivulets of his enemies' blood across verdant soil.

Calming the bloodlust rising within him, he silently vowed to start with the fools taking rabid pleasure in watching noble warriors waste away before their eyes. Fools so lax in their over-confidence that it was preferable to mock and torment dying men than guard their charges. Once that score was settled, he would handle the lord of this impressive demesne. Watching him slowly, painfully die knowing everything he held dear was destroyed before him would avenge the good men dishonorably slaughtered after a truce was called.

In the interim, he would pander to his guards' foolish assumption that he was a dead man crawling. That his will to live was gone. They weren't entirely wrong. Or they hadn't been. He had no reason to live when he didn't know who or what he was. Now that he did, hell would freeze over before he gave up the fight. He had a life to live and a king to serve. Death was not an option. He would escape this place.

When he did, may God have mercy on de Vescy's soul...

CHAPTER ONE

Menteith, Scotland 1138 A. D.

Alexandria stared over the moors. This spot felt haunted though puir Eddie never joined her anymore. He'd been laid to rest when the MacLarens fell. As difficult as it was to admit, her unease came more from the royal messenger emerging from the mist than visitors from the other side. Although not his intent, Greggorius's arrival signaled changes in her life that she wasn't ready to embrace.

Not when she knew his purpose and didn't like it. Not when Drummond was at peace and her life was everything she hoped it could be. Yet, from her experience, that was when the bogills appeared. She'd be more surprised if they didn't.

However, her displeasure wasn't Gregg's fault. It was her godfather's. David was up to something or he wouldn't send his trusted servant to summon her husband to service. As usual, he wanted his Wolf by his side for the planning and execution. There was nothing strange about that. However, that he'd sent Greggorius on such a menial assignment was.

She'd seen enough of these lone riders over the years to know a herald when she saw one and Greggorius wasn't just any herald. He was the king's official messenger. Deciding she needed to find Thor, Alexandria turned from the window to find herself staring into her husband's favorite golden-brown tunic instead.

"How do you do that?" Sneak up on her without making a sound. "It shouldn't be possible with how bloody huge you are."

"No, it shouldn't." Thor dropped a kiss on the top of her head. "But my father taught me well."

"As you are teaching our bairns." Alexandria resisted the urge to punch a taunt belly for that little trick. "The beasties are as good at sneaking as you are."

Laughing softly, Thor pulled her close. Glancing out the window, he instantly noted why the woman in his arms was in such a foul mood. She knew as well as he what the man dismounting in their inner bailey signified. Heart racing in anticipation, he was torn by unexpected emotions.

The warrior within relished the coming battle for that was all Greggorius's appearance could mean. The husband and father didn't wish to leave his wife and lover...His people or his cubs...However, he was honor-bound to do just that. His king needed him and his bloodlust needed an outlet. While Alexandria soothed the animal within, she had yet to tame him.

"Come, lady, we have a guest to greet." Thor draped his arm over her shoulders. "Don't get that look on your face." He dropped a reassuring kiss on her lips. "We both knew this day would come when I became David's man."

While true, this was much sooner than expected. He'd heard no talk of raids on his last visit to court a scant month ago. Not the faintest whisper. He wondered briefly what had changed his sovereign's mind and knew his questions would be answered soon.

"It would come were you not;" She retorted. "So don't try to soothe my ruffled feathers with unnecessary truths."

"Yes, it would." Thor agreed. "David needs all of his men in the service of Matilda."

"Aye." Alexandria agreed. "But that doesn't mean I like it."

Shaking his head, Thor laughed. He would never tire of the fire in her eyes. Though Zan's beauty was undeniable, her resilience and spirit first drew him to her side. Her devotion and love kept him there. Knowing this woman was his greatest strength and his greatest weakness humbled him. Almost losing her when they lost their son taught him to value the life he now had above all else, even duty to his king and country.

"Come, we must go below." Thor rested his hand on his wife's shoulder. "Hiding up here won't make Gregg disappear as much as we might wish it so."

"You're right but," Alexandria rested her hand over his. "Do you?"

"Do I what?" Thor pretended not to understand as he guided her towards the door.

"You know what." Alexandria halted midstep. "Do you wish you didn't have to go?"

"Truthfully?" She wouldn't like his answer. "Are you sure you want to know?"

"Aye." Alexandria nodded. "The truth."

"Your husband has no wish to go," Thor admitted. "To leave you and our babes."

"But the warrior is chafing for the fight." She finished for him.

"Aye." There was nothing left to say. "He is."

"While I didn't expect anything different," Alexandria nodded. "I'm glad part of you doesn't wish to go."

"Why would I?" Thor turned her to face him. "While I enjoy a good fight more than most, I am content with my life at Drummond."

With his bride, his cubs, and his people.

"Good." Alexandria headed for the door. "Make sure that never changes."

Shaking his head at the expected response, Thor followed Alexandria down the stairs smirking at every exaggerated sway of her hips. He didn't need reminding of the pleasures he was leaving behind. His bride was never far from his thoughts. Whether working the fields or on campaign he counted the hours until they were together again. He'd done that almost from the start. Resisting the urge to laugh at the final saucy look Alexandria cast over her shoulder, Thor decided she was a delightfully strange creature.

One he didn't regret taking to wife though he had questioned his sanity soon after he'd agreed to wed the woman. He could have just as easily snatched that sword from her hand and impaled her with a twist of his wrist instead. However, he hadn't questioned his sanity in the years since. He now knew only a dalcop would have refused the lady of Drummond or harmed a hair on her head. A fool was something he had never been.

Shaking his head at the man he'd become Thor silently acknowledged that while he'd never lacked female companionship, he never knew what was missing from those relationships. That oversite was quickly remedied when he discovered the illusive "what" in an unwanted union with an unusual woman not to his usual tastes.

Watching his wife head for the kitchen as he entered the hall, Thor noted the royal messenger already seated by the lord's chair breaking his fast. While his visits were few and far between, Bertie had a soft spot for Greggorius of Grontabricc. Something about his deceptively good looks tugged at her shriveled heart and fueled the desire to spoil him much as she did her lord.

Settling in his chair, Thor glanced at the laden trencher and the filled goblet before the other man. Catching Greg's eye, he made a loud sound of disgust. That old woman acted like she owned Drummond and everything in it, not just her domain. From what he'd heard, Bertie always had. Maybe that was why he let her get away with her hubris. She was a tough old busard, and he admired strength, even in a woman.

Shaking his head, Thor laughed thinking that while he had to bribe his wife's cook with bolts of fine fabric to get the same treatment, the king's messenger boy had but to smile at the stingy old hag to receive her choicest morsels and a goblet or two of his finest wine. While he'd like to inform Bertie that her pretty boy wasn't just the royal messenger, he was the king's pet assassin as well, he suspected she already knew. Like him, she appreciated power and strength, even in a man.

"I assume you bear messages from our king." Ignoring unnecessary pleasantries, Thor cut to the chase. He didn't need the missive sealed with David's signet lying on the table beside Greggorius to know the truth of his words. "We are preparing for war."

"Skirmishing at the least." Gregg agreed. "If I don't miss my guess, the king wants you in on the planning." He nodded in the direction of the letter. "He wants to catch King Stephen by surprise."

"I doubt that is possible." While he may not know the exact day David's warriors would pour over the border, Stephen knew they were coming. "No good ruler is ever caught totally off guard."

Not that Stephen was a good ruler. Nor a good man for that matter. Stephen of Blois wouldn't sit on the throne of England instead of Empress Matilda if he were, and he would still be bouncing his son on his knee instead of riding off to war. Not that he minded too much.

The leaving, yes. The fighting, no. He would assuage the blood lust within him in a matter of days. He could then refuse the king's invitation to celebrate their victory at court and return to his wife and family more at peace for a bit of battle play.

"Tell my liege I will join him as soon as I consult with Lionel and see that my family is safely settled." He would do all of that as soon as he read the king's letter and knew the lay of the land. "I should be at the royal keep before you are."

"I doubt that." A blonde brow rose in question. "You are the only warrior the king has summoned. He wishes to have your advice before final decisions are made."

"I see." Then this skirmish was more serious than just harrying the borders. His king had an objective in mind. One he needed guidance in deciding how best to achieve. Interesting. "Then I will see you at the royal keep as soon as possible."

Nodding his goodbyes and grabbing the sealed letter, Thor rose to his feet, distracted by the words he needed to say to his wife. While Alexandria knew what Greggorius' appearance meant, she wouldn't expect him to leave so soon. There was usually a matter of days, if not weeks, between the summons and the departure. However, she wouldn't try to stop him either. She knew the ways of a warrior as she was a warrior, too.

CHAPTER TWO

Exiting the hall, Thor broke the seal on the vellum in his hands. Scanning the brief message, he immediately understood his king's intent and how best to prepare for his departure. He would start by meeting with Alexandria and Lionel. From there, he would alert his men and his messengers they would be needed soon.

While he couldn't give anyone a definite time frame, he could ensure his men were in peak fighting form when the time came. And he would. They knew the routine: eat well, sleep well, abstain from overindulgence in distilled spirits, and practice battle-play until summoned. When that happened, they'd fight as though their lives depended on it. None of them would survive if they didn't.

Looking around him, Thor huffed thinking of the whispers he'd heard over the years. Not that he would share, but there was nothing magical about his successes. The secret to his seeming invincibility was preparation, not mystical spells or incantations as some thought. While he wasn't above dreams and divination, they weren't common tools in his arsenal.

He'd learned long ago that self-discipline, self-awareness, mental fortitude, and constant practice ensured a good warrior became a great one. His vassals were cut from similar cloths or they wouldn't be his sworn men. Times were turbulent. When called to service without warning they were always ready. Their overlord expected nothing less and he returned the favor. The Golden Wolf stood by his men and his men stood by their Wolf. Mutual loyalty and constant training were why the Sheriff of Lothian had the best fighting force in the land.

Heading for the kitchen, Thor knew his unhappy mate was hiding so she didn't have to face what was coming. He knew as well that she'd finished discussing the menu with Bertie hours ago. She was more likely perched on a stool burying her sorrows in toasted bread slathered with fruit spread, crispy strips of bacon, and cider instead.

If he didn't miss his guess, she'd also had a few nips of cook's lethal strong ale to fortify her against the words she didn't want to hear. Stepping into the kitchen, he caught Bertie's eye and motioned for her to leave. Watching the woman depart to check on Greggorius, he silently rested his hand on his wife's shoulder. While confident she was aware of his presence before he touched her, Alexandria refused to look at him.

"This won't help." Thor drained Alexandria's goblet unsurprised he was right. "Strong ale is the last thing you should drink when I need your help." He dropped a kiss on the top of her head. "Here, read this."

"Why?" Alexandria glanced at the letter in Thor's hand. "It will only say what I don't want to see."

"Are you sure about that?" Thor placed the letter on the table beside her. "Maybe you were expecting the king to send you a personal message in my summons, but I wasn't."

"Fine." Alexandria nodded as she accepted the document. "I wasn't either."

Skimming the whole missive, she smiled as she read her godfather's words at the bottom of the page. While it stated exactly what she expected, his words of open affection and vow to release her husband as soon as the battle was over soothed her ruffled feathers.

As displeased as she was with this latest turn of events, her loyalty lay with her king and Empress Matilda. If that meant putting her husband and her comfortable life at risk, so be it. She would do what she had to do. That was the way of the warrior and of the warrior's wife. Handing the vellum back to Thor, Alexandria rose to her feet and looped her arm through his.

"It seems we both have work to do." He needed to meet with Lionel while she needed to raid Bertie's emergency stores for enough viands to pack for his journey. "Let me know what you and Lionel decide as soon as possible. I'll need to make arrangements for the extra men."

Thor stopped midstep and looked down at her. "That won't be necessary." He shook his head. "Not yet anyway. As you have already read, I'll be leaving later today but Lionel will remain. He will see to alerting our vassals that war is imminent. As soon as our plan of attack is decided, I will send you an update with the king's seal. Check that it isn't tampered with before you open it. If all is well, do as it says."

While he knew the king's messengers were loyal, he trusted no man implicitly. It wouldn't be the first time a seemingly loyal servant flipped to the other side. While complicated seals were a great deterrent, they weren't infallible. He'd been on the receiving end of more than one such message. He was fortunate he knew what to look for since he'd been known to intercept and tamper with messages himself in the past.

Nodding, Alexandria knew that a sealed missive would contain her final instructions. While he might not trust any man completely, her husband knew she would only act once she determined the message was real. If events followed the usual plans, she would send messengers alerting their vassals to where and when to meet their overlord. They, in turn, would do the same with their men and so on.

Once the men were notified, they would likely converge on whatever royal residence the king occupied and go from there. Once they amassed enough men, David would lead his army into battle with Thor flanking him on one side and Prince Henry on the other. While there would likely be stragglers joining the fray late, none would be from among Thor's vassals.

His men understood the importance of being at the right place at the right time. Many still retained their lands because the Golden Wolf and his warriors aided them at that pivotal moment when all should have been lost. That meant they weren't casual in their loyalties. To their overlord or their king. Alexandria was grateful for that. Their dedication meant greater security for everyone.

"I need to meet with Lionel." His second in command was likely working with the squires in the north bailey. "I'll return when I've finished."

"Aye, and once I've raided Bertie's stores," And received an earful for her trouble. "I'll be in the sewing room working with the girls on their stitches." She now had three rambunctious young charges in her care. "When I'm sure they've settled down, I'll leave them in Adela's hands and retire to our chamber to repair Sweyn's tunic."

The one already stretched across her frame. Rather than trust the tiny garment to less skilled hands, she'd decided to mend the tear herself. The outcome would be better for everyone. A smaller replica of one of his father's, the shirt was one of her son's favorites. Unfortunately favorite didn't mean a thing when it came to a rough-and-tumble boy.

Heading for the kitchen, Alexandria pondered everything she would lose if anything happened to Thor. He had brought more to her life than affection and protection. She recognized that now. While unorthodox, their union gave her legitimacy she'd never had.

One that grew when Thor put Ruthven in her hands. While meant only as an opportunity to rest and recuperate, her exile from the keep where she'd lost so much presented her with a healing challenge instead. One that allowed her to prove herself a worthy mate to the Golden Wolf.

In the end, no one expected the miracle she and Reina pulled off at the derelict estate. Especially Thor. Ensuring everyone knew the turnaround at his keep was due entirely to his wife and her more unusual attributes caused society to view the crossdressing firebrand with new respect. That he had the foresight to wed such a woman had only enhanced the Golden Wolf's reputation as well.

Somewhat unexpectedly, aristocratic parents now clamored to send their sons and daughters to Drummond to foster. While none of them expected their delicate flowers to return riding massive destriers attired in men's clothing, they did expect them to have insights into running a household most young girls lacked.

She and Reina did their best to fulfill that obligation. If anyone knew how competitive the marriage market was, she did. The MacLarens had ensured she remained unmarriageable until her father's death forced her to take matters into her own hands.

As much as they might protest otherwise, any lord worth his salt appreciated any edge that made beneficial marital alliances more attainable. While rare in their world, her husband knew many men such as himself who would appreciate a wife who could do more than run their household and birth children. A strong woman capable of leading their men in times of crisis would be a godsend.

Thor knew that firsthand. He had no qualms about leaving their lands in her hands. His men respected her. They would follow her to the death as they followed him. If he ever felt that wasn't so, Lionel would remain behind to take her place. She expected nothing less. However, that had yet to happen and she doubted it ever would.

Deciding she had better things to do than dwell on possibilities she'd rather not contemplate, Alexandria prayed Bertie remained in the hall with Greg. The last thing she wanted was to get caught raiding the pantry. She'd never hear the end of it if she did. Looking around, she decided so far, so good.

TURNING THE CORNER, Thor decided he could easily find his wife when the time came. The sewing room and their chamber weren't that far apart. Right now he needed to talk to Lionel. Catching the other man's eye, he watched the warrior inspect a final piece of armor before dismissing the pages and squires in his charge.

From his smiles and nods, the boys had done well maintaining their assigned pieces of armor. Thor reached out to pat one blonde head in passing. He was fortunate to have Lionel in his ranks. A deadly warrior in the field, he was an equally talented teacher who took great pleasure in instructing the boys how to be men of both honor and war.

"From the look on your face, I don't need to ask why Greggorius was outside our gates before the haar dissipated." Lionel fell into step beside his lord knowing the longer they stayed in motion the less likely it was that anyone would overhear their conversation. "When do we leave?"

"I leave shortly." Thor corrected his false impression. "The king wishes to take advantage of my tactical skills before the battle."

"I see." Lionel nodded. "That leads me to think his objective is in an area you are intimately familiar with."

"I suspect you are right." Thor agreed. "Once I know the lay of the land, I will send instructions."

"In the interim, I know what to do." Send messengers to their vassals alerting them that war was imminent. "Once you give leave, I will join you with a contingent of men."

He already knew which men he would choose and which he would leave behind. While he'd prefer leaving their best men to guard Drummond, that wasn't how his lord operated. He had a system in place that he'd followed for years. One that ensured he always had the freshest warriors at hand. Their best men would be rotated between the keep and the king. The men fighting in the last skirmish would remain behind to guard Drummond while the guards would now fight.

"That sounds like the plan." Thor stopped and looked Lionel in the eyes. "If anything changes, and it may, you'll know what to do. I suspect we won't be fighting together. I have an idea what David's up to. If I'm right, we will need you leading our men into battle from a different direction."

"Then I await your instructions." While he preferred fighting beside his lord, there had been many times when that wasn't possible. "Until then, I will watch over Drummond in your absence."

Thor nodded his thanks knowing the man would watch over his wife and family as well. Just not too closely. Where other men would feel threatened by Lionel's unwavering devotion to their mate, he was grateful for his presence. The story would be different if the warrior were a less honorable man. As it was, he trusted his wife and her ardent admirer until there was reason not to.

"Good." Thor nodded. "Now I have to beard the lioness in her den. I'm afraid my wife isn't happy with my coming departure."

"She has grown used to your presence."

They all had. His overlord had proven surprisingly hands-on with every aspect of his demesne. His people love him because he wasn't above joining them in the fields and his family adored him because he adored them. While strict with the security of his estates, Thor was fair and generous to everyone.

He kept his finger on the pulse of his lands and rewarded his people well for their service. Keeping his villages provisioned was a priority. In return, his villagers did their best to ensure his storehouses overflowed to the benefit of everyone.

"Reina won't be happy when I depart either." Lionel shook his head.

"No, she won't." Thor agreed. "But Reina and Alex know we must fulfill our duties to the king."

"No matter how they feel." Lionel stopped by the entrance to the keep. "I will see that your mount is ready when you are."

Standing in the open doorway, Thor nodded before turning toward the stairs while Lionel headed toward the stables. There was no reason to stop by the great hall. He knew exactly where his wife would be. She'd already told him. Glancing into the sewing room, he nodded to the tittering women before closing the door behind him. As usual, Adela had her charges, and his wife's ladies, well in hand. They wouldn't be disturbing them any time soon. There was too much sewing to be done whether they wished to do so or not.

The thought brought the familiar twinge to his heart. Bridget pretended to hate every moment she spent in the sewing room. He suspected she secretly craved the companionship of the other women instead. Though his daughter's memory was still bittersweet, the darning of the clothes was a necessary evil.

Not only for practical reasons but because it was an opportunity for young ladies to perfect their stitches. Once they did, they could move on to bigger and better challenges like creating beautiful new bliauts. Fortunately, Adela ensured her charges were proficient before they touched the finer fabrics lining Drummond's coffers. Not a bad idea in his opinion. Some bolts were irreplaceable.

Pushing gently on the door, Thor was surprised when it swung open. In her petulance he expected Alexandria to lock the door against him. While not something she'd done often since the memorable night he'd learned of Siward's existence, he no longer shattered the door on the rare occasion she did.

He'd quickly discovered her anger burned hot and quick. It was more rewarding to let Alexandria's moments run their course. She was far more likely to reward him for understanding if he did. Locking the door behind him, Thor saw that Alexandria was true to her word. The tiny tunic stretched on her sewing frame was the one his son had caught on a twig running hell for leather across the heath two short days ago. From the finely wrought stitches already in place, the small tear would be all but invisible when the repair was done.

"I assume you have spoken with Lionel," Moving the frame to the side, she rose to her feet. "And he is getting your mount ready for the journey."

While she knew the animal in question would be a seasoned destrier or a courser, she didn't know which it would be. She did know that the horse he left riding would be the one he rode into battle. However, that animal wouldn't be Wotan. Not anymore. The main reason was to avoid being readily identified.

While Thor's size ensured he stood out in a crowd, several fair-haired warriors of similar height and build had joined the king's forces over the past year. More would likely come from the Isles in the future. While not something she would admit aloud, Alexandria was grateful for anything that made her husband less of a target as both of those things did.

"I have," Thor smirked. "And you have assumed right." But he would take his time about it. "However, Lionel knows I won't depart without a suitable goodbye."

"Is that what we're calling it now?" Alexandria rolled her eyes as she released his locks from the familiar leather thong. "A suitable goodbye?"

"Something like that," Pulling his tunic over his head, Thor slowly backed her against the wall not surprised when her thighs automatically encircled his hips. "I suspect he will act similarly before his departure."

Burying his face in her hair, Thor knew that event would come sooner rather than later. He knew as well that Reina would appreciate her husband's attentions as much as Alexandria was appreciating his. He knew as well that both men would eagerly anticipate being welcomed home in much the same way.

CHAPTER THREE

Dragging a hand through his unbound hair, Thor rolled on his side, kissed Alexandria's shoulder, and rose to his feet. Washing up, he quickly dressed before turning to face his wife. Watching her stretch in a way that left nothing to the imagination, he contemplated succumbing to temptation before dismissing the idea.

If he didn't leave now, he wouldn't make it to the royal keep before nightfall, and traveling alone after dark wasn't wise even for the Golden Wolf. Besides, his king expected him sooner rather than later from the tone of that letter. However, worshipping his wife had already shot that plan to hell. Not that he regretted it. He didn't. But he mustn't do it again.

"As much as I'd like to take you up on your offer," Thor kissed her lips. "We both know I can't."

"As much as I wish things were different, we do." Alexandria wrapped her arms around her sheet-covered knees. "I'll get the bairns and meet you in the bailey."

"I'll be waiting." Thor grabbed the bag abandoned just inside the door and glanced inside. Just as expected there was a leather flask of ale, a cloth-wrapped loaf of bread, and a chunk of cheese neatly packed inside. He didn't need anything more. Any clothing he might need for any occasion was already in their clothes trunk at the royal keep. Any weapon he might need was safely locked away in a separate trunk. The keys to both were tucked safely inside the pouch at his waist. "Don't be too long."

"I won't." Alexandria watched him leave before she quickly dressed and headed for the nursery.

While none of their offspring was old enough to understand what his leaving meant, they would realize their father was gone soon enough. Especially Siward. He was his father's favorite little man.

No, that wasn't fair. Thor adored Maryse and Sweyn just as much, but Siward was older. He could do more with his firstborn son than with the other two. That was closer to the truth. Opening the nursery door Alexandria saw that everything was exactly as she expected. Maidlin and Annas were rocking Sweyn and Maryse while Sweyn played with his tiny wooden sword. One day he would be as big and strong as his father. Maybe bigger. She already saw the resemblance between them in looks and mannerisms.

"Thor is leaving for the royal keep." Setting his toy aside, she lifted Sweyn in her arms. "He'd like to say goodbye to the bairns before he goes."

"Yes, my lady." Rising to her feet, Maidlin finger combed Maryse's fiery hair grateful she wasn't expected to curtsey at home as she did at court. "Are we going now?"

"As soon as you are ready." Alexandria smiled. "I don't know how long the Sheriff will be gone, so we're meeting him in the stables."

"Do you want us to go with you?" Copying Maryse, Annas propped Sweyn on her hip. "Or should we follow in a few minutes?"

"We'll all go together." There was no reason to do otherwise. "Then we'll let the bairns play in the South bailey for a while."

There was nothing they could get into there. While Siward preferred remaining in the stables with the horses, that wasn't a good idea. He was a bright, adaptable child capable of getting into far too much mischief on his own. Her younger brothers were the same at his age. Walking down the stairs, Alexandria glanced over her shoulder satisfied her nursemaids were taking every step with care.

Respectfully inclining her head in Greggorius's direction, Alexandria exited the keep and headed for the stables. She would have been offended to know she reminded the royal assassin of nothing so much as a mama duck leading her ducklings down the garden path. Then again, wasn't that what a mother did? Lead her offspring to safety? Everyone knew there was nowhere safer than in the presence of their father.

Stopping just inside the stables, Alexandria looked around. Her husband was nowhere in sight. Not sure which horse Thor would ride to the royal keep, Alexandria decided her husband must be in a stall farther back.

Unfortunately, there were no stable hands around to ask. They were likely exercising the animals. Seeing several empty stalls, she knew she was right and used the only option left to her. She called out hoping Thor heard her over the snorting and whinnying around them.

"I'm here." Thor entered the stables from outside. "I saw you coming." Reaching out, he took Siward from her arms. "Your Uncle wanted to show me the colt he's training for this guy. He is a magnificent animal. When Siward is ready for his first horse, Heimdall will be ready to be ridden."

"Heimdall?" While the source was obvious, she'd never heard that name before.

"The guardian of Asgard." Thor supplied. "And a fitting name for the golden mount that will guard our son."

Heimdall was a worthy name for the zebra dun with the dark mane and tail. Much as Wotan suited his destrier and Loki fit that mischievous, nipping kelpie his wife called a horse. However, Wotan rarely went into skirmishes anymore. While his old friend had served him well, he'd earned his right to live the rest of his days siring future war horses and training young knights for battle. He would ride his son, Caturix, instead.

As dark as his sire, Battle-King was as formidable and foul-tempered as Wotan on his worst day. However, in his favor, he was a well-trained destrier who relished the battle as much as his rider. When Alexandria asked where he'd heard such a name, she learned that he'd read it on an ancient inscription in Burgundy years ago. The locals had been happy to share that Caturix was the war god of the Helvetti. Locking the name in his memory, Thor had known even then that one of Wotan's offspring would bear that name.

"If Angus is involved, Heimdall will be perfect for our son." Her Uncle had a way with animals of any kind, especially horses. "Are you almost ready to leave?"

"I am." Thor agreed. "If I don't leave soon, I won't arrive at court before nightfall."

"Then you must go." Alexandria motioned for Maryse and Sweyn. "However, the bairns wish to kiss their Papa goodbye."

While he wouldn't say it, their Papa wished to kiss them goodbye, too. Nodding, Thor ran his fingers through Siward's long, unruly curls. "Here."

He handed Siward to Alexandria before he took Maryse from Maidlin. Spending a few minutes talking nonsense to his daughter, he kissed her fiery curls and handed her back to her nurse. He then took Sweyn from Annas and repeated his prior actions.

He couldn't do anything more. His offspring were too young to understand their father was leaving. Or that he might never return. Draping his arm around his wife, Thor watched Maidlin take Siward from Alexandria before both girls carried their charges away to play. Pulling Alex close, Thor kissed her temple.

"If I had a choice, I wouldn't go." Unlike other times, this departure weighed heavily on him. "I would organize a hunt instead."

"That wouldn't begin to sate your bloodlust," Alexandria placed her hand on his chest. "You've been a man of war too long to find long periods of peace comfortable."

"Aye, but I am willing to learn." Thor realized his words were true. "I doubt there will be an opportunity to come home between meeting with the king and going to war. While I will return as soon as possible, we know I will be gone far longer than we wish."

"Aye, we do." Alexandria agreed. "However, we will be here when you return."

"I know." While he would die for his cubs, all he cared about was this woman waiting with open arms when he returned. "I will send word as soon as I can."

"If you can," While he meant every word, the likelihood of that happening wasn't good. "That would be wonderful."

However, the only word she expected was a royal messenger informing her it was time for their men to meet the king at the royal keep.

"I will try." He would do it, too. Unbeknownst to his bride, he already had a short note tucked in his pouch to be delivered when Greggorius summoned his men. "Now I must go."

Caturix and the king were both waiting for him. Glancing over her shoulder, Thor laughed seeing his favorite stable boy standing by the massive destrier quaking in his boots. Insides warring, he'd procrastinated as long as he could.

Leaning down, he kissed Alexandria before taking her by the hand and leading her to his mount. Swinging into the saddle, he nodded at his wife before riding through the castle gates. Watching the gates swing shut behind him, Alexandria smiled at the stable boy before heading towards the South bailey.

While her bairns were clueless today was different from other days, she knew better. It was a day that would forever change their lives. She felt this deep inside. She suspected Thor sensed it, too. However, neither of them would admit it. They both knew giving voice to their deepest fears only invited the untenable into their lives.

CHAPTER FOUR

Looking at the landscape around him, Thor knew he wasn't far from his final destination. He'd traveled this route or a similar one so many times over the years that he barely noticed the passage of time.

While his senses were on high alert, he was preoccupied with thoughts of everything he'd left behind. That wasn't good considering the reason he was making this journey in the first place. While he doubted the king would convene in the war room tonight, he would expect the Sheriff of Lothian by his side first thing focused on the upcoming skirmish. Thor knew he would likely fail his overlord unless he made peace with emotions he'd never felt.

Shaking his thoughts, he contemplated each step of the coming battle. First, he must determine their final target or targets which he couldn't do until he learned the king's true intent. Once that was done, he'd decide the most effective means of ensuring an uninterrupted supply chain was put in place. The next step was determining the logistics and military tactics they needed to accomplish their goals. Once the rudimentary decisions were made, the pieces would fall into place.

However, that was only half of the battle. Flawlessly implementing their plan would be much harder. That took a seasoned leader to accomplish. Fortunately, David had one. While the king would lead his men into battle, no one was under any illusions about who the real commander was.

Thor was fortunate most of the king's men had fought under his command for so long they'd developed a rhythm ensuring they didn't outstrip their supply chain. Armies without adequate food and water were sorry armies indeed. He'd seen that happen far too often among less disciplined troops. It wouldn't happen on his watch.

While not an unconquerable mistake, doubling back to meet up with their supplies used energy his men couldn't afford to expend. It was better to cover less territory in a day and conserve their strength for battle. He'd drilled that reality into everyone's head to the point they automatically adjusted their pace as needed.

Unless they met an opposing army on the heath in route, their target wasn't going anywhere. While that wasn't always true, he suspected this was a land grab. Not outright war. David was going after keeps, villages, and land, not openly challenging Stephen's right to the crown. That would likely come soon enough. Not sure how he felt about that possibility, he hoped this skirmish wouldn't be as dangerous or last as long as past campaigns.

Seeing the gates opening before him an hour later, Thor rode into the bailey and dismounted. Saluting the watchers on the wall, he handed Caturix's reigns to the stable hand and headed for the great hall. Confident his mount would be well tended, he needed to inform the king he'd arrived before nightfall as commanded. It wouldn't hurt to fill a trencher on his way to the high table either. His sack had contained a light repast to hold him until he arrived at his final destination. It had been many hours since he'd eaten his fill.

As he did at home, he'd stop by the royal kitchens to give the cook a small token of his appreciation. His gift, while modest, would ensure he was well-provisioned for the foreseeable future. Like Bertie, Amalise ran a tight ship. She knew everything in her kitchen including what came in and what went out. Usually nothing without her permission.

Entering the corridor, he veered left lured by delectable aromas wafting from pots cooling on the hearth and meat dripping on the spits. He wasn't surprised to find the sturdy cook alone in her immaculate kitchen carefully taking inventory before locking her spices away. He knew the rest of her staff was busy clearing tables and restoring the hall for the evening's entertainment since the evening meal had recently ended.

"My lord." Amalise nodded in his direction. "It's good seeing you. We heard you were coming in tonight, so I saved some of your favorites."

"I appreciate that." Laying the small pouch on the counter, Thor took the plate she handed him and loaded it with seasoned vegetables and the slabs of meat Amalise had set aside along with hearty chunks of rustic bread, a generous serving of pork pie, and a sliver of her legendary spiced cake. "This smells so good."

Amalise nodded as she poured three cabochon rubies onto her palm. Lifting each one to the light, she recognized that while small, each was a fine specimen worth far more than a larger stone of lesser quality. She knew also that they were likely from the stores accumulated in Lord Thor's mercenary days. Tucking the pouch in her pocket, the cook bobbed a quick curtsey and poured him a tankard of hard ale. Lord Thor was a generous man. He'd been very kind to her over the years and she'd kept an eye out for him in return.

Unlike other people she served, he never demanded anything. He asked instead. If that wasn't enough, he frequently brought her trinkets of gratitude for little things like ensuring he had a warm plate of food waiting when he arrived. The gifts meant naught to him, but an extra coin here or a small ruby there greatly impacted her family. While she knew the king would provide when she grew too old to run his kitchens, Lord Thor's gifts ensured they had no worries if the unforeseen happened.

"I'm off to see His Majesty." Watching him lift his trencher and tankard of ale, Amalise snorted at the idea of the Sheriff of Lothian calling anyone "His Majesty." The Nordic giant was far more likely to call the king by his given name. She'd heard him do so more than once. Not that the king minded, or if he did he didn't correct him. He wouldn't dare. "Thank you for thinking of me."

"Anytime." Amalise watched him leave before wiping at an imaginary spot on her counter. Those rubies were thank you enough and he knew it. Then again, he might know it, but she wasn't telling him so. She didn't want him rethinking his generosity anytime soon. Not that she thought he would. She and her family were far too valuable to the crown.

Heading for the great hall, Thor appreciated how similar both cooks were. While he bribed Bertie with luxury items like bolts of fine cloth, the old woman had been provided for by Lord Ian before his death and she would continue to be provided for in his daughter's household. Amalise was a different matter.

Her situation was more tenuous. If anything happened to David or Henry she could find herself with nothing. The trinkets he'd slipped her over the years would ensure she was never penniless no matter the upheaval in the royal keep. In return, the kitchen was always open and his favorites were always available when he was in residence. No matter the time of day or night.

Making his way to his usual seat by the king, Thor set his plate and tankard on the table smirking slightly at the familiar goblet filled to the brim with his favorite wine setting by the king's hand. While good enough for David's palate, he preferred hard ale. He'd savor that rich flavor over oily Bordeaux pretentiousness any day.

"I see you've been bribing my cook again." David glanced at the loaded plate noting the succulent pork pie that never made its' way to him. "What did you give the woman this time? A gold coin or some rubies you won't miss."

"What do you think?" While the king acted disgruntled he knew what his Sheriff was up to. He'd occasionally slip a small jewel into Thor's gift in gratitude for his servant's unwavering loyalty. While anyone in the know assumed the Sheriff's bribes ensured the tenderest cuts of meat and the most expensive sauces, he and his king knew better.

He paid the wily woman for acquisitions far more important than the food that filled his belly. Amalise, her husband, and her two sons were a veritable font of information that couldn't be acquired any other way. Beneath the notice of the people they served, David's loyal servants saw and heard things he couldn't. They had apprised him of fomenting rebellion more than once.

"Three small cabochons. Substantially less than my wife paid to get your blessing on her iniquities." Thor tipped his tankard in the direction of the jewel-encrusted goblet.

Laughing at Thor's audacity, the king lifted the offending glass to his lips.

"I have enjoyed Zan's gift more than you will ever know." Owning the beautiful set meant he no longer repented of covetousness every time he visited Drummond. "As for your impudent suggestion that my goddaughter bought anything, she didn't need my forgiveness for her iniquities. There was no iniquity to forgive."

Her marriage to Thor gave them what they both needed. No matter how it came to be. Both men knew that. Alexandria got her savior and he'd eventually received the sworn oath of his most powerful warrior. He would never have received that binding if not for the unsanctioned acts of his goddaughter.

As for the gift of her father's favorite goblets, that was merely the fulfillment of his heart's desire. What could he say? His goddaughter loved him. She wished only to repay his kindness by putting a smile on his face.

"Exactly as I thought." Thor shook his head. "That woman can do no wrong in your eyes."

"Not when that wrong is wedding you." The king laughed softly. "How never mattered; only that she did."

Thor's laugh filled the great hall. If he didn't know better he would think the king was in cahoots with his goddaughter. He did know better. While David wished for their marriage and encouraged it, he was completely in the dark until after the deed was done.

However, he wasn't surprised that the how didn't matter. For a saint, his lord was cunning and ruthless when the need arose. The survival of Drummond and his goddaughter was nothing if not a need. With hindsight, he saw that with more clarity than he had at the time.

"Ah." Thor toyed with his knife. "That's good to know."

"Is it?" David stared him down. "Is it good to hear what you already knew?"

"Yeah, I think it is." Thor stared back. "It's good to hear you're still as ruthless as you've always been. That being said, what are you contemplating?"

"What do you think?" David sat back in his chair. "Newcastle and Carlisle and everything in between eventually."

"I see." Envisioning the landscape, Thor mapped possible routes to accomplish the king's goal. "It's not impossible if we plan well."

Although not doable in a day, who knew what the coming weeks held? They'd start by taking what they could get for now. The future would take care of itself.

"I thought you would see things my way." He wouldn't have sent for his Wolf if he'd felt otherwise. "Relax tonight. Tomorrow is early enough to plot."

"If you say so." Thor laughed as the king rose to his feet. "We both know that isn't likely to happen."

"We both know you already have the major campaign planned in your head." The king patted his shoulder. "We'll refine the particulars tomorrow."

Rising to his feet Thor watched the king leave knowing he was right. He did have the major campaign mapped out in his head. It all came down to attacking the most vulnerable areas first. As for the rest, they would have the finer points worked out in a few hours. If all went well he would be home before he had time to miss Drumond.

After that, he prayed his life would be quiet except for his royal duties for the next few months. He prayed also that his family would have grown by another bairn or two by this time next year. With his wife, one never knew. The woman was full of surprises.

However, he liked the idea and he thought Alexandria would as well. He'd run it by her when he got home. Watching a servant clear his dishes Thor nodded and headed for the stairs. While his king liked to move around his domain, David was staying put in the royal keep for a while. That meant he wouldn't need to sleep on a bench in the great hall as he often did. Not when a comfortable bed with soft sheets and warm furs that smelled like his wife awaited him near the top of the stairs.

Taking the steps two at a time, Thor arrived at the chamber, unlocked the door, and stepped inside. Locking the door behind him, he was pleased to see a fire in the hearth and several beeswax candles sitting on a clothes trunk. Lighting a couple of candles, he stripped down and washed the dirt from his skin. After all these years, the royal servants knew the Sheriff of Lothian's habits well.

Drying off, Thor emptied the basin, blew out the candles, and slipped between lightly scented sheets. If he looked hard enough, he would find the sachets that Alexandria tucked amongst the bedclothes and under the pillows at every visit. Lifting the sheet to his nostrils, the Golden Wolf closed his eyes and breathed deeply of the spicey perfume his wife favored.

Opening his eyes, Thor knew he wasn't likely to fall asleep soon. His thoughts were too tumultuous. Leaning back against his pillows, he covered his eyes with his arm contemplating his last sight of his flame-haired vixen. He'd casually draped his arm around her shoulders and stared down at her.

Compared to him, she was such a tiny, fierce thing. A wily fox to his savage wolf. There were times when he didn't understand how their lives fit together. He just knew they did. When he tried to see his lady as nothing more than his bedmate and the mother of his children, the warrior within would rise to the surface reminding him that she was so much more.

Today was no different. Though she tried her best to remain calm and supportive, he knew Alex bristled within. If she could have stopped him from leaving, she would have. If he'd dared refuse his overlord, he wouldn't have come. But he couldn't do that despite feeling an unease he'd never felt before.

Not when the king summoned him for a purpose only he could perform. Shaking his head slightly, Thor recalled leaning down from Caturix's back to drop one last longing kiss on her lips before riding out the front gates without a backward glance.

Shuffling, Thor sat up a little straighter and looked around the chamber at the shadows on the wall. He remembered a similar night of light and shadows and the events that changed his life. Most occurred here in this room. Not all of them, but the pivotal moment setting his life on a different course.

Had he not given in to his animal urges, he would have stayed his course and kept his vow to never wed again. Once he'd sampled the forbidden fruit, he knew he'd lost the battle. While he would never admit it, he knew the truth deep inside. The woman would haunt him until he finally gave in. However, he'd intended to resist her charms as long as he could.

Not all that surprising his resistance didn't last long as he'd hoped. His bride was nothing if not unpredictable. Several years into his marriage, he admitted his initial acceptance of that sword to his throat was due more to the titles, wealth, and power coming with the heiress of Drummond than from fear or affection.

Thor laughed acknowledging the woman quaking before him had known that more than him. She'd recognized their carnal compatibility was a mark in her favor and she'd played that card every chance she got. However, her strongest weapon was her acceptance of who and what he was joined with her unwavering loyalty.

Alexandria of Drummond had won him over quicker than he'd believed possible. While it was true that he became restless during times of peace, he wouldn't trade the life he'd built for the life he'd had for anything the world had to offer. Closing his eyes, he drifted off to sleep knowing tomorrow would be a busy day.

CHAPTER FIVE

Staring around the hall, Thor looked at the extra bodies already milling about. He wasn't surprised by how quickly the campaign had come together. David was known for his military acumen and strategic mind, so his preliminary ideas were good. The king just wanted a second pair of eyes to see the holes in his plan. There weren't many and he had quickly taken a solid foundation to the next level with minimal effort. As amazing as it seemed in hindsight, messengers went out two days after his arrival.

Truthfully, once he'd known Carlisle was the main objective, mapping the course of the coming battle wasn't complicated. Nor was it a simple skirmish as he'd assumed. Parameters in mind, he'd studied the rough maps on hand and worked out the proper routes to use. Intimately familiar with the landscape around their mark, it didn't take long to decide what siege machines to use and how many knights, soldiers, and archers would be needed. The king agreed with his assessment and the plans were done. He'd sent messengers to Drummond and Alexandria had done the rest.

Heading up the stairs, Thor wasn't surprised more men than they needed were waiting to mobilize behind their king. Chuckling to himself, he knew why. He and Lionel weren't the only warriors ready for a good fight. Peace was hard on seasoned men of war. Channeling that energy into other enterprises worked for a while but the day always came when a fighting man needed to do what he did best.

Entering Alexandria's chamber, he unlocked a rarely used trunk to remove rarely used armor. Quickly donning the various pieces, he gazed at his reflection deciding he looked like nothing so much as a Norman warrior when he was anything but. While not a stranger to chain mail, he rarely wore anything more than the occasional byrnie, not finding anything more necessary.

Like all true warriors, he expected to die on the field of battle even if Alexandria refused to accept that thought. She believed his mindset had more to do with his knowledge of the old ways and less to do with the reality that it was a fact few warriors lived to be hoary old men. Not that he intended to expire anytime soon. He didn't.

He had a wife and a family to raise before he called his life done. Not that his bride would be amused to know he considered her a child still needing raising, but she was. A courageous, sensual child less than half his age witnessing far more of the dark side in her short life than she should have, but an innocent nonetheless when compared to him.

Staring at his reflection, Thor contemplated the king's reaction to seeing him attired in the kind of armor he never wore. However, a promise was a promise and he was a man of his word. He would endure his leader's ribbing before he would betray his vow. Tightening his belt around his waist, he lifted Móði, ran through a repertoire of moves from parries to ripostes, and satisfied he was still familiar with the heft of the weapon, inserted the sword in his sheath.

Like Avenger, Wrath was made of the finest Damascus steel and void of excess ornamentation. There was naught save the pattern on the blade and the elongated ebony-eyed pine martin decorating the hilt. While few knew why such an insignificant creature was associated with a Norse god of battle or with his sword, the pine martin was as relentless and fierce as the entity inspiring his weapon. It was a beast worthy of association with both Möði and the Golden Wolf.

While he would prefer to have Avenger by his side, he'd left the sword with his wife as she'd asked. He'd wanted to deny her request but something urged him to do as she wished. Feeling at a loss, he'd finally decided it was better to endure a brief separation than lose his favored weapon.

While Alexandria hadn't voiced her fear, Thor knew that was it. He had similar reservations and he didn't know what he would do without his father's sword. Losing his most valuable treasure wasn't something he was prepared to risk.

Known as Hevnarmaðr in his father's day, he'd quickly learned that "Revenge Man" in the old tongue didn't strike fear in the soul of his opponents as readily as the word Avenger in their native tongue, so he'd changed the name many years ago. Now he could happily say the sword was almost as feared and revered as its bearer. Making a sound of disgust at the foolishness of men, Thor knew there was nothing mystical about Avenger. A sword was only as good as its wielder.

However, this wasn't the first time he'd fought with a different blade and it wouldn't be the last. He could confidently say the sword in his hand had little impact on the outcome of a battle. His strength and skill did. Unlike most warriors, he was adept with every weapon used in hand-to-hand combat and passably lethal with a bow.

That dedication to prowess more than anything had led to his towering reputation. When he'd committed to becoming a man of war as a page, he'd committed whole-heartedly. Nothing had changed since. Shaking his head in silent confirmation, Thor locked the chamber door and headed for the stairs. The coming battle waited for no man. Taking the stairs two at a time he arrived at the landing long before he was ready. Rolling his eyes, he steeled himself for his sovereign's reaction to a sight he would likely never see again in his life.

—⁓—

WATCHING THOR ENTER the great hall, the king choked back a laugh. Coughing, he ignored the nasty side eye cast his way. Since when did the Golden Wolf wear full armor? Never. Not as long as he'd known him. A byrnie and chausses, yes. Full armor, no. While he should look foolish, he didn't. He was more intimidating than ever instead.

"Zan?" Picturing his goddaughter's face in his mind, David smiled at the answering nod. "I thought so."

"And the babes." Thor nodded. "She fears I will not return this time."

"Gruoch?" He knew of the Drummond phantasma. "Did she see the spirit again?"

"Not since the MacLaren's demise," Thor admitted. "Nor poor Eddie."

"Then something else has her on edge." That wasn't a comforting thought. "Her mother was like that."

"Like what?" Thor removed the conical nasal helmet. "Strange?"

BACK FROM THE SHADOWLANDS

"Given to knowing." That was all the king was willing to say. "You are wise to take precautions."

Thor nodded. While he didn't like being encumbered with a helmet, coif, itchy gambeson, thigh-length mail hauberk, and chausses, he had no desire to tempt fate. Not when his wife asked him to have more care. It was the least he could do for his family.

Besides, he knew he would shed all of this as soon as the campaign ended. Maybe he'd wear a byrnie but that was all. There was no need for such protection once the truce was signed. Everyone would be on their way to joyfully reunite with friends and family. Fighting would be the last thing on their mind.

"Perhaps." Thor nodded. "Now, I think it is time we get our men on the road. The sooner we finish what we set out to do, the sooner we return home."

He ignored the knowing look the king cast his way. "Don't start that again."

"Have it your way." King David fell in step beside the blonde giant fully aware of the commanding presence he made with the sun glinting off his red hair. "For now keep your mind on the coming battle."

"You know me better than that." Thor glanced at his king. "Carlisle and Newcastle will fall as planned."

The king nodded. His Wolf had spoken. So be it.

CHAPTER SIX

A few weeks later, Thor motioned for Lionel to fall into step beside him. While the battle was over, the politics weren't. He wasn't leaving the battlefield for home as soon as he'd hoped. Though displeased by the thought, his overlord wanted him by his side while the final agreements were recorded. Not just by his side, he wanted his signature and seal to witness the conditions of the treaty.

Snarling at being so thoroughly snared when he wanted nothing more than to return home for a hot bath, a warm meal, hugs from his babes, and a torrid night getting reacquainted with the only woman in Christendom who could kidnap him and live to tell about it, Thor knew his presence was a silent threat no one could mistake. Crossing the King of Scotland meant crossing his Golden Wolf. No one wanted that. Not in their right mind they didn't.

Picking at the snarling wolf rampant decorating his signet ring, Thor knew there was no way out of the diplomatic web David had expertly woven around him. It didn't matter they'd taken numerous garrisons and hostages, and effectively harried the countryside for a span. Nor did it matter that Newcastle and Carlisle had fallen through crafty planning. Only fools would open the gates to a neighboring king and his army. None of that satisfied his king.

As frustrated as he was, Thor couldn't refuse the crafty spider's command. They both knew he would have done just that in the past and the king would have let him. Those days were over. He'd sworn his freedom away and allayed any fears his lord harbored that wedding his beloved goddaughter put thoughts of rebellion in his head. It hadn't, but he didn't blame the man.

That his loyalty never wavered with his marriage was the exception, not the rule. Unlike so many men, he was content where he was with what he had. He possessed wealth and power few men ever attained thanks to hard work and his monarch's favor. He had no desire to be anything more than he was. He hoped the king knew that.

All that had changed over the last three years was that he now had a family to protect. However, swearing fealty to his king lessened the temptation his enemies would try to use his family against him. They would regret it if they did. Being the king's sworn man added another layer of protection around what was his that they wouldn't have otherwise.

"What has happened?" Breaking the other man's concentration, Lionel knew there was a significant change by the tensing of Thor's jaw. "The terms of the treaty have not changed?"

New borders were drawn, hostages released, and oaths sworn not to break the truce until spring. After that, it was anyone's game. All standard give and take or so he'd believed.

"No, they have not." Thor agreed. "But my king's willingness to navigate the terms of the treaty have."

Studying the Sheriff's demeanor, Lionel immediately understood what had happened. Only one thing would stress Thor so. He saw that now.

"You won't be leaving with us?" He hadn't anticipated that. "The king wishes you to witness the terms of the treaty."

"He does," Thor confirmed. "And we both know why he wishes for my presence."

"As a silent promise of the repercussions of breaking the treaty." Unless their king broke the treaty first. "I will let Zan know you will be home as soon as loose ends are tied up."

"Tell my wife I am not the only lord staying behind to witness the truce." Although he had traveled alone to the royal keep, Alexandria wouldn't like him returning through hostile lands the same way after a battle. While he worried little about his safety, like any good wife, Alexandria would not rest until his return. It didn't help that something about this excursion made her uneasy from the start. "Let Alexandria know that I will travel with Moray's party until I head North and they head West. I can handle the last few hours through friendly territory without an entourage."

Few would dare tangle with the Golden Wolf even alone. His reputation had long preceded him. The destruction of the MacLarens had done the rest.

The fact that Fitz Duncan, Mormaer of Moray, remained behind to discuss personal business with his king was nothing his wife needed to know. Half his retainers were returning to the Northland ahead of their lord as planned. That was the party he was joining.

"I'm sure you can." Lionel laughed at the memory of what happened the last time anyone tried to take the Golden Wolf captive. Their men had feared for their lives until Thor finally reassured them that he wouldn't kill them in their sleep. That had taken months, rather than weeks, to happen. Alexandria's continuing contentment with her mate had finally reassured her men that a dangerous situation was satisfactorily resolved. "I wouldn't want to fight you on the heath."

"Nor I you." Thor countered. "While we both know who would win, it would be a worthy challenge."

While that remark coming from any other man would have made him bristle, Lionel laughed because he knew it was true. While of comparable size and strength, Thor was both more ruthless and skilled on the battlefield. He had superior endurance as well.

While such a match would be well fought, the Wolf would prevail in the end and they both knew it. For many reasons. Not the least of which was the Norse blood flowing through his veins and his ties to the old ways. If sufficiently challenged, Thor would cut his throat without a second thought and watch him expire in a pool of blood. Or drape his lungs over wide-spread ribs before calmly walking away feeling fully justified in his actions. While she'd done an admirable job taming the beast, there were parts of her Wolf that Alexandria would never conquer.

"Perhaps, but we will never know will we?" That was true as well. "You are loyal to our king and I am loyal to you."

Thor nodded. He and Lionel had fought well together many times over the years. They still fought well together. He wouldn't be his right-hand man if they didn't. A mercenary of long-standing like him, he'd been surprised to find the warrior settled at Drummond.

While the idea of de Montluzin in the service of one family was disconcerting, the knowledge he'd sought to wed his lord's daughter and settled for the niece instead surprised him more. He would never have seen that coming. Like him, Lionel wasn't a man given to compromise when he desired something deeply. Thor knew he had wanted his lord's daughter more than anything.

Though his loyalty wasn't in question, knowing his tendresse for his wife, Thor kept an eye on his second in command where Zan was concerned. While Lionel loved his wife deeply, he'd loved Alexandria fiercely once upon a time. Thor was under no illusion who would step into the gap should anything untoward happen to him.

No matter how innocent the comfort offered, the thought of the other man getting that close to his mate didn't sit well. A man of the world, he knew how quickly emotions once laid to rest could resurrect in trying times. Lines were crossed in ways that could never be undone before either party realized what they'd done. Seeing that such opportunities never occurred was the best way to ensure nothing untenable happened.

"Aye." Thor agreed. "You are a man of your word."

"As are you." Lionel quietly agreed. He and Reina still resided at Drummond because Thor knew he would never cross that line of honor. Nor would Alexandria. If possible, she loved her husband more than he loved her.

Adding to the emotional complexity of the situation, the impossible occurred not long after Thor's marriage. The Golden Wolf unexpectedly fell for his fiery bride and fell hard. While everyone tried to appear oblivious, it was no secret the Wolf returned his wife's affections more deeply than any believed possible.

Lionel caught Thor's eye. "I will ensure Zan knows you are well, detained by royal business, and will be home as soon as the king releases you from his service."

"You are right." Thor glanced in the king's direction. "I will return as soon as I am free."

The Wolf nodded his thanks as he turned to rejoin the royal party. He didn't need to watch Lionel mount his destrier to know he was heading for the castle gates. While he'd rather join the other warriors returning to Drummond, his duty was to remain by David's side. That meant the quicker his work was done here, the quicker he would be free to return to his family.

While Alexandria wouldn't be happy the delay meant he'd be home a scant few weeks before leaving on his rounds as Sheriff of Lothian, they would have ample time to get reacquainted. Nodding at King David and the lingering nobles, Thor was unaware he wore that rare smile that, while not displeasing when worn by other men, struck the fear of God into the warriors around him.

CHAPTER SEVEN

Shaking hands with Fitz Duncan, Mormaer of Moray, Thor was glad the prince had given him leave to travel with his party. A wily character, Fitz Duncan had wasted no time in wedding Alice de Romilly, heiress to Skipton Castle, in Yorkshire after his wife's death. While he would have appreciated getting to know the other man better, he wanted to see his family more. There would be time to form new alliances later when both of them were more settled.

Joining the other men in the party, Thor swung into Caturix's saddle and looked around him. While he recognized a couple of the men, they didn't know him. The handsome fair-haired boy was Gervais de Blois and the weakling was Theobald de Calais. As for the others, they were strangers to him and he to them.

Following the men out of the royal keep, Thor decided it was better that way for now. He would observe his companions and decide whether to reveal his identity when they stopped to rest. As it was, no one had taken the time to identify themselves to the others. They were too interested in hitting the road to take time for idle pleasantries. He could respect that since he felt the same.

Falling in line at the rear of the party, Thor allowed his mind to drift over the past few weeks. While he would never admit the truth to his wife, he'd eagerly anticipated the coming skirmishes. No, he'd prayed they weren't just skirmishes but would become more. They had.

In truth, David intended that from the start. The idea of a simple skirmish or two was put out there to lull Stephen into a false sense of security. It worked. Thor wasn't surprised that everything fell into place to give them the upper hand leading to the favorable treaty his king wanted. His overlord was considered a formidable foe for a reason. He was a master tactician who kept his cards close to his chest.

---— ❧ —---

COMING OUT OF HIS REVERIE, Thor noticed the sun was high in the sky casting a warm glow over the rolling hills of the countryside. Everyone had fallen into a relaxed formation several hours ago under the direction of their self-appointed leader, Cedric Annarsson, Fitz Duncan's second in command. He, nor any others, had felt the need to challenge the man's authority.

The warrior was an alert, seasoned knight whose keen eyes constantly scanned the horizon for potential threats. Studying the man, Thor knew his position in the Mormaer's army was hard won. The wicked scar running from forehead to chin coupled with his immense build testified to many years of active battle experience. Most, if not all, likely in the service of his current overlord. From his observations, Thor saw no reason not to respect Annarsson as his equal.

In truth, he had no desire to be anything more than he was. Another unnamed member of an armed fifteen-man party traveling together for added security. Had he not promised his wife otherwise, he would have made the trip alone as he usually did. That being said, no one was that concerned with a coming attack. Not even him. Nothing around him indicated danger.

Instead, the men rode in a loose group enjoying the rhythmic thud of their horses' hooves striking earth as they scanned open land as far as the eye could see. While vigilant, his companions weren't on edge. There was no reason. They'd participated in a successful battle that ended with a favorable treaty with both sides pledging not to attack until fresh shoots were bursting from the ground. It didn't get much better than that for fighting men.

"Keep your wits about you." Lord Cedric glanced at the men behind him. "We may be crossing neutral territory, but that doesn't mean we're out of danger."

Bringing up the rear, Thor couldn't agree with him more. While they were surrounded by open land, it was only a matter of time before they reached that stretch of forest up ahead. Unfortunately, they had no option except to get through the dense underbrush as quickly as possible. If this were back in his mercenary days, he'd consider that a perfect place to ambush his unsuspecting quarry. Or even suspecting quarry for that matter. His familiarity with the area would give him the upper hand either way.

However, this wasn't his mercenary days and this wasn't his neck of the woods. That meant while he wasn't overly familiar with this area, others were. Resting his hand on his sword, the thought made him uneasy. Anyone could hide in that copse of trees waiting to catch them unawares.

Dismissing the thought, Thor found small comfort in the idea that attacking his party would forfeit the treaty. It would be tantamount to declaring war. However, that didn't mean there weren't fools out there lacking the foresight to see the future repercussions of their actions. He'd brought many such men to their knees over the years.

Feeling the hair rise on his arms, Thor heard every crack of a branch and rustle of the leaves as the group rode past the thicket. Something wasn't right. He knew it. Hanging back even more, he wasn't surprised when a band of warriors sprang from the trees swords upraised. While not caught fully unaware, their party was easily outnumbered four to one. Hearing Annarsson's cry of, "Ambush!" Thor watched the retinue quickly form a defensive circle with upraised shields to deflect the initial onslaught.

Hearing the clash of steel as the two groups collided, Thor joined the fray easily hacking through the outer perimeter with practiced ease. Satisfied he'd lessened their opponents by five strong men just getting to his current position, he fought with fierce determination easily killing the man intent on stabbing him through the back. The dishonorable cur deserved to die for his actions. Sword cutting through the air with deadly precision, he parried a blow from an enemy rider and countered with a swift strike, unseating his opponent. Running the warrior through, Thor pulled his sword from his body before lifting Móði yet again.

Senses on high alert, Thor continued his relentless attack on their attackers feeling that for every man he killed, two more took his place. That was likely true. Not only were they fatally outnumbered, but their opponents were seasoned warriors equally, if not more, skilled than most of them were.

Watching his comrades fall to the sword or ax Thor doubted he would make it out of this melee alive. He doubted as well that anyone would ever find their bodies when they didn't return to their loved ones. Not in any identifiable state. They'd likely rot in anonymity falling prey to the beasts of the field and birds of the sky. It wouldn't be the first time he'd come across the signs of such carnage, but it would be the last as he would be amongst it.

The thought of Alexandria's anguish and the potential vulnerability of his lands if that happened galvanized Thor to action. Drawing on his bloodlust he hacked through the men without realizing what he'd done. He was fighting for his life and the lives of his remaining comrades. What did he care if an enemy's innards spilled from his belly or his head rolled from his shoulders? He didn't. In truth, the more times that happened the better.

As they tired under the never-ending assault, Thor watched his companions fall all around him and fought with renewed fury. He cut down one attacker after another, his sword a blur of motion. But even his strength and skill couldn't turn the tide. One by one, he saw nine of his party fall to the sword or the ax. The cries of the dying and the cloying scent of fresh blood and offal permeated the air mingling with the clash of steel and the thunder of hooves all around him.

Gervais was the first to be unseated and disarmed. Theobald remained in the saddle along with him and several others. Annarsson held his own against two warriors for the moment, but it didn't look good. While he would come to his aid if he could, Thor wasn't sure he would make it in time. Breaking through the line of fighting, he saw the arc of the Danish axe and watched Annarsson's head fall away in a bloody spray as his body toppled from the saddle.

Reaching out, Thor grabbed Annarsson's sword in passing, sheathed Modi in his saddle scabbard, and lifted his new sword liking the heft in his hand. As mercenary as his action seemed, it was practical instead. The dead man didn't need his weapon anymore, and a second sword was always good if you could get one.

Fixing Annarsson's killer in his golden sights, Thor hacked the warrior across the neck before thrusting his sword through his companion's gut and giving it a practiced twist. While an extra layer of cruelty he rarely employed, bastards breaking good-faith treaties deserved what they got. Urging Caturix back into the thick of battle he decided the dishonorable curs may have succeeded in killing Annarsson but he'd succeeded in killing them...

CHAPTER EIGHT

Alexandria stared over the moors. Something wasn't right. She felt that deep in her soul. Were Gruoch not laid to rest by the demise of the MacLarens, she would have awakened long ago to discover the distressed spirit standing by her bed wringing her long white hands. As it was, she'd felt uneasy before Thor left. She felt the same now. However, she was powerless to stop her mate from leaving. She didn't try. It wasn't her place. Not knowing both Lionel and Thor longed to join the battle. Any battle. Anywhere. They'd been idle too long. Bloodlust roiled through their veins night and day with a thirst that wailed to be quenched.

If restlessness wasn't enough to warrant a more savage outlet than sparring with his men, the king's summons meant they dared not turn him down. Not when Thor was David's sworn man and Lionel was his. While she didn't like it, she never protested their departure. She understood a warrior's life. Was she not a warrior in her own right? Besides, from what was said, the battle was a minor skirmish over the border to seize a swatch of English soil for the Scottish crown. It wasn't a major offensive. It was a masterful two-step forward, ten-step back board game enacted on verdant land. One that should have ended weeks ago.

Staring over the moors a final time, Alexandria turned to enter her room. If she didn't appear in the great hall soon, Reina would come looking for her. While she would rather brood in solitude, she didn't have that option. She was the lady of Drummond. She must put on a strong, brave front. Her people expected nothing less from her. Thor and Lionel weren't the only husbands and fathers to heed their king's call. Or the only warriors still missing.

Not missing; returning later than expected. That sounded better. They were returning later than expected. That wasn't true either. Only Thor had yet to come home. Lionel had ridden through Drummond's gates three days ago sporting minor injuries half-expecting his lord to have arrived before he did. Rejoicing at his return, everyone was glad to see him. Yet that joy was tinged with silent fear.

Quickly changing into a clean bliaut, she combed her hair, stopped by the nursery to drop kisses on tiny noses, and headed for the stairs. Arriving on the bottom step, she was greeted with more commotion than expected streaming in from outside. While Drummond was a noisy place teeming with activity, whatever this was, it wasn't normal. She didn't like it. Opening the door, Alexandria headed for the outer bailey.

Now that she was outside, she liked the sound of that ruckus even less than she had from the inside. Not when it shouldn't be happening in the first place. Staring at the men gathered around the familiar mount she pushed through the crowd attempting to stop her and froze in place. Caturix stood before her riderless wearing a blood-drenched saddle.

Walking up to the quivering horse, she wiped two fingers over the brownish stain. Drawing her fingers to her nose, she noted the faint coppery smell most wouldn't detect. It was undeniably blood and it wasn't fresh. If this blood was her husband's, Thor had been injured days ago. Most likely on the journey home since she knew he wasn't hurt in the battle.

While it was possible the blood wasn't his, the fact his mount came back without him indicated otherwise. Removing his sword from the saddle scabbard she inspected the blade for dried blood. Finding none, she knew Thor was likely immobilized before he could fight back. Likely by whatever trauma bloodied his saddle.

"Take Caturix to the stables." She petted the destrier's nose. While not a pet or even an everyday mount, he still appreciated the affection of his riders. That meant only her and Thor as he would accept no others. "Give him feed and water and tend him well."

Watching the young groom lead Caturix away, Alexandria was glad Thor didn't take squires into skirmishes. Under the circumstances, that wouldn't have been wise. Besides the fact that he didn't want the distraction of protecting his charge, he preferred to tend his armor and his destrier himself. While he instructed their pages and squires in weaponry, he left taking them into actual battle to his men.

Should a squire prove worthy, her husband would take him under his wing. However, that was rare. Roderick had been his last squire. Thor had trained the boy well. He'd been knighted soon after Drummond was restored and now served as a royal messenger.

Shaking her head, Alexandria suspected Roddy was a whole lot more. The last she'd heard the boy reported to Greggorius personally. That was a feat that hinted at darker assignments. She wasn't surprised to learn this. From what she recalled, the boy preferred lurking in the shadows to basking in the light. Both were good character traits for an assassin in training.

"Lionel, get Reina and meet me in my chamber." Turning, Alexandria motioned to the men standing around. "The rest of you can return to work, and we'll update you when we know something. Osgar, please stay."

Alexandria watched the men disperse in every direction while the young knight remained behind. Since Osgar was her messenger, the king would know who sent him the minute he appeared at court. He would know immediately that the young knight wouldn't be there if his mission weren't of the highest importance. His goddaughter didn't send unnecessary distractions his way. She understood he was a very busy man.

"I don't need to tell you what I need." She smiled at his knowing nod. "Get your mount ready and I'll return in a few minutes."

Hearing his, "Yes, my lady." Alexandria watched him head for the stables while she headed for the keep. Silently composing a brief note in her mind, she made her way to her chamber knowing she would return with the coded message long before Osgar appeared in the bailey.

Once she saw her messenger off, she could return to the master's solar in plenty of time to compose herself before Lionel and Reina appeared. Her cousin was working with her ladies in the herb garden, so she would need to make herself presentable before their meeting. It wouldn't do to appear in her lady's chamber covered in dirt and grass stains. It wasn't appropriate. It mattered little that her lady was her cousin as well. She was still her lady and the wife of the Sheriff of Lothian.

Unlocking her trunk, Alexandria removed her enameled writing casket and opened it on a small table. Sitting in a chair, she laid a small paper rectangle on the table, opened her ink pot, and used a sharpened quill to jot a brief, coded message. While not complicated, it was the code she'd used over the years to update her godfather on events at Drummond. Since every note was burned as soon as it was read, she was fairly confident her code remained unbroken.

Her husband's disappearance was the last thing they wanted common knowledge at this moment. While it wouldn't remain a secret once the king's search parties went out, they would have a brief period to prepare for potential attacks before the vultures started circling the keep.

Fortunately, her husband was never unprepared for such an eventuality, so there wasn't much they needed to do. Nothing beyond ensuring they had the manpower to handle anyone foolish enough to attack the Golden Wolf's demesne in his absence. The fall of Drummond was much harder to obtain now that there was no Bridget to open their gates to the enemy.

Folding the note, she applied a dark green glob to the vellum before pressing her lead seal matrix into the tinted beeswax. Satisfied with the impression of the mounted female warrior, she covered the seal with a tiny silk bag. Confident her missive was in order she carried the letter downstairs. Entering the bailey she was pleased to find Osgar waiting patiently for her to appear. She was equally pleased to see him flanked by four seasoned warriors.

"You know where to go." Alexandria gave him the sealed vellum and watched him tuck the document into his belt. "Find Greggorius or Roland. Have them arrange a private meeting with my godfather. Act as you always do until the king sends for you. Once he does, release this into his hands."

"Yes, my Lady." Osgar nodded before swinging into the saddle. "We shall return as soon as possible."

"Have a safe journey." Alexandria watched the small party depart before heading back inside.

Entering the great hall, she took her seat by the lord's chair and contemplated her next move. There was little she could do until the king responded. But little didn't mean nothing and nothing was the last thing she would do. Looking up, she wasn't surprised when Lionel slid into the seat to her right.

"What are you contemplating?" Lionel took her hand. "Taking the men out to search a day's ride in all directions?"

"Perhaps." Alexandria nodded. "I know my godfather will send men out to do the same when he receives my note."

"I'm sure he will." Lionel agreed. "The Sheriff of Lothian is his most valuable servant." As well as a trusted friend. "The king's reach will far exceed ours by the time he is done, but we can make a start."

"We can." Alexandria agreed. "What I'm thinking is that we form a search party made up of you, me, Eaun, and Colban. Each of us will take two men and head in a different direction." She nodded liking the way that sounded. "If anyone thinks I will sit by idly wringing my hands when I could help find my husband, think again."

She expelled a deep breath and pulled her hand from beneath Lionel's as she rose to her feet. While the gesture was meant to be comforting, it was anything but. No matter how innocently meant, that was the kind of thing to set tongues wagging and the last thing any of them needed.

"Let's get moving." Lionel fell in step beside Alexandria as she headed for the stairs. "The easiest plan of action is to head out from the four corners of the keep and meet back in the great hall before dusk to compare our reports."

Glancing up at Lionel, Alexandria shook her head in disbelief. While he didn't openly contradict her, she saw the truth in his eyes. He didn't think she should lead a search party for whatever reason. Most likely because he didn't think she could handle what they found. Nothing could be farther from the truth and he needed to get over his need to protect her from the truth.

"You might as well get that look off your face. I won't stand around while my husband is missing so you best forget the words hovering on your lips. I won't listen to whatever you wish to say nor will I stay here while Thor is God only knows where enduring God only knows what."

Hearing that determined lilt in her voice, Lionel knew this was an argument he couldn't win. Nor did he want to. While he didn't like Alexandria being out there with only two men to protect her; he knew as well that nothing would deter her from participating in the search.

He would feel the same way in her shoes. While his lady hadn't been to battle since the twins were born, she hit the training yard regularly. From what he'd seen, she was still in fine fighting form. If knowing that wasn't enough to reassure him, he had no right or reason to interfere with her plans. Only the not-so-secret desires of his heart that everyone wisely chose to ignore.

"Then I'll get the men together while you change." He already had eight loyal, discrete warriors in mind. "Zan, we will find Thor. You have my word." While spoken with confidence, Lionel prayed he wasn't making empty promises. "We will."

"If we don't?" Alexandria stood her ground. At this point, empty promises were meaningless. "He may be dead."

That was possible, even probable, given the amount of blood coating that saddle. They both knew that.

"He isn't." Lionel firmly believed she would know if that were true. "But if we're wrong, you will be fine."

The love in his eyes conveyed he'd make sure of it. Resisting the urge to walk into his arms and take the comfort he offered, Alexandria opened her chamber door instead. Knowing he was dismissed Lionel silently stopped to rest his hand on her arm.

"I'll get everyone ready to leave while you change." Then he would order Loki saddled. "We'll meet in the bailey when you're ready."

Alexandria nodded as she closed the door behind him. Saying a silent prayer they found Thor in time, she quickly donned a long black tunic, black leggings, and the black boots she usually wore in the training yard. Touching the embroidered wolf rampant on her tunic, she heard her husband's laughter in her head.

He'd been greatly amused that she so openly labeled the lady of Drummond his when she'd displayed her latest creation a few weeks ago. Her saucy response was that she'd not labeled herself his, but rather labeled the Golden Wolf hers. That had amused him even more. Closing her eyes, she recalled the tender seduction that followed before exiting her fantasy.

Fastening her belt around her waist, she sheathed her sword and the familiar jewel-handled dirk in their scabbards before adding her throwing knives to the eclectic mix of weaponry hanging from her waist and lurking in easy grab pockets throughout her attire. She'd much prefer having Avenger at her side, but that wasn't possible. She lacked the size and strength to wield the weapon effectively so the sword would stay safely locked away in their weapons trunk.

Taking a moment to contemplate her hair, she decided to leave well enough alone. The intricate coils and plaits would work as well as a tucked braid to deter anyone from grabbing her hair. Fastening her mantle, she bounced down the stairs, not surprised to find Reina lurking near the bottom step.

"You're doing this?" Reina shook her head over her cousin's revealing attire. "Lionel said you were, but I didn't believe him."

"Believe him." Alexandria rested her hands on her cousin's arms. "I can't sit around here waiting impatiently for my men to return."

"Are you ready for this?" Her cousin was surprisingly calm. "Truly ready?"

"As ready as I'll ever be." Huffing, Alexandria's response was honest. "As ready as anyone can be."

"What if you find what you don't wish to find?" They both knew that was a possibility. "What no one wishes to find."

"Then I'll bring my husband home," As she had with her father and brothers a lifetime ago. "And do what must be done."

"You are stronger than I." They both knew she would fall apart if anything happened to Lionel. That was one reason Alexandria walked away so long ago. Though she'd loved Lionel with a young girl's love, she'd known her cousin loved him more. "I don't think I could stand it if anything happened to Lionel."

"Perhaps." Alexandria knew Reina was stronger than she believed. "However, I have no choice. Thor expects me to bring him home."

Whether riding a horse or draped over his saddle.

"Yes, he does." Reina agreed. "Just as he would find you."

"He would." Alexandria smiled softly. "We'll return before nightfall. Pray we don't return without our lord. Preferably among us in the land of the living."

"I will." Reina nodded already planning to gather the women in the chapel for an afternoon of prayer along with Father Eustace. "I'll also watch over the cubs and keep everyone calm."

While she might not be good warrior stock, she excelled at keeping the household on track when their lady was away. Her reliability was her contribution to her family, people, and home.

"I can't ask for anything more." Alexandria hugged Reina. "I'll see you in a few hours. We all will."

Turning, Alexandria walked out the open doors into the bailey. Glancing at the men congregating in groups, she decided Lionel had done well. There wasn't anyone she was uncomfortable with participating in the search party. Instead, she thought he'd chosen exceptionally well as the men had already fallen in line with the partners they worked best with.

"Lionel, take Aymer and Gamelin and head South. Lowrans and Odart, you're with me heading East. Johnne and Adamnán, you're with Eaun going West. Colban, you take Ludan and Hendrie through the North country. Search as far and wide as possible before nightfall and return home before dark. I don't want to send parties out after you."

"Yes, my lady." Colban motioned for Ludan and Hendrie to swing into the saddle. "We'll return before dark hopefully with our lord between us."

Alexandria nodded knowing that none of them expected to bring Thor home uninjured. Nothing about that idea made sense. He would already be home if he were not hurt or worse. She knew also that no hostages were kept in this truce between David and Stephen. Lionel told her so.

Instead, each side left the battle with their armies intact knowing they would return home only to fight again another day. While her godfather's victory wasn't as decisive as they'd hoped, he seized valuable land with valuable keeps for the Scottish crown. How long he would keep either remained to be seen.

The next skirmish would decide whether they were moving two steps forward or ten steps back. It always did. The two kings had honed land grabs back and forth between the two counties to a fine art as had the kings before them and as would the kings after them as well. None of that mattered right now.

What mattered was Thor should have returned right before or right after his men. He hadn't. Since he'd helped the king plan the battle, her godfather had no cause to detain him at Court after the treaty was signed. He knew her husband was anxious to return home and that she was anxious for his return. There was no good reason for Thor's continued absence. Caturix's sudden appearance confirmed her fears.

Watching Colban and his men exit the bailey, Alexandria watched Eaun follow. Falling in line she knew Lionel and his men would take up the rear. Once they were well without the gates, each team would head in their assigned direction. While going North of Drummond made little sense, she knew Colban would guide his team more Northwesterly than actual North. That did make sense.

Then again, it wasn't impossible Thor had decided to check in with a neighboring lord in an official capacity. Nor was it impossible that he was helping a wounded lord home. He had done both in the past. However, she didn't think that was true this time, not with that bloodied saddle. That had a far more ominous feel.

One she didn't want to contemplate. Alexandria urged Loki towards the coast, motioning for her men to follow. Perhaps Thor had stopped at a keep for help and their messenger had yet to reach Drummond. While plausible, she wasn't holding her breath on that one either.

CHAPTER NINE

Leaning against the wall in hopelessness, the warrior contemplated falling from his saddle all those weeks ago. Bleeding profusely, he'd prayed his mount escaped the fray and made his way to the royal keep. If he did his bloodied saddle would tell the tale that none of them might live to share. If he failed no one would ever know of the betrayal. Fifteen good men would disappear off the face of the earth as their attackers wanted.

Growling to himself, the prisoner recalled that day with renewed hate. Outmanned and overwhelmed, he'd lain on the hard ground hovering on the edge of consciousness. While his eyes were closed and his body limp his other senses were highly engaged. Tapping into the same sensory efficiency a sightless person used to map their environment he had a fair grasp of everything and everyone around him.

"Locate any of these fools unfortunate enough to linger and load them up." From the grunts and groans around him, he'd realized he wasn't the only man to survive the attack. Though not likely for long from the man's cruel laughter. "Tate and Bescomb will appreciate having new toys."

Although his heart rate accelerated in recognition the more the brute talked, he remained limp. The one mark in his favor was he knew this man by his voice, but the monster didn't know him. One of Stephen's less scrupulous minions, Ricard de Vescy was a soulless bastard known for his pointless cruelty and treacherous ways. Feeling his body lifted and tossed over a horse's back, he'd known they were nowhere near the nightmare's end. He was right. Nothing had changed in the weeks since.

Watching Bescomb and Tate lock the bloody, brutalized body back in his manacles, the golden-haired giant hung his head in sorrow. Gervaise was naught but a boy. A handsome, courageous, silver-haired boy recently knighted who would have become a fine warrior in time. Ever valiant, he'd known nothing of the king's plans.

Why should he? He was but a fledgling warrior intoxicated by the excitement of war. He knew nothing of the gore, the stench, or the cries of dying men. Or he hadn't before now. He should be home with his family celebrating his bravery and the king's victories instead of drowning painfully in his blood.

Tate and Bescomb had taken malicious pleasure in beating the youngest member of their party to death bruise by painful bruise, break by painful break, over the last weeks until he'd finally reached the end of his endurance. If he didn't miss his guess, and he didn't, the boy would succumb to his injuries in a short while. He suspected the final beating shattered a rib that pierced his lung and sealed his fate. He'd know the moment his spirit departed his body by those final shuddering rattles.

Closing his eyes, the man lamented being one of only three still living. Nine of their party perished outright in the ambush. Two died within the first week from their injuries while another lingered a few agonizing days before infection claimed his life. A third warrior he didn't know succumbed to starvation two weeks ago and Gervaise was drawing his final ragged breaths if those wet gasps were any indication.

He knew the torturers would go for Theobald next. The demons preyed on the weakest link and Teddy was it. Not that the poor fool knew anything. He didn't. He hadn't before. He knew even less caught in the thrall of madness. The warrior knew he was fortunate the trolls had ceased to torment him a while back. There was no pleasure in whipping a man who made no sound.

Truthfully, he had no sound to make. Not anything they wanted to hear. He'd quickly learned the moans, groans, and cries of his fellow prisoners did nothing to ease their suffering. Begging for mercy made the torture worse. Even had he been a man to make those sounds, he wouldn't have. He learned from others' mistakes.

Besides, how could he tell them anything? He didn't know his name. He'd realized that soon after his fever finally broke a while back. Nor did he know the names of his companions. He'd learned a few from the brief snatches of conversations he'd overheard the last few weeks.

There hadn't been an opportunity to get acquainted before the attack. No, there had been. They'd preferred to ride hell for leather toward home instead. There would be time for small talk over a light repast of bread and cheese while their horses rested. Unfortunately, or perhaps fortunately for him, everyone who knew his identity died outright. Or he hoped they had. Closing his eyes in weariness, the man waited for an end not yet come.

⸻ ᪣ ⸻

ONE WEEK LATER

Eyes adjusting to the inkiness around him, Thor knew it was night. Faint glimmers of light penetrated his prison during the daylight hours which added a deeper dimension to the impenetrable darkness once the sun went down. A dimension filled with unsettling creatures and sounds.

While common sense told him this torment was but the skittering and gnawing of rats and the slithering of snakes or newts, he understood why Theobald lost his mind long before they suspended him in that cage. Suggestion was a powerful tool in the hands of the enemy. It was an effective weapon he'd used many times to his advantage. Immobile within his newest prison, his final companion expired in a torrent of spit, gibberish, and bodily fluids on the third day.

While Theobald's passing wasn't unexpected, the added stench of rotting flesh grew oppressive within hours of his death. His passing signaled as well that as the only surviving prisoner, the torturers would come for him next. His only option was to escape or die.

Thor would have known that with or without his memory. This wasn't his first sojourn in hell's hostel. He doubted it would be his last. However, being surrounded by rotting corpses wasn't healthy mentally or physically, so it was time to go. Knowing who and what he was had given him an edge he didn't have even a day ago.

Overhearing the guards discussing a breach in the walls that couldn't be repaired for days energized him in ways he hadn't been since his capture. Just knowing there was a window of escape gave him hope. Rising to his feet, Thor carefully pulled against his manacles.

Ignoring the sting of metal grating flesh, he slowly worked both hands out of the restraints as quietly as possible. While he lamented the agony of shredding skin, he appreciated the slick lubrication of blood against iron. Grateful his guardians no longer found it necessary to bind his ankles, he carefully stepped away from the wall glad to be free.

Heading towards the breach, Thor used his hands to guide him along the lichen and nitre-encrusted tunnel ignoring the feel of slime beneath his palms. Snorting at the skitter of rats running over his feet and the slithering of snakes and newts nearby, he continued through the darkness praying for the faintest shimmer of light to illuminate the opening before his strength was gone.

Sliding down the wall he rolled over to drag his body along the floor stopping every few feet to catch his breath. While a lesser man might find his condition shameful, this wasn't the first time he'd propelled himself across the rocky ground on his belly, usually through far more unpleasant substances than filthy groundwater and sewage.

Hanging his head and leaning against the wall to rest, he caught the faintest glimmer of light from the corner of his eye. Taking a few deep breaths, Thor summoned a fresh wave of strength from deep within his gut. Forcing his legs to support him, he dragged himself along the wall to the edge of the jagged break.

From the debris littering the massive hole, it was evident the ground had given away beneath a section of the inner wall due to underground instabilities easily detected by a good engineer. It was equally apparent that step was bypassed here. Knowing de Vescy was either too arrogant to use the services of good engineers or too shallow in the coffers to hire them would play in his favor down the road.

Slipping through the breach, Thor flattened himself against the wall blending easily into the shadows. Scoping the guards milling about, he realized no one considered the breach of an inner wall a liability. Even a breach accessible to the prisoners languishing in the dungeon.

Oh, that's right, the only prisoner still alive was on his last leg. Barely breathing much less moving the last time he was seen. Since there was no danger from that quarter guards near the breach weren't necessary. While a common mistake, it wasn't one he would have made. If there was one thing he knew, it was the little things one ignored that came back to bite one on the arse. He'd learned that lesson early on.

Noting the guards playing dice and being lax in their duties, Thor slipped along the wall a few feet at a time until he reached the outer wall. As he expected, there was a small breach in the corner yet to be detected. Again, another breach suddenly appearing not far from the first break wasn't unexpected either.

Mistakes were made in constructing the keep that compromised the foundations. He'd noted that from his prison cell. However, he never expected to use those errors to his advantage. While it was unlikely his captor knew of this latest breach, he would learn soon after daybreak on the morrow.

Stopping to glance at his wrists and hands he was pleased to see he was no longer bleeding and the ground water had washed the last of the blood away. Satisfied he wouldn't leave telltale droplets behind to give his route away, Thor slipped through a crack he would have never fit through at his most robust. Literal skin and bones were another matter.

Flattening himself against the wall yet again, he listened to the talk above him. He needed to pinpoint where each sentry was to the best of his ability while he edged ever closer to the clump of trees nearest the keep. While it was a cloudy night, being seen weaving across the open land between the keep and the cover of brush was the last thing he wanted to happen.

If he survived, he would end up trapped in the dungeon he'd just escaped. He'd likely be offed with a short bow arrow to the back instead. Seeing the forest looming before him, Thor stopped and leaned against the wall. From the commotion above him, it seemed some fools were getting into a scuffle over weighted dice while others were trying to stop them.

Deciding it was now or never, he headed for the forest listening for the soft, high-pitched whistle of arrows flying towards their target. Hearing nothing, he penetrated deep into the thicket and collapsed against a tree. While unable to prevent leaving tracks, he'd zigzagged over grass hoping to leave as few footprints as possible.

Once he exited the other side, he'd use Polaris and the moon to get his bearings. He didn't believe he was that far from where they were ambushed. That they were attacked on Alba's soil added to the heinousness of the attack, but it also signaled he wasn't far from the borderlands either. Knowing that he had a rough idea of which direction to go and how many miles stood between him and his king.

CHAPTER TEN

Maccus Keep, Roxburghshire

Stopping to rest against a tree while he caught his breath, Thor refused to admit he'd crawled over more rugged terrain the past few days than he'd walked. Forget the people he'd scared witless or the scraps he'd stolen along the way. He was quickly reaching the end of his endurance. He would die where he lay unless he could find the strength to rise and wobble from the forest around him.

Grabbing the trunk of the hazel tree, he pulled himself to his feet inch by painful inch. Leaning into the branches, he felt the bark and the leaves beneath his cheek. Gathering his strength, he sternly reminded himself he was but the distance of the no man's land between the forest and the outer walls of the keep from salvation. All he had to do was get from here to there. Forcing one bloody foot in front of the other, the lone figure emerged from the ticket silently praying to whatever god chose to listen that one lone sentry would recognize him wavering in the breeze.

Staring over the countryside from his post on the battlement, a Norman sentry noted the figure emerging from the fog. Ignoring the cries of draugr or aptrgangr uttered all around him, he knew better. While impossibly tall and clothed in filthy tatters, the skeletal being weaving in the mist was a living, breathing man. He was sure of it. One he was intimately familiar with. Not an evil undead returned from the barrow to rip them limb from limb bare-handed as his companions feared. This was real life, not some bard's tale to scare enfants into obedience. How could they be so foolish? Shouting to his captain, he hurried down the ladder and motioned for the gates to open.

Unsure what threat awaited them in the mist, the guards watched the figure shuffle through the entrance to the inner bailey as they swiftly closed the massive gates behind him. Not daring to leave their posts for fear of an

English trap, the men watched the emaciated warrior covered in rags, blood, and filth confidently enter the keep. Trudging through opened doors, he hobbled towards the great hall knowing the nightmare ended at the end of the corridor in front of the high seat.

Surprised that the outer gates opened to him much less the inner doors to the royal keep, he knew he had Roget to thank. He was likely the only guard familiar enough with the man he used to be to recognize the shadow of the man he'd become. He was also the only sentry willing to ignore the ridiculous cries of draugr he'd heard all around him. Fools. As though he had the power to create fog to shield himself or the supernatural strength to rend a mighty warrior from end to end. Perhaps in his berserker days, he may have come close. Not now. Not when it was a struggle to ease one foot in front of the other.

"Your Majesty," Thor uttered the title that seldom passed his lips as he fought to remain standing. "Dauíd." That was more like it.

Staring at the apparition before him, the king snorted at the thought that few men dared such intimacy in private and lived to tell about it. There was but one who dared such a feat in public. The one so inelegantly trembling before him looking like something recently dragged from the grave. If what he suspected was true, that thought wasn't as far off the mark as it seemed.

"Thor?" Stepping closer, David ignored the breath-stealing stench of pus and death wafting from the black-skinned wight. "Prepare the bathing chamber, summon the healer, and bring this man something to eat and drink. He who was lost is home again."

Nodding his gratitude, the Wolf knew there were better uses for his rapidly fading strength than words. While he would prefer viands to a bath his wounds needed tending first. That couldn't happen until he was clean.

However, he did accept the cloth-wrapped trencher and the goblet of wine. Staring at the piece of bread folded over a bite of sauced lamb, he knew two things: this bit of sustenance would but whet his appetite, and to eat his fill would prove disastrous. Even deadly. His body had grown unaccustomed to regular feedings. As much as he hated the thought, gruel and thickened broths would sustain him for the foreseeable future instead of the meat and bread he preferred. Once he'd sufficiently recovered from the detriments of starvation, he could eat again.

Allowing himself to be led away, Thor knew better than to sit. He wouldn't rise again. As it was, his strongest desire was to fall to his knees and crawl. He wouldn't display such weakness. Not in the presence of his allies or, more importantly, his enemies. He was the Golden Wolf. He bowed to no one even his king.

He would get through the next couple of hours before he allowed himself the rest his body craved. Once he was down, he was done. He wouldn't awaken for hours. Perhaps days. Glancing at the vacant bench nearest the king, he wouldn't sleep in that space anytime soon. He would lay on a bed in the infirmary recuperating from his wounds and regaining his strength instead.

Entering the bathing chamber, Thor watched as the massive tub was filled before he stripped and tossed his tunic and trousers into the fireplace. Watching what was left of putrid rags go up in smoke, he lowered himself into the tub and reached for the soap. Using the last of his energy he scrubbed one arm staring in disbelief as filth gave way to pale skin he hadn't seen in months.

Collapsing against the tub's rim, he closed his eyes and breathed deeply. He was grateful when other hands resumed doing what he no longer had the strength to do. Allowing himself to be scrubbed with soap bearing a hauntingly familiar scent, he laid his head back against the tub and surrendered to the detached ministrations of the healers. While the sensual touch of feminine hands would be more appealing, he laughed out loud knowing seductive intentions would get the unlucky female nowhere. It would be much longer than he liked before he resumed his lecherous ways.

Looking around him, Thor appreciated the comfortable familiarity of the room. Something told him that he'd bathed here many times. Not only him but his men as well. Visions of masculine comradery flashed through his mind as he moaned softly at the feel of strong fingers kneading the muck from his hair. It was more than he could do for himself at the moment. Accepting aid to rise, he stood as water sluiced over him. Watching the tub emptied and refilled, he slowly lowered himself into the clean water knowing the process would likely happen several more times before the water ran clean. Months in a pit was filthy business.

CLOTHED IN A LONG LINEN tunic and settled comfortably on a trestle bed, Thor surveyed the room as he set his empty cup aside. While the last few hours of scrubbing, cleaning, stitching, and debriding of wounds had been unpleasant, it was necessary if he stood a chance of surviving much less becoming the man he used to be.

He didn't need the healers to explain that. He'd been a warrior long enough to know how the game was played. He knew also that while he could hold his cup of broth today, the same might not be true tomorrow. He was far from out of the woods and he wouldn't be for weeks to come. If he survived the infections and fevers ravaging his body, it would be a miracle.

Now that the desperation that fueled his escape had dissipated, he knew how ill he was. He knew as well that this was where many valiant warriors died. When the skirmish was over. When they thought themselves safe. He didn't intend to die so ignominiously. Unlike them, his battle had just begun and he refused to die. Like all good warriors, he would live to fight again.

Cocking his head, Thor listened to the activity all around him. If he didn't miss his guess, and he didn't, the king would appear any second now. He'd recognize that tread anywhere. Watching the door swing open, he wasn't surprised to see he was right.

"How do you feel?" The king settled in the vacant chair by the bed. "You look better than you did when you entered the hall."

"Draugr...right." Thor barked at the thought. "As for looking better," He glanced at the king. "I'm clean and free."

Either of those things could account for the change in his demeanor.

"We feared you were lost," David answered honestly. "When you didn't return when your mount did, I sent a search party out to find you."

While Thor didn't know it, those words weren't strictly true. Yes, he had sent a party out searching for the Golden Wolf; but his wasn't the first. Alexandria led several attempts to find her husband before he knew he was gone.

"They found the rotting corpses of my traveling companions instead," Thor growled at the disgraceful memory. "We were ambushed by one of

Stephen's lords just over the border." It was a simple statement of fact. "There were too many to fend off...Six of us survived the rout...I survived captivity."

David nodded. "What happened to the other men?" While he had his suspicions, he needed to know.

"Gervais succumbed to the torture chamber." Thor stared at the ceiling as though he was hearing the man's agonized screams reverberating through his head. He'd been tormented to death for nothing. The poor boy had nothing to betray. Not even Thor's identity. He hadn't known it. "Theobald went mad." He wasn't long for this world when mad ravings turned to mindless gibberish. "The other three succumbed to infection and starvation."

"And you?" The king stared him straight in the eyes.

"I had the mental and physical fortitude to withstand the deprivations." Thor stared back. "You don't look surprised."

"I'm not." David's lips turned up slightly at the corners. "You've survived situations making other warriors shudder."

The Golden Wolf was so feared and revered for a reason. While it seemed unlikely, he was fortunate to be captured by one of the only lords in the empire not to recognize who he had at his mercy. Maybe his poor physical state helped obscure his identity. He would have been slaughtered outright had he known.

De Vescy made it clear from the start that there would be no ransom. They would die in the pit, decreasing David's army by six strong warriors. While some of the men could have possibly betrayed his identity, they didn't. They'd known that nothing positive would come of it. Nothing save denying them their only hope of escape. Or vengeance. Even if they didn't make it, those men were confident one of them would survive to share their fate. They knew as well that the Wolf would avenge their betrayal as only he could once he did.

"You are right." It was that knowledge that had pulled him through. "When my companions broke at learning we wouldn't be ransomed, I vowed vengeance deep in my soul."

That determination pulled him through dark days when all hope was lost. When he didn't know his name. When he wished to die as his companions had.

"Where were you?" That no ransom demand was made for the return of the Sheriff of Lothian was disturbing. His captors should have known he would pay any amount for the return of his most formidable warrior. "Zan nor I received ransom demands."

"That doesn't surprise me." And he knew why. "Who is this Zan? Have you wed again in my absence?"

David schooled his features at his unsettling words. Fortunately, he had learned long ago not to betray his thoughts. There were times when that was much too dangerous. No matter how shocked he was.

"I have not." The king shook his head. "However, Lady Zan is a dear friend." Catching Thor's lecherous expression, David clarified. "Not a mistress. She is much too young."

"I see." Thor snorted softly. "Like that ever stopped anyone before."

"No, it never stopped you, but we can leave that for another day." Warning bells were ringing in his head. Something terrible was awry here and he needed to know what. "I am glad you are here; however it will be a while before you can resume your duties. Perhaps you would like to go home as soon as you can travel."

"I prefer to remain here," Thor stated bluntly. "You know Ruthven is not my home."

While he wished he felt different, the keep was much too cold. Literally and figuratively speaking. One wife had died screaming in the master's solar, and the other had died in a fall from her horse not that far from the castle gates. He didn't know why he remembered either of those things. It wasn't like he'd held either woman in great affection. Lady Brigetta turned his stomach once he'd learned of her intimacies with her brother. Lady Julia's indiscrete indiscretions would have made a laughing stock out of a lesser man. As it was, he'd felt nothing at her death.

"I see." David leaned forward. "Thor, what are you hiding?"

"I am Thorauld Sweynsson, Sheriff of Lothian, and Lord of Ruthven," Thor stated bluntly staring him down. "I am the Golden Wolf in the service of my king. I call you and Prince Henry my friends. That is all."

Reading between the lines, the king immediately knew what he was saying without saying anything.

"I see." The pieces were starting to fall into place. "You have lost your memories."

"Aye." Thor agreed. "Most of them. I remembered who and what I was a week ago. That knowledge gave me the strength to scurry through a breach in the dungeon wall like a rat from a hole in the middle of the night. It took most of the day to free myself from the manacles."

David glanced at his hands and wrists knowing the skin was shredded and inflamed beneath bloodied bandages. He refused to imagine the agony the man had endured to free himself. That he had was a miracle and a personal testament to Thor's intestinal fortitude. To his willingness to do what must be done. Rising to his feet, David prepared to take his leave.

"I'll check on you later." He patted Thor's shoulder knowing he was one of the few men allowed such liberty. "We will talk more. For now, rest and recuperate. In time your memories will return and you can resume your duties. What you have experienced is not uncommon with head injuries."

From the healer's words, that wound alone should have killed him without months of deprivation spent underground in a frigid, dank oubliette. Staring at the man, the change in him was unimaginable. It was evident he'd received just enough sustenance to prolong his suffering while barely sustaining life. There was no denying his vassal was a dead man walking. Taunt skin stretched across protruding bones was all that differentiated him from the bleached carcasses on the moor. From limp hair to sunken eyes to his emaciated body this man was but a whisper of the man he used to be.

Leaving the room, the king pondered his next move. The situation was tricky on several fronts, not the least of which was his mightiest warrior may not pull through. His organs could still seize up. Oswald admitted not long ago that there was no guarantee the Sheriff would survive this ordeal even with his exceptional care. His condition was much too grave. Then there was the issue of Thor's memory. Or rather his lack thereof.

While his strongest desire was to inform his goddaughter that her husband lived, David's instincts urged caution for the foreseeable future. It was clear Thor recalled neither his bride nor his family. However, that didn't mean he wouldn't eventually summon de Montluzan for a secret meeting.

He would wait until he knew the Wolf would pull through then he would dispatch his messenger. Once he talked with the other warrior, he would plot his next move. Satisfied his dilemma was resolved for now, the king made his way back to the great hall to enjoy the evening's entertainment satisfied he had done all he could do for the present.

CHAPTER ELEVEN

"**M**y King, is it true?" Aimee FitzAlan walked over to stand beside the monarch. "Has the Wolf returned?"

"It is true." Reaching out, David draped Aimee's arm over his not surprised the woman had learned of her ex-lover's return. "Oswald believes he has finally turned the corner. He is fairly confident that he will live."

"That is good." Aimee nodded. "Then why is Alexandria not by his side?"

"Because nothing is as it seems." David led her down the hall. "Perhaps you should see for yourself. While the court knows our Golden Wolf is here, that is all they know. I prefer to keep it that way for a while. However, you and Thor are close. I believe it will do him good to see you."

If the meeting went as he hoped, Aimee's help would be invaluable in convincing his Sheriff that some of the more unpalatable things he would soon learn were true. Otherwise, he doubted Thor would believe him. He wouldn't readily accept that he was not only wed but bound to his sovereign by an oath of fealty. The man he was now would cling to the man he had been. He would believe his word was his bond. That was enough for his king in the past; it was enough for now.

Shaking his head against the futility of that coming argument, David decided to allow that sleeping dog to lie as long it would. He would have to confront him soon enough. Once Thor was back on his feet there was little he could do in the way of damage control.

By its very nature, the royal court was a sewer of rumor and innuendo. Stopping to knock on the door, Oswald or one of his helpers should be just about through changing Thor's bandages. Seeing the healer's lined face appear in the doorway, he wasn't surprised when Oswald exited the chamber with a nod as they walked in. He would get the latest update on his Wolf's health sometime in the late afternoon after the healer finished his rounds.

"Good morning." David gently pushed Aimee forward. "I've brought you a guest far prettier than me."

Wincing as he pushed himself up a little higher on his pillows, Thor studied the ebony-haired beauty through piercing amber eyes. Those stormy violet eyes gazing back at him in open disbelief made him think he knew her. Not only knew her, but that her name balanced precariously on the tip of his tongue.

The not knowing wasn't pleasant. However, looking at her was. The woman was a feast for the eyes. Tall and lithe with deep violet eyes, full red lips, an aristocratic nose, and the most luxurious raven curls he'd ever seen she embodied everything he admired in a woman. She was delicate and feminine in every way.

"Hello, Thor." The woman stepped forward. "I was worried about you."

"While that is good to know," No man in his right mind would find a beautiful woman's concern amiss. "I am doing well as you can see."

Something about the soft 'hah' that passed her lips betrayed she felt differently. Her opinion aside, compared to his last accommodations he was doing wonderful. A lavender-scented down-stuffed mattress and pillow beat the hell out of hard, urine and feces-stained rock. It certainly smelled better.

"I am glad." Aimee studied him openly knowing instinctively that something was very wrong.

Something more ominous than his emaciated form or infected injuries. If she didn't know better, she would think the Wolf didn't know her. While hedgy at the best of times, this felt different. Before, while she knew he trusted her as implicitly as she trusted him, she'd known he was a man of few words for a reason.

The stoic guardian of invaluable state secrets, the Wolf refused to risk casually betraying the information he was entrusted to retain. However, the glint in his eyes conveyed that while carefully navigating the situation, this man was lost in every possible way. She'd known him intimately long enough to recognize what others would miss.

"I will leave you to get reacquainted," The king's voice pierced their thoughts. "I fear I am needed in the great hall. I have a meeting with Abbott Boniface. I suspect he wishes to fleece me yet again to make the same unnecessary repairs to the monastery I approved last year. In truth, he is hoarding coins until he can commission that ornate gold reliquary for the big toe of St. Rule that he believes will bring the pilgrims flocking."

Thor laughed out loud at the thought of that doddering old fool fleecing anyone. The king was onto him years ago. While he'd outright refused to give the man the astronomical sum he wanted to have a solid gold and gemstone reliquary commissioned for the questionable bit of bone, most likely procured from the graveyard behind the abbey, the king wasn't above toying with him. If he didn't miss his guess, Boniface would have his reliquary by this time next year. It would have only taken a handful of years to lie his way to acquiring his heart's desire.

He only hoped King David would feel half so generous when funds were needed to make real repairs to the monastery roof in the coming years. If his reliquary was half as successful as he believed it would be, the old monk shouldn't need to ask the crown for anything. Thor wished him well. The Norse in him appreciated Boniface's cunning while the royal servant would gladly send the old man packing. Watching the king pat Aimee on the shoulder as he walked out the door closing it behind him, Thor waited patiently for his opponent to make her next move and expose her hand.

"We both know Boniface is no fool even if you refer to him that way in your head." Her words told Thor she knew him better than he'd thought. "A swindler and a cheat, maybe. But never a fool."

"All right." Thor nodded. "Perhaps you are right."

"I know I'm right." Aimee leaned forward. "And I believe I understand what the king meant now."

"What the king meant about what?" Thor leaned back against his pillows. "Has David been talking behind my back?"

"What do you think?" Aimee's words were light but her tone was not. "I believe I know what he meant when he said nothing is as it seems. While you look like the man you've always been, you aren't."

"Really?" Thor dismissed her words deciding for all her beauty the woman had lost her mind. "I am nothing but the man that I have always been."

"Are you?" Aimee leaned forward. "I don't think you are. More importantly, I don't think you know who I am."

"It is clear that you are a friend." David would never let her near him if she wasn't. Not with his vulnerabilities. "You wouldn't sit there if you weren't."

"You are right." Aimee agreed. "But we were more than friends. Much more."

Ah, she was a discarded lover. That would explain her change in attitude. That, and he'd all but admitted he didn't remember her. While he was reluctant to confirm her suspicions, this woman was in his room because the king was privy to intimacies he wasn't.

"Much, much more," Aimee admitted. "If you remembered me, you would already know."

"You are right." Thor tipped his hand. "I would, and I don't."

"I thought as much." Elbows on her thighs, Aimee rested her chin between her thumbs and forefingers. Inhaling a deep breath, she looked away visibly upset by his admission. Pondering what to do next, it wasn't long before she fixed him with her purple gaze. "I'm beginning to see what you do remember." She blinked in a wide-eyed way and shrugged. "But I'm lost when it comes to what you don't."

Thor nodded. "Why don't you start with us?"

"Fine." Aimee removed a violet gemstone pendant from beneath her chemise and pulled it over her head. "Do you remember this?"

Taking the gold chain from her hand, Thor studied the deep violet sapphire cabochon mounted in an elaborate gold setting. Closing his eyes, he remembered accepting the jewel for services rendered to Geoffrey le Breton in Rouen. He remembered commissioning the setting and the heavy gold chain soon after. It was an opulent piece he'd worn with pride for many years. Opening his eyes, he wondered briefly how such a rare gem came to be in the possession of Aimee FitzAlan. He couldn't imagine giving it to any woman. However, it appeared he had, and to the one whose name just popped into his head.

"I remember it well." Thor watched the pendant swing on the chain. "It was a gift for convincing an enemy that harrying my client's family wasn't in his best interest. Once the assignment was done, Geoffrey didn't feel I was adequately compensated for my trouble, so he gave me this stone. Who was I to argue with the Archbishop of Rouen?"

"Who indeed?" Aimee laughed knowing the Golden Wolf would challenge the Pope if he felt it was in his best interests. "You put that pendant into my hands for safekeeping not long before..." Halting midsentence, she realized what she'd almost said. "You left for your rounds four years ago." Not quite four years, but close enough. "We'd been together several years by then."

"You were my mistress?" Thor laid the pendant on the bed between them.

"Sometimes." Aimee nodded. "When you were at court and my husband was away."

That there were other women when he wasn't away remained unsaid. Thor nodded thinking that sounded like him. While he knew he was married in the past, he wasn't married now. It hadn't been necessary for the king to tell him that. He remembered both of his wives. He remembered their deaths as well.

While both women were overjoyed to wed the Sheriff of Lothian, neither truly wanted him. They wanted his wealth, his power, and his position. Nothing else really mattered. He'd been more relieved than grieved when both had passed away long before they should have.

"How did we meet?" Thor sat up a little taller ignoring the twinge in his ribs. "At court?"

"Yes." Aimee smiled. "I was watching the night you beat the king at chess. Our eyes met across the table."

Thor's laugh turned into a cough. He was sure more than their eyes met later that evening when a table was no longer between them. Aimee's laugh confirmed his suspicions were right.

"How long ago was that?" He didn't expect the sudden shuttering of her eyes. "Two or three years ago?"

He tended not to stay with one woman that long. However, a woman like Aimee FitzAlan may have changed his mind. He could see himself sharing her bed for more than a season.

"Six maybe more." Aimee took a moment to think. "Gilliard and I had been wed a year or so when we met...I'd turned eighteen the day before, and I'm twenty-five now...I guess it was seven years ago...So, we were together almost four years."

Off and on.

"What happened to change that?" From the way she sounded, they had been over for a while. "Why aren't we still together?"

He wasn't a man to cast beautiful, intelligent women aside for no good reason. Then again, he might not be the one who ended it. While he remembered her name, he remembered little else about Aimee FitzAlan. Nothing beyond a few images flitting through his head confirming they were lovers. He would never have seen her naked if they weren't.

While tempted to believe he was merely imagining the woman that way, he knew better. His mind couldn't concoct the small scar on her abdomen. The one she'd laughed off as the memento of a childhood fall. He would only recall such an insignificant thing now if he'd seen it in the past.

"Because you...tired of hearing me lament over the husband I loved who didn't love me in return." Though the words tripped easily off her tongue, Thor knew that wasn't what she'd meant to say. Aimee FitzAlan was hiding something. While he longed to call her on it, he decided to play along instead. "And because I finally conceived Gilliard's heir. When my husband learned I carried his child, he realized he visited Hereswyd out of habit not love."

That he could believe; there was comfort in familiarity.

"You should know that we were friends first and lovers second." Aimee gently informed him. "We spent as much time talking and playing chess as we did in bed,"

While that wasn't the usual way of things with him, Thor could see where that might happen with Aimee FitzAlan. The woman was more than just another pretty face. She was bright and engaging. Daring and different. He'd likely found her fascinating in any setting. He still did.

"I don't know why," Thor shrugged slightly. "But I believe you."

"Good." Aimee nodded. "From what I can see, you need a friend...You'll need one even more as you try to navigate court without your memories."

"Perhaps." Thor agreed. "However, I will need a friend I trust while my memories slowly return even more."

"I believe you will." Aimee agreed. "I will be here until Gilliard returns from France in a few weeks. I will help you as much as you let me until then."

"That is good." Thor lifted the chain and put the pendant around his neck. "This feels like it is back where it belongs."

"It is." Aimee laughed. "My husband will be glad to see you wearing it again, although it would have been returned long ago had it belonged to any other man." Gilliard would never have countenanced her keeping it.

In truth, she hadn't been holding the necklace for him. Thor had given it to her in remembrance of their friendship when he'd realized her husband had come to his senses. That Gilliard was finally home where he belonged. He'd wished her all the best and been glad her hopes were finally coming true. He'd then slipped the pendant over her head, kissed her cheek, and left to find his wife.

She'd kissed the pendant, tucked it under her collar, and joined Gilliard at the high table. While she often secretly wore the pendant to honor the man who finally made her husband see sense, she'd never worn it in Gilliard's presence after that first night. It didn't seem prudent to remind him of their past discontent.

"I don't know whether to feel relieved," Thor shrugged. "Or insulted your husband finds me no threat."

"You should feel honored." Aimee stood up and dropped a kiss on his cheek. "Gilliard considers you the man who brought us together."

"You are leaving?" He would miss her presence. "You will return?"

"I will visit soon." Aimee smiled softly. "I fear I have overstayed my welcome and Oswald will scold me if I don't leave soon. He doesn't want you overtired."

"I fear you are right." Thor suddenly realized how exhausted he was. "And I fear the healer is right as well."

"Perhaps I will join you for dinner if you would like?" Aimee stood in the open doorway. "I am sure Cook will prepare your favorites."

"I would like." Thor agreed. "Now, I believe I will rest."

Watching him lay back and close his eyes, Aimee quietly closed the door behind her and headed for the stairs.

———— ⚭ ————

HANDING THE REINS TO a stableboy, David patted his mount before heading for the dark-haired woman walking through Oswald's herb garden as though she knew what she was looking at. He doubted she did. His goddaughter was the only person he knew, other than the healer, who might come close to identifying all those plants. The old monk-turned-healer prided himself on cultivating rare medicinal plants that were difficult to grow and finding new uses for each. He considered himself fortunate to have such a man as the royal healer.

Alexandria seemed to feel the same. She'd spent years learning everything he was willing to share and never left the keep empty-handed. Oswald was delighted to share his medicinal blends with another talented healer especially if she was young and attractive. While he never stepped out of the line, the man had an eye for a pretty lass and his goddaughter was lovely to gaze upon. David shook his head as he focused on another young woman lovely to gaze upon.

"How did your visit go?" Looking up from the rose she was sniffing, Aimee shrugged as she smiled at her king.

"That good?" David laughed.

"The Wolf is the Wolf." As much as she wanted to pluck that sweet-smelling blossom, Oswald would have her head if she did so she wouldn't. "He is different yet the same. He knows of me, but he doesn't know me. However, I believe bits of his memory are returning."

"Yes, I believe so, too." David glanced around and was pleased to see they were alone as far as his eye could see. Oswald's garden was laid out in neat rectangular plots with walking paths in between and benches to sit on. The nearby well provided the water source the gardeners needed to maintain healthy plants and trees. Fortunately, at this time, he and Aimee were the only visitors enjoying the garden so he wasn't worried about anyone eavesdropping on their conversation. Besides, anything they discussed now would be common knowledge when Thor was well enough to rejoin the royal court. "I assume you plan on spending time with Thor while your husband is away?"

If history repeated itself, that was their usual pattern. Despite being happily wed, their relationship hadn't ended. No longer sexual, they remained close friends and confidants with the blessing of both their spouses.

That was why he had taken the woman to see the Sheriff and urged her to spend time with him. If anyone could coax Thor's memories to return, Aimee could.

"Cook has already agreed to send two trays to Thor's room for the evening meal." Aimee fell in step beside the king. "I intend to spend as much time as possible with him until Gilliard returns."

"Good." The king nodded. "You question why I haven't sent for his wife."

David stated what she dared not ask. If she were making the decisions, it would be Lady Alexandria seated by Thor's sick bed. Not a bedmate from years gone by.

"You are right." Aimee watched a stable boy exercising a horse across the way. "However, I suspect you have already sent for de Montluzan." The confirming nod was no surprise. "And you are waiting to see how much of Thor's memory returns as his wounds improve." She leaned over to smell an apricot rose. "Lastly, I suspect the Wolf doesn't know he is married and, when the time comes, you will wish me to urge him into his bride's waiting arms."

Something they both knew would be far easier said than done.

"Your suspicions are correct." Looking around them, the king sat on a bench confident no one loitered nearby. "There is nothing to gain by introducing Thor and Alexandria to each other right now. It will do more harm than good to both of them."

Thor would resist the idea of having a wife out of hand. When that happened, his goddaughter would be destroyed. He was navigating a delicate situation he had no idea how to handle.

"I fear you are right." It would certainly decimate his wife. "It is early yet. Who knows? Perhaps everything will be all right in a few weeks when Thor's injuries have healed."

"Perhaps." He doubted it. "Oswald seems to think some of his memories will return."

"But not necessarily the ones about his wife and family." Aimee plopped inelegantly beside the king. "You fear more than just the physical has robbed Thor of his memories."

"It has happened before." David agreed. "He remembers little more than he did when he first arrived and nothing about his family. He recalls who he is and the duties of a Shire Reeve. He recalls Ruthven as the place it used to be. Not as the home Zan made it. He remembers his youth, his father's murder, and being sent to Normandy. He remembers his glory days before he returned to Scotland with Henry. He even remembers his last judicial rounds and the skirmish that led to his imprisonment. He remembers everything that happened in that dungeon and how he escaped. What he doesn't remember is anything to do with Drummond.

"Then we must gently remind him of what he has lost," Aimee nodded as though that was the most brilliant plan she'd ever heard. "And ease him into his wife's waiting arms as soon as possible."

"Perhaps." David agreed. "I fear Alexandria will get hurt badly before that happens."

"Not by me." Aimee smiled softly. "I was as happy to see Thor content in his life as he was happy to see the same with me."

"Ah, but you are different from other women, my dear." The king smiled fondly at the woman. "Thor wouldn't value your friendship so if you weren't. However, other women will be less scrupulous. They will feel entitled to the opportunities they lost when Thor and Alexandria wed. As for the Wolf, if he remains the man he is now, he won't hesitate to accept their offers."

"I fear you are right." Aimee agreed. "As I fear Lady Zan will certainly hear of his infidelities."

"Once she understands the circumstances, she will forgive his transgressions for a while." He prayed he was right. He would have a mess on his hands otherwise. One he hoped to avoid until he had no other choice. "However, I fear what will happen if Thor crosses a line that cannot be uncrossed."

"Then he will lose everything he once held dear." Aimee said what they both knew. "Your goddaughter is not a weak woman. She will endure what she must for as long as she can. If Thor chooses to mistreat her rather than bowing to common sense as he did the first time, she will petition for dissolution of their vows."

"Which I will ensure happens." Favors of long-standing would be called in if need be. Somehow, he doubted that it would be necessary. "Once she is free, Zan will choose a new husband of her free will."

Not one born of desperation.

"It sounds like you have a plan in mind." Aimee rose to her feet. "One that can alter as circumstances change."

"I do and we shall see how well it works." The king agreed. "I trust you will keep what you have learned close to your chest until it becomes common knowledge."

"Not even Gilliard will hear a whisper until you give me leave." She promised. "As for wagging tongues, our friendship is well-known as is my loyalty to Gilliard. No one will believe we have rekindled what we once had."

Not even Gilliard. Especially not Gilliard so she had no worries there. He knew she counted every moment they were apart. She always had.

"I will do my best to dissuade such talk," David promised. "As much as I have enjoyed our time together, the Bishop is heading my way."

Turning slightly, Aimee realized the king was right. The Bishop was headed their way with a very determined look on his face. Respectfully taking her leave, she greeted the elderly clergyman in passing as she headed for the kitchen. After she met with Cook, she'd freshen up a bit before making her way to Thor's room. With any luck, Oswald would be through checking his bandages and clucking over his patient like an old woman by the time she made her presence known.

CHAPTER TWELVE

Riding into the bailey, Lionel dismounted and handed the reins to the waiting stable boy. Watching the lad lead the animal away he was confident the king knew of his arrival. His sentries were nothing if not alert, and he was instantly recognizable at a distance by size alone. Looking around him, he wasn't surprised when the doors suddenly opened to reveal King David. From the wording of his summons, he'd expected nothing less. Bowing, Lionel headed in the direction his monarch indicated.

"Thank you for coming so quickly." The king fell in step beside him. "The matter is urgent."

"Sire, you gave me no choice," Lionel stated bluntly. "We both know that."

"Perhaps." David agreed. "However, I have good reason for summoning you here."

"I am sure." Lionel agreed. "You would not have left Drummond vulnerable otherwise."

"You are right." The king nodded. "I wouldn't have."

"Have you learned something of my lord?" A part of him dreaded the king's response. "Is he dead?"

"Far from it." David shook his head. "Not physically anyway."

"What does that mean?" That wasn't what he expected to hear. "How can one be both alive and dead?

"Go to the training grounds and see for yourself." David stopped abruptly. "We'll talk when you return."

Nodding, Lionel silently did as his king commanded. Intimately familiar with the royal keep, he contemplated the best route to get to the training grounds unseen. Lurking behind a column he studied the man practicing a disciplined range of motions as though he were battling an opponent. He wasn't. He was practicing elementary swordplay with a blunt-edged training sword.

Unsurprising, the warrior was bare-chested despite the cool temperature. Not only shirtless, but sweat-drenched, emaciated, and weak. Barely able to wield the child's weapon clutched in his hands, he could never lift Avenger if he tried.

Lionel doubted he would ever lift the hallowed sword again. Thankfully, given recent events, he'd chosen not to risk his most valuable treasure in a lowly skirmish. He'd left the beloved heirloom behind at Drummond choosing to carry Móði instead.

While nothing like the warrior of old, the Wolf was still formidable from the fluidity of his movements and the assurance with which he dispatched his imaginary enemies. Once he'd recovered lost strength, he would be a worthy lord for his lady and a competent protector of his lands. But he'd never be the warrior he once was. Lionel was confident of that.

It wasn't possible to bounce back from such injuries if the scars littering his chest and back were any indication. Without the scar on his forehead that his hair had yet to cover. Even the most feared and revered warrior in the land was no match for the ravages he'd suffered.

Confident he'd seen enough, Lionel headed for his meeting with the king. If things went to plan, he would take his leave before this day was over. He'd been away from Drummond long enough. While he trusted the men he'd left behind to protect everything they held dear, Reina wasn't well.

Though she would never admit it, her health had slowly deteriorated since the fall of Drummond. Weaknesses plaguing her since childhood had grown worse and more persistent over the past few months. Though she hid it well, Alex was worried. If she was concerned, so was he. Heading back the way he'd come Lionel silently prayed the king would be brief. He needed to return home as soon as possible. There was nothing he could do here. While his lord was safe for the moment, his wife needed him.

"Your majesty," Lionel approached the king. "He is not the man he once was, nor is he likely ever to be."

The king nodded. "Perhaps." He couldn't shake the thought that Lionel was wrong. "However, if any man can return from the abyss, the Golden Wolf can."

"Perhaps." It was Lionel's turn to nod. "As there is nothing I can do here, I must take my leave. My wife is not well, and Drummond is vulnerable."

While his men were more than capable of protecting the keep, they could do nothing for Reina. Only his presence comforted her. While he didn't fear her dying anytime soon, the good periods had grown less frequent and farther apart. He wanted them to enjoy every good moment together that they could.

"You may go." There was no reason for him to stay. "You have seen what I needed you to see."

"I will inform Alexandria that Thor lives." He wasn't looking forward to that. "She will wish to be reunited as soon as possible."

"You will not," The king placed a restraining hand on his arm. "And she cannot."

"What?" Lionel recoiled slightly at his words. "You don't expect me to lie to Zan. To keep that her husband lives a secret?"

"I expect just that." The king ignored his outrage. "More than Thor's body has been damaged." The words were quiet. "He doesn't remember becoming my man." Seeing the slight widening of Lionel's eyes, David knew his words were gradually filtering through. "More importantly, he doesn't remember Drummond, Alexandria, or their children."

"You are saying..." Lionel couldn't finish the sentence.

"That Thor is back to being the man Alexandria married." That wasn't quite true either. "No, he is the man he was before he married Brigetta."

While that marriage scarred him deeply, it had softened him as well.

"Oh, my Lord." Lionel didn't know what to say. "If he doesn't know he has a wife and family..."

"Then he is the man he used to be." That was enough to convey what he didn't want to say. "While I am sure he will learn the truth despite my best efforts, I don't think he will care."

He was too busy living his life as a free man.

"Will his memories return?"

"No one knows." David shrugged. "I'm not sure it would matter if they did." He was confident it wouldn't. "The Wolf is the Wolf and he bows to no man."

"I didn't expect to see Thor in that shape when you summoned me." He didn't expect to see him at all. "If you had told me this was possible, I would never believe it. Given this change in circumstance, I will wait for further instruction before I do anything."

"Good." The king nodded. "Give my goddaughter my love and tell her to remain strong. She will get through this. Tell her to send word if she needs anything and I will send word if anything changes here."

"It is done." Lionel accepted the king's nod and watched him walk away before heading for the stables muttering, "My God, what are we going to do?" repeatedly under his breath.

Taking the reins of his horse from the stable boy, Lionel urged his mount towards the gates. While his spirit rebelled against keeping what he'd learned from his lady, he'd given his word. Even if he wanted to, he dared not expose the truth. To do so would cause more pain than it would salve. He knew that deep in his soul as well.

CHAPTER THIRTEEN

Four months later

Tamping down on his disgust, Lionel wondered why the king had sent for him again. Surely not to watch the massive blonde mountain cut a swathe through the bevy of court beauties from the shadows. While it was evident the past few months had made miraculous physical changes in the Wolf, it was equally clear that little had changed mentally. It was apparent that Thor either didn't know or, more likely, didn't care that he was a married man.

Dread roiling in his gut, Lionel knew with certainty why his presence was demanded at the royal keep. His liege felt it was time for his lady to learn the painful truth she had yet to learn. Against his will, he would be charged with informing Alexandria that her husband lived. Thor not only lived but thrived from what he saw before him.

As impossible as it seemed, the giant was more daunting and muscular than before his capture. That shouldn't be possible. The last time he'd seen the Wolf he was a walking cadaver, a revenant, a shadow of his former self. Broken in mind, body, and soul, the shire reeve should never have recovered from the havoc wreaked on his person. He'd not only recovered. He'd become more than he'd ever been.

Nothing about the man cutting confidently through the crowd harkened to the weak, wounded warrior he'd viewed all those months ago when he was first summoned to court. He was far from it. While he'd foolishly believed all was lost that day, he should have known better. The Golden Wolf wasn't bested by anyone or anything. Not even his body. This miraculous recovery attested to that fact.

While he'd respected the king's request he observed the traumatized warrior from afar the first time, his plea was no longer valid. Not when the Sheriff was stronger than he'd ever been. Taking a step forward, Lionel decided he was done accepting the obvious. It was time to discover how much of Thor's forgetfulness was real and how much the desire to start over unhindered by his wife and family. From what he'd seen tonight the man had done an admirable job of that already.

Following Thor out of the great hall into the bailey, he contemplated how best to corner his lord without being observed by David or his men. Seeing the Wolf halt in his tracks, he knew cornering him wasn't necessary. He shouldn't be surprised. It appeared the warrior was as adept at sensing he wasn't alone as he'd always been.

"Step into the light." Thor's hand instinctively rested on the pommel of his sword though Lionel made no threatening overtures. "Do I know you?"

"Aye." Lionel nodded. "You know me well."

"I see." Believing the warrior, Thor studied him while he wracked his brain for any memory of the sepia-haired giant. "We have fought together in the past...You are de Montluzan...I recruited you when Lord Oliphant hired me to recapture his keep a few years back."

That event was far longer than a few years back, but he wouldn't correct him. From what he'd been told, and what he could see, Thor was missing more than just bits and pieces of years long past. He was missing large chunks of time and the people who populated them.

From what the king said, Oswald believed he might recover more memories with time. Or he might not. What wasn't in question was that the man had no memory of his wife or family. Nor was he keen to regain the missing information. Instead, the Sheriff of Lothian seemed content to live in the present and resume his duties as his health improved.

"I am." Lionel agreed. "And we did."

He repressed a shudder at the memory. A hard-won battle, that fight wasn't dissimilar to the struggle to reclaim Drummond from Jamie MacLaren. Thor had gone berserker then too. Not only been berserker; but relished the violence and the carnage. Closing his eyes, he relived sights, sounds, and smells he'd hoped never to recall. It was a kind of madness he never wished to see again. He hadn't until Drummond. Although a while back, he had yet to wipe those memories from his mind.

"You are recalling past battles?" Thor nodded. "It is hard to forget some of them. Oliphant's was difficult for all of us."

"Yes, it was." Lionel agreed. "Although I never knew you felt that way."

"Sometimes the trance is a pleasure." Thor fixed him with that unsettling amber gaze. "Sometimes necessity."

Nodding his head, Lionel watched the man depart without another word leaving him staring at his back. From Thor's tone, Olifant was more necessity than pleasure though he'd believed otherwise at the time. Walking in the opposite direction, Lionel knew he'd learned something he probably should have guessed long ago. While an efficient killing machine, the Thor he knew wasn't a murderous marauder. He wondered why he ever thought he was. The man had always operated within his code of honor.

Stopping by the great hall Lionel poured a goblet of hard cider before jogging up the stairs to the battlement overlooking the training yard. If he had to guess, that was where the Wolf had gone when he departed. No, not to the observation bridge where he was, but to the training yard as a combatant.

Shaking his head he knew life at the royal keep wasn't that different from Drummond. Not when he discounted the puffed-up flatterers sitting at the king's table. While his lord's overlord tolerated the sycophants, he took them with a grain of salt. David possessed the wisdom to see through their tricks. Watching two soldiers sparring, he caught Thor's influence in some of their moves. So, the Wolf had been far from idle while he recovered. No wonder he was in such good shape. He'd been training the king's soldiers to be more effective killers while he worked at getting back in peak fighting form.

"I see you have talked with my Sheriff." Lionel resisted the urge to jump as the king sidled up behind him. "He has made a remarkable recovery wouldn't you say?"

"In some respects," Lionel agreed. "If not in others."

"Ah, yes, there is that." The king made a noise. "Oswald no longer believes Thor will recover his lost memories. Not the most important ones anyway."

Reading between the lines, Lionel knew the king meant his memories of Drummond and his life there. Oswald didn't discount the return of memories similar to ones he'd already recalled, or that his mind would fill in gaps in those stories with time.

What he didn't believe would ever come back was Thor's memories of his wife and family. As much as he didn't want to accept the possibility, the healer was probably right. The warrior would likely never remember his wife and family. Whether the result of the trauma or the injury, they would probably never know and Thor couldn't tell them. However, from where he sat, it was like the last three years had never been.

CHAPTER FOURTEEN

Lionel stared around him at the daunting landscape regretting what came next with every part of him. The king made it clear the time had come for his lady to learn what she never wished to hear. He made it equally clear it was his place to tell her. While he understood why he was given this role, that didn't mean he liked it. He didn't. The clammy gray mists rolling in from the sea echoed the dread roiling in his soul.

Why Alexandria wanted to meet here beneath the shadow of the mighty cross was beyond him. Then again, it wasn't. She sensed he had something life-altering to share. He would be amazed if she hadn't. He shouldn't be surprised she'd want to hear such a revelation within the mystical presence of the monument revered by Drummonds past and present.

Looking up, he watched his lady dismount. He smiled at how efficiently she dealt with the stallion's antics and silently acknowledged that he'd expected her to arrive wearing a man's tunic and hose. She didn't. What she wore wasn't much better though.

The dark green slitted calf-length bliaut over tan hose worn with familiar brown leather boots was a recent creation that allowed her to ride astride rather than sidesaddle without baring her legs. While he appreciated the practicality, wearing such attire just wasn't done. Not unless you were the lady of Drummond thumbing your nose at society.

"I'm sorry I'm late." Alexandria apologized for making him wait. "The bairns were fussy and Reina needed help in the sewing room."

"The girls were in high spirits?" The three youngsters fostering at Drummond were a handful at the best of times. "That doesn't surprise me."

"Me, either." She'd been rather high-spirited herself. "They're a little much for Reina at times but Adela is more than capable of reigning them in."

"That old hag is tough enough to scare seasoned warriors," The Golden Wolf said something similar in another life. "And I didn't mind waiting. I needed time to gather my thoughts."

"Why?" Alexandria felt the hair rise on the back of her neck. "What's going on? Whatever it is, just spit it out."

"It's not that simple." Lionel dropped on the grass beneath the cross as he'd done many times before and patted the ground beside him. "The king wished to do this himself; however he is in the midst of royal business that cannot be left in another's hands."

The king was monitoring activities at court. He dare not leave the Golden Wolf unattended. Only God knew how detrimental something he heard might be. While unable to prevent Thor from learning what he shouldn't, David could deal with any fallout if he was present. That was why Lionel was tasked with a revelation he'd hoped to make himself instead.

"So he has charged you with telling me what he cannot share?" She wasn't sure how she felt about that. "Have they found my husband?"

She and her parties had searched as far and wide as they dared without causing a diplomatic incident. However, that didn't mean they hadn't overlooked Thor's body or where he was being held. There were places they could not go and everyone knew it.

"Yes." Lionel nodded. "Thor has been found."

"Dead?" She prayed not. "Or alive?"

"Alive." Lionel expected the tears of relief. "Zan, wait." His hand on her arm stopped her from rising. "It's not that simple."

"What do you mean?" Settling back against the cross in a half-crouch, Alexandria fought the urge to shake free and scurry away. "If Thor is alive, I must go to him."

"You can't." Lionel ignored her wide-eyed gaze as her legs shot from beneath her. "The king demands you wait until he sends for you."

"Why?" There was genuine fear in her eyes. "How badly is he hurt?"

"Thor is doing well." Lionel knew it was time for hard truths neither wished to hear. "He was more dead than alive when he arrived outside the gates of the royal keep. He wasn't expected to live at first."

"Not expected to live?" The pieces were falling into place in a way she didn't like. "If he is doing well now, just how long has my husband been in my godfather's care?"

"Six months, perhaps longer," Lionel admitted. "Don't look at me like that. Thor was near death for weeks."

"How long have you known he lived?" Alexandria turned to stare him down. "A half year or more..."

She'd tried to ignore the distance in his manner, but it was impossible to deny. She'd dismissed the change in attitude as concern for his wife. As a need to care less about her and more about Reina. She'd been fine with that idea. Now she knew it was the lies between them that he couldn't stomach instead.

"Not that long." Half that time wasn't much better. "I wanted to tell you, but the king forbade it. He thought it best to wait and I agreed with him." He could see that she wanted to storm off, but she wouldn't. "You need to listen to me. I saw Thor from across the bailey. Even at that distance, it was easy to believe that he might still die."

Lionel closed his eyes against that vision. He never wanted to see such a thing again. The man was a walking skeleton.

"What do you mean?" Gradually calming down, Alexandria chose to get as much information as possible before deciding her next move. "It was easy to believe he might still die?"

"I saw him from afar in the training yard practicing with a blunted sword." Lionel opened his eyes. "Thor was nothing but scarred skin stretched taunt over bones. Oswald believed the infection still raging through his body would eventually kill him. Should that happen, the king wanted to spare you the pain of watching him die. Of losing him twice. However, that was but one of the reasons the king didn't want you to know Thor lived."

"What were the others?" Alexandria took a deep breath. "You've gone too far to stop now."

"I guess I have." Lionel agreed knowing he couldn't stop if he wanted to. The king had given him leave to do what must be done. "The Wolf is not the man you wed."

"War changes a man." Alexandria plucked a blade of grass. "Captivity changes him more."

"I never mentioned captivity." She was moving faster than he was comfortable with doing. "Why would you say that?"

"Because it's me that you're talking to." Alexandria shook her head. "And I'm a warrior, too. The only way the Golden Wolf wouldn't return to us is if he was dead, injured, or in captivity. Since you saw him after the skirmish and he wasn't hurt, that means he was likely injured when his companions were killed. If Thor appeared outside the royal keep, that means he was either in hiding or in captivity for months. We both know the Wolf doesn't hide so that only leaves captivity."

"I'd forgotten how reasonable you can be." Lionel's laugh was ugly. "You are right. Thor was in captivity, but it's more than that. We both know a few months in a dungeon would only piss the Golden Wolf royally, not change him."

"You're scaring me." This man wasn't the stable rock she knew. "What has happened to Thor?"

Staring into her face, Lionel knew his time was up. He had no choice but to jab a sword through the heart of the only woman he'd ever truly loved.

"Thor suffered serious head injuries not unlike the one that claimed your father." Not unlike it, yet not as severe. "While he has recovered from the physical trauma, he hasn't recovered mentally."

"What does that mean?" Alexandria prayed it wasn't what she feared most. "Is his mind affected?"

"Not in the way you fear." Lionel reassured. "Thor's mind is good. He knows who and what he is, but there was a time when he didn't know either."

"That can happen with head injuries." Her godfather knew she knew that so why hadn't he sent for her? "Memories return as the wounds heal."

She'd yet to encounter a case where they hadn't. Not one where the patient lived anyway.

"Normally, yes." Lionel agreed. "From what I have been told, Thor's memories suddenly returned one morning and he escaped that night through a breach in an inner wall that also cracked the outer wall. I don't know the specifics beyond it was a miraculous escape." Hopefully, she would get the details from the Wolf's mouth one day. "After escaping, Thor made it to the forest without being seen under the cover of darkness and used the heavens to make his way to the royal keep."

That the king was in residence when he finally arrived outside his walls was another fortunate break. However, the Sheriff of Lothian was nothing if not an organized, methodical man. He was intimately familiar with how his lord moved around his kingdom.

Since he'd kept a calendar on the dungeon wall, he knew where the court and the king should be this time of year and he'd used his navigational skills to get there. Were his timing off and the king not in residence, he would be sent for. The Golden Wolf's return was too important to ignore.

"From what I understand, it was a difficult journey that took several days that further drained his strength." Lionel picked idly at the grass. "While able to walk to the king's table, Thor was more dead than alive although he managed to stay conscious long enough to get cleaned up and have his wounds treated. When he finally slipped into unconsciousness, he didn't awaken for days. Oswald feared he'd slipped away several times, but Thor fooled everyone. He survived starvation, fevers, and infections to emerge a shadow of his former self. What didn't survive is his memories of this place," His gesture encompassed Drummond and all her lands. "The bairns, or you. As far as your husband is concerned, he never wed again. The Sheriff of Lothian is a widower and has been since Lady Julia's death."

"You're saying Thor is the man I forced to wed with me." The thought was too horrid to contemplate. "No, you're saying he is the man he was before that."

"Yes, I am." Lionel agreed. "While you never knew this man, he is one that I knew well."

Rising to her feet, Alexandria strolled to the edge of the cliff. Staring out over the sea, she ignored the swell and crash of the churning waves below her. If she understood what Lionel conveyed correctly it may have been better for Drummond if Thor were dead. If he had no memory of her, their family, or their people what practical use was he?

From her perspective, it would be better if she were free to wed a man who would protect his people and lands. Being tied to a man who no longer remembered what he once treasured did not bode well for them. Hearing the crunch of dried grass under booted feet, Alexandria turned to face Lionel.

"My husband has moved on with his life even knowing he has a wife and family here at Drummond." She caught the involuntary flinch and knew she was right. "Who is the newest bedwarmer? Thor always preferred willowy, fair-haired women without a real thought in their heads. I assume that hasn't changed."

However, despite what she thought she knew, Lady Aimee was still out there and she didn't fit that mold. Fortunately, the exception and not the rule, she was also happily wed. The worst threat Alexandria expected from that quarter was the renewal of a very close friendship. She seriously doubted the other woman would invite the Wolf back into her bed at the risk of her marriage. She knew better. If FitzAlan wasn't threatened by Thor, she wasn't threatened by FitzAlan's wife.

"You are right." He wouldn't lie to her. "From what I've heard, Thor has cut a swathe through court. He doesn't have a favorite yet although there are whispers he has more than a passing interest in Lady Rosalynd."

"Ailred's fair-haired blue-eyed daughter." Alexandria nodded. "I can see where she would catch Thor's eye."

The girl was a golden-haired stick who wore fancy pleated bliauts well.

"Perhaps." The only thing that could be worse would be if he installed her at Ruthven. "Perhaps not. Don't look for trouble where there is none."

Lionel offered comfort in the only way he knew how. By reminding his lady that his lord had yet to make a move he couldn't take back. However, he feared that it was coming.

"Did you just tell me not to look for trouble where there is none?" Alexandria absently wrung her hands as she watched gannets dive for fish. "Seriously? My husband is alive and I'm not allowed to see him. I'd call that trouble enough."

"That man isn't your husband." Lionel spoke quietly. "And he isn't anyone you want to see. Not right now."

"Oh, you know that do you?" Alexandria shook her head. "Don't you think that should be my decision?"

"What I think doesn't matter." Lionel raised his hands in surrender. "The king has asked that you give Thor time to make peace with the idea he is married. At the moment, that knowledge isn't sitting well. He will let you know when the time is right for you to meet."

"I don't believe this." Alexandria tossed a stone over the cliff's edge and watched it splash into the sea. "My godfather wishes to determine where and when I'm introduced to the man who shared my life until his damnable skirmish took him away." Her tone was bitter. "I don't think so. Does he expect Thor to remember his wife and family without prompting?" Tossing her head, she stared at the top of the cross. "Again, I don't think so. I should have been summoned when he first arrived. He would have found me easier to accept if I was."

If she had been there to love and nurse him through his injuries as a wife should be Thor would have become familiar with her if nothing else.

"Perhaps." While he agreed, neither of them dared cross the king. "Or perhaps your presence would have only made things worse. The king did what he felt was best."

"While that may be true, I don't like how this was handled." Alexandria resisted the urge to scream her frustration. "I should have had a say in my husband's treatment." While she would have been treated as other wives were; she was far from just another wife. Her godfather knew it. She was a recognized healer, too. "What am I supposed to do while I wait?"

"What you do every day." Lionel shook his head. "Lead your people and strengthen yourself for the day you meet again."

"It won't go well, will it?" She expected the shake of his head. "I suppose that shouldn't surprise me."

"You are right." Lionel agreed. "It shouldn't."

"Then I will do what must be done." Alexandria took a deep breath. "I'd like to be alone for a while if you don't mind." The raised palm said, 'Even if you do.' "Reina needs you and I need to be alone with my thoughts."

Nodding, Lionel silently departed knowing there was nothing he could do to change her mind. While his first instinct was to remain on the perimeter to ensure her safety, he knew Alexandria could defend herself. More importantly, with the MacLarens gone, there was little threat to the well-being of the lady of Drummond. Not like there used to be. Giving his mount his head, he headed toward Drummond knowing leaving was best for everyone.

Walking along the cliff Alexandria contemplated her next move. While denying her the opportunity to be by Thor's side from the start was wrong, she understood why the king did what he felt was best for both of them. It was hard to remain angry when she didn't know if her presence would have done more harm than good. Perhaps her godfather had seen something she hadn't leading him to handle the situation as he did. She didn't know.

What she did know was that not being by her husband's side from the beginning would make reestablishing their relationship more difficult. Had she arrived as soon as possible after his return, Thor would have opened his eyes to learn his wife was by his side. Whether he remembered her or not, he would have had six months to get used to the idea.

As things stood, he'd had six months to get used to living like he wasn't married. From what Lionel said, he'd easily fallen back into old habits. If things were as they'd always been any number of women at court were standing in line for their shot at the Sheriff of Lothian. If she knew Thor, he had taken them up on their offers.

Shaking her head, Alexandria knew her best line of attack was fighting fire with fire. Lust had brought them closer in the beginning and lust would bring them closer together now. However, she would have to get past the man Thor used to be as she had done before. The one who claimed he wasn't attracted to her although his actions that night in her chamber belied his words.

However, unlike events from all those years ago, she wasn't fighting a man with no wish to wed again. She was fighting a man who believed he no longer loved the woman he had married. The coming conversation played out in her head against her will.

Given what she knew of the man her husband was now, he would likely tell her how he truly felt. She ran every eviscerating word through her mind. She wasn't sure she could handle them. Not yet. She'd just learned her husband was alive. She couldn't imagine being rejected any time soon. Perhaps Lionel and her godfather were right. She should give herself time to accept the situation before adding to her pain.

While she did, she would ponder her next move. One that likely involved the physical. Forget the likely. It did. The one place they'd never had trouble communicating was in bed. She knew that. The battle was already lost if she didn't do whatever had to be done, whenever, and however it had to be done, to reawaken the Wolf's loving devotion.

within hours of the truce being signed. "However, I didn't want Thor to depart when he did and I could have stopped him."

But he'd known how badly he wanted to get home to his wife and family so he'd ignored his uneasy feelings and allowed him to leave instead.

CHAPTER FIFTEEN

S taring out the window, Alexandria couldn't believe her eyes. If she didn't know better she would swear history was repeating itself. Like it or not, that was Greggorius emerging from the mist. Feeling her gut drop to her knees, she prayed he came bearing word from her godfather. With any luck, she was being summoned to court. These past few weeks knowing Thor was alive but unable to see him was more than she could bear. Running down the stairs, she met the royal messenger at the door.

"Is Godfather sending for me?" She hung on the door frame. "Is that why you're here?"

"Perhaps." Greggorius handed her the sealed document. "You will have to read that to see."

While he knew the gist of the message, it wasn't his place to tell the lady of Drummond what she needed to read for herself. He wasn't privy to his king's every thought. Or to the full contents of that letter. He knew it was an invitation to court. He didn't know what other warnings or counsel the king might have shared.

It would be a shame if Lady Alexandria missed some important advice because she listened to him instead of reading David's words for herself. Watching her break the seal, he wasn't surprised by her changing facial expressions as she read each line. It was clear she'd hoped some of Thor's memories had returned and it was equally clear she was bitterly disappointed that they hadn't.

"Come inside." Alexandria motioned for him to follow her into the great hall. "I'm sure Bertie knows you are here by now. She's probably sending a trencher of viands and a tankard of ale to the high table as we speak."

"I hope so." Greg nodded. "It's a hard ride from the royal keep to Drummond and a tankard of Bertie's ale would hit the spot."

While he wouldn't mind eating a bite as well, Bertie's ale was the best in the country. Far better than anything offered at the royal keep. It was what he looked forward to when he visited Drummond and everyone knew it.

Looking up from her letter, Alexandria smiled at the expected plate of viands and ale suddenly appearing at Greg's side. "I need to meet with Lionel and Reina so I'll leave you to your meal."

"I'll be here when you finish." Greg poured a tankard of ale.

If things went as expected, he'd likely accompany Alexandria and her party to the royal keep. He could do with an extra day or two in the countryside. Being the king's private messenger kept a man busy. Being his secret assassin, well, he didn't talk about that. Loose lips weren't in anyone's best interest.

Watching the lady of Drummond link arms with de Montluzan as they headed off to find his wife, Greggorius decided she was a fine woman and Lord Thor was a fool. Most men would give their fighting arm for a woman like Alexandria of Drummond. However, few of those men were willing to sign their execution warrant by challenging Jamie MacLaren's imaginary claim to the heiress of Drummond. The ones who dared met a swift end under questionable circumstances until the Golden Wolf turned the table on his wife's tormentor.

However, that man and the one he knew today weren't the same person. While he wasn't among Lady Zan's romantic admirers, he likely would be if it weren't for his wife of ten years. Kayte would kill him if she suspected he so much as looked at another woman. An adept poisoner, his child bride was more lethal than he in the right circumstances.

Fortunately, those situations were few and far between. Leaving the killing to him, his lovely Kayte was far more useful at gathering information from unsuspecting marks. Savoring a sip of ale, Greg hoped the tide turned soon for Alexandria's sake. Although she didn't know it yet, it wouldn't be long before she knew the truth: Rosalynd and her ilk were winning.

CLOSING THE DOOR TO the master's solar and locking it behind them, Alexandria turned to Reina and Lionel. Breaking the seal on the letter she quickly scanned the contents before passing it to her cousin. After reading the king's words Reina passed the vellum to her husband.

"This isn't unexpected." Lionel handed the note back to Alexandria.

Shrugging she tucked the letter into her belt. "No, it isn't."

"But you don't know what to do next?" Reina said what she wouldn't. "That's easy. Go. Do what you've wanted to do since you learned Thor was alive."

"It's not that simple anymore." Alexandria sat on her window sill. "Going to court now isn't as appealing as when I expected to be welcomed with open arms. Why can't Thor come here instead?"

Now that she knew the truth it would be much easier to deal with their initial meeting in private. She knew to her toes it wouldn't go well. How could it? She was an unknown quantity to the Golden Wolf.

"Because he won't." Lionel stated what she already knew. "Why would he when he has no interest in this place?"

He couldn't bring himself to say what they all knew. Thor had no interest in his wife, his family, or the life he'd built at Drummond. The thought was too painful to express.

"He wouldn't." Alexandria agreed. "It appears there is no choice but to go to him."

"I would say you are right." Reina nodded. "When do you want to leave?"

"As soon as possible." There was no point in delaying the inevitable unpleasantness to come. "We should be able to leave tomorrow or the day after at the latest."

"The day after." Lionel spoke firmly. "We need time to pack and you need time to compose yourself. If we leave the day after tomorrow, we'll arrive at the keep within a reasonable time frame."

"You're right." Alexandria agreed. "I must gather my thoughts and the horses could use another day to rest." They would be in top traveling form by then. "Godfather will still expect us no matter how long we take."

However, the sooner the better remained unsaid. While the king was fairly lenient with her, David would know if she put off answering his summons. She couldn't do that. Her godfather expected better of her and she refused to give the twittering idiots at court anything more to laugh about. Meeting Thor in front of all of them would be fuel enough.

Rising to her feet, Reina brushed her hands on her gown. "Then we have a plan. We take a little longer than necessary to pack and go slower than we otherwise might. I'm sure Greg will appreciate the extra day out of the saddle."

"I'm sure he will." Alexandria agreed. "Let the men know we're leaving in a couple of days and ensure our mounts will be well rested. I need to meet with Bertie and let her know we'll be gone a while."

Nodding, Lionel left the room with Reina in tow. They both knew that meeting had more to do with getting her surrogate mother's advice than leaving instructions. Bertie was more than capable of overseeing Drummond while they were gone. Between Bertie, Adela, and his second-in-command the keep was in capable hands.

All he needed to do was bring Arnulf up to speed, inform the stablemaster that they were leaving the day after tomorrow, and choose the men accompanying them from the training yard while Reina met with Adela in the sewing room. When that was done, they could pack and leave.

Once they did, they would arrive at the royal keep before they were ready and Alexandria would confront her unknown future much sooner than she wanted to. Heading for the stables, Lionel decided he didn't envy her things to come. Each day would be harder than the one before, and every event would be more difficult than she anticipated. He knew that. He'd felt that way himself. He knew also that Zan would muddle through one way or another. They all would as they always did.

CHAPTER SIXTEEN

Giving Loki his head, Alexandria lost herself in thought. This journey was reminiscent of the life-altering one she'd undertaken a lifetime ago. Too reminiscent. The same trepidation she'd felt that day gnawed at her belly like a tenacious worm.

The same trepidation, desperation, and determination. No, not the same. This was different. More than her family, her people, and her fantasy lover were at stake...Her heart was, too, and that peril felt far too real...far worse than that first frantic effort to win at any cost.

Soon after Lionel shared the news he'd been forbidden to share on royal command, she'd sent a letter to her godfather begging to see her husband. While usually welcome anytime, it would be unwise to show up unannounced this time. That wouldn't go anyway but bad.

When the king urged her to wait a few weeks until travel was easier she read between the lines. Things were worse than she'd feared. Her godfather needed time to convince a stubborn warrior that he had a wife. One he would meet much sooner than he wanted. None of that surprised her under the circumstances. It couldn't be any other way.

While her attire was a calculated risk and likely to fail, she refused to be who she wasn't. It wouldn't be fair to her or Thor. As much of her life was spent in men's clothing doing manly things as it was femininely attired managing her household. Things might have been different had there never been a feud.

As it was, she'd adjusted to living between two worlds at an early age. She saw no reason to stop living that life because the feud had ended. She loved her family and she enjoyed her wifely duties. However, that didn't mean she wasn't as up for a good hunt and challenging battle play as the next warrior. Fancy bliauts and embroidered chemises were impractical for both.

Forget riding Loki hell for leather as she was wont to do. Long skirts were an unnecessary impediment in her life. They could prove deadly as well.

However, since her preferences didn't count at court, she kept a trunk filled with beautiful gowns at the royal keep for occasions that demanded she look like the lady of Drummond. It was a role she couldn't escape. It was also a role she would play with consummate ease when the time came.

THOR STOOD ON THE BATTLEMENTS surveying the king's domain. Life was good. Better than good. It was exciting and more fulfilling than it had been in years. His only dissatisfaction was that while he was fully recovered from the ordeal he'd suffered at de Vescy's hands, he'd yet to exact his revenge.

That reckoning would come soon enough. He had but to wait for the perfect opportunity. Until then, royal duties filled his days and delicate court flowers filled his nights. The only threat to his comfortable existence was a wife who refused to remain out of sight and out of mind one day longer. The one he'd first learned he had a while ago.

The king wouldn't lie to him as revolting as the idea was, and as badly as he wanted to deny such a prospect. Not about something like this. Nor would Aimee. He trusted the woman with his life as she trusted him. If his old friend said he was wed, he was. Whether he liked it or not. He didn't. But he couldn't change what was already done.

He could, however, send the nuisance back to her keep. It was the best solution for everyone. His unwanted bride wouldn't be subjected to his indifference and he could live as he pleased. He had no reason to alter his life for a woman he didn't remember and he wouldn't. He'd found a partner who pleased him. He didn't need one who didn't.

He'd already approached Lady Rosalynd's father about installing her at Ruthven. While he couldn't offer her marriage and wouldn't if he could, such an official alliance with the Sheriff of Lothian was a major accomplishment for the daughter of a minor lord. Lord Ailred eventually agreed to his offer. He would be a fool not to.

Both men knew her time as his mistress would only increase Rosalynd's value in the eyes of future suitors. If the Golden Wolf found her compelling enough to move her into his home, there was something special about the woman. He agreed with that assessment.

Rosalynd was comely in that fair-haired, blue-eyed way. She was charming, and a good conversationalist who knew when to speak and when to be silent. She was a skillful lover as well. Deciding not to question how one so young had come by her carnal expertise, Thor shrugged off the doubts pecking at his brain.

She was pleasing to the eyes and satisfactory in bed. What more did he want or need? He was a man of war. He had little need for anything more than Rosie had to offer. Not when he had servants to darn his drawers, a cook to prepare his meals, and a trove of trustworthy servants to keep his home in order.

Staring over the bailey, he contemplated his next move. While her father knew what the future held Rosalynd had yet to learn of his plans. It wasn't in his best interests for her to fully comprehend her new position until after he'd dealt with this latest problem. His mistress crowing about her place in his life and his bed would not bode well for tactfully dismissing an unwanted wife from his life. Not when he considered how close she was to the king.

While he refused to accept he'd broken his vow to never wed again, that didn't mean he didn't. He had. He knew that now. However, that didn't mean he was willing to accept this unwanted interloper into his life either. He wasn't.

That was why he was standing on the battlement looking down at the bailey waiting for his first sight of this unknown woman. Aimee and the king refused to describe Lady Alexandria preferring to say only that he would know her when he saw her since the woman was impossible to ignore. While meaningless to him now, he knew their words were too significant to dismiss.

It would do no good to ask anyone else. There was a royal command against anyone describing his wife. No, not a royal command, one from the royal healer that few dared disobey. Oswald was a law unto himself, and he believed it would be better if he didn't know who he was looking for.

The healer believed the shock of seeing this unknown woman might suddenly break his memories free and restore him to the man he used to be.

Thor snorted loudly. The idea was ridiculous. He was perfectly content with the man he was now. He had no wish to be who he used to be. He wasn't sure he believed that was even possible.

Hearing the sudden commotion below him, he glanced towards the massive gates only to see them swing open to admit a large party with a rather peculiar rider at their head. Watching the warrior dismount, he couldn't believe his eyes. What he'd thought a slight Gaelic warrior with a tall flame-red topknot flowing into a waist-length ponytail was no man. She was instead a small female with an arrogant carriage and loud mouth.

Stunned into silence, Thor smacked his forehead praying there was no way in heaven or hell *that* was the mysterious lady of Drummond...

CHAPTER SEVENTEEN

U rging Loki to a halt, Alexandria felt her skin crawl. Looking up, she wasn't surprised to see the Golden Wolf staring down from the battlements. Just as he'd done the first time. Studying him from afar, Thor's hair was much longer than she remembered and his tunic wasn't one she'd made for him. Beyond that, the same cold amber eyes stared down at her that she'd seen before.

Hearing her godfather's voice behind her, she tore her gaze from Thor's and slid out of the saddle. Landing elegantly on booted feet, she wiped sweaty palms on her hips as she turned to find the king giving her a thorough once-over from head to toe.

Seeing one auburn brow cock questioningly as he studied her high ponytail and masculine attire, she cracked the familiar mischievous smile. The one that said she knew she was setting his court on its ear and didn't give a fig. Shaking his head, the king resisted the urge to laugh out loud. The girl, no, the woman, would never change. She'd always be daring and incorrigible.

"Hello, my dear, while I wish this were under better circumstances, I am delighted to see you." David engulfed his goddaughter in his arms. "Thor stared down on you much as he did that first time?"

Alexandria laughed softly, "Aye."

David glanced up and saw nothing. Shaking his head, he wasn't surprised the Wolf was gone. Thor never lingered once reconnaissance was done.

"As I looked up at him. While my husband is far from predictable, some things will never change." Like his habit of surveying an opponent from afar. "The man disappeared just as quickly as he appeared."

As he had the first time.

"That doesn't surprise me." Snorting softly at the unnecessary folly of the whole situation the king offered his arm to his goddaughter. "Settle in and rest a while. I'll have some blackberry wine sent up along with some bread and cheese. Thor will wait until you've composed yourself."

"That sounds good." Alexandria allowed herself to be led inside. "I'm sure Lionel is hungry and we can all rest."

"I think that's best." The king stopped by the stairs. "I'm sure Reina is waiting in your chamber already."

"I'm sure she is." Looking for the perfect bliaut to wear to dinner. "As I'm sure you'll send Lionel with that blackberry wine as soon as you finish talking with him."

"You have my word." The king patted her arm. "Take as long as you need and I'll see you at the evening meal."

"Yes," Alexandria nodded. "You will."

The king watched her jog up the stairs before entering the great hall and taking his seat. Sending a servant for blackberry wine, he wasn't surprised when Lionel eventually took the seat to his right. He'd be more surprised if he hadn't. He'd requested the warrior meet him in the hall once their mounts were stabled to his satisfaction. Like Thor, Lionel was very hands-on about their mounts and weaponry.

"I overheard what you said to Zan." Lionel watched the servant set a tray with three goblets of wine beside him before handing the fourth to the king. "You know she won't rest until the evening meal."

"I know." David studied his wine. "She'll be out and about when she shouldn't be and run into Thor before she's ready."

"Yes." Lionel agreed. "She will and you expect me to be there when it happens."

"I do." It wouldn't be pretty. "I'll try to be there as well."

"That is probably a wise idea." Lionel agreed. "If there isn't anything else, I'll take this upstairs and try to dissuade Zan from rambling about."

"Good luck." The king laughed. "I doubt you'll be very successful."

"You are probably right," Lionel lifted the tray. "My lord."

David watched him leave not looking forward to the coming mess. While the reunion was necessary, he expected things to get worse before they got better. For one thing, he doubted that the promiscuous lordling's daughter would give up without a fight. For another, he doubted Thor would give up his bit of nothing without a compelling reason. One he prayed would manifest in time to save their crumbling marriage.

THOR SCOFFED. HE HAD carefully avoided the recent arrivals since they rode through the gates. It hadn't been difficult. The two women had retired to an upper chamber soon after their arrival. De Montluzan had joined them a short while later. He'd noted the warrior carrying a tray of wine and cheese upstairs and didn't expect them to emerge again until the evening meal.

It wasn't uncommon to rest after a long journey so he'd gone about his day as he normally would. He never expected to run into the party exiting the keep as he entered. Since he'd done just that, he took advantage of the unexpected opportunity to eyeball this so-called wife.

Studying her from head to toe, he immediately decided the woman standing before him wasn't to his usual taste. Not in any way. While common sense said he would never marry such a creature, it was common knowledge that he had. He couldn't deny that truth as hard as he tried. Yet, it seemed impossible that he would break an oath to never wed again over such a disgusting wench...No matter the titles, wealth, or properties coming with her hand.

Again, this didn't make sense. His late wives were all fine-boned court beauties desired by every man. His current lovers were the same. Given what he knew about himself, he had no words to describe this Lady Zan. She was like nothing he'd ever seen. A diminutive flame-haired child, she was too vivid and lush to ignite his loin. Too arrogant in carriage and person to appeal to his senses.

Added to that, no lady would dare arrive at court astride a snorting, pawing fawn beast dressed as a man with a battleworthy sword strapped to her side. But she had. Unexpected and unannounced. While he was taken aback, he couldn't say the same for others.

It appeared the lady of Drummond's audacity was no surprise to many. Especially his king. He wouldn't have embraced her with such affection were things otherwise. He acted as though such behavior was acceptable instead.

That he expected nothing different from the auburn-haired wench. Thor felt differently. This woman was no wife of his. Scoffing again, he turned on his heel and walked back inside.

Staring at his back, Alexandria shrugged at the king. She refused to run after the man. There would be time enough to confront her husband without an audience. The words they had yet to say would be better spoken behind closed doors. Catching Lionel's eye she nodded in the direction of the practice yard. A few rounds of battle play would allow her to work off the stress of the last few hours and be better prepared to face what lay ahead.

"Do not fear." The king glanced in the direction of the keep. "He will come around in time."

"Whether he comes around or not, we will talk before I leave." Alexandria sounded more confident than she felt. "Thor can come to terms with my arrival over the next few hours. In the meantime, Lionel and I are going to practice our swordplay. Your practice grounds are much larger than ours at Drummond."

"Yes, it is." David patted her shoulder. "I have a few things I need to do myself. We'll meet in the great hall for dinner if you're up to it."

"I wouldn't miss it for the world." Alexandria made a rude noise. "Don't worry, I already see it will not be a pleasant experience."

"No, it won't." The king agreed. "But now you know what you're up against."

"I guess so, but then again, when has court ever been that pleasant for me?" Save for the last couple of years with her Wolf by her side. "I know the odds are not in my favor, but if I can win I will. If I cannot..."

"I have your back," David promised. "You have my word. You will be happy again." If that meant the Golden Wolf exited her life and a better man entered, then so be it.

Alexandria nodded before walking in the direction of the training yard. She could talk with her godfather after she'd worked off the bitterness of her despair. While she'd remained poised and calm, Thor's reaction was devastating. She needed time to work through the pain and she couldn't do that until her churning thoughts were under control.

A few rounds of beating the hell out of Lionel would do more towards calming her than anything else. Glancing over her shoulder she saw the castle doors close behind the king before she turned the corner to see her opponent across the training yard warming up. Heading in his direction, she took a blunted training sword from the rack and began practicing her moves.

Once they were both ready, the sparring would begin. One look at her face would alert Lionel that she held nothing back. She expected the same from him. They would both be bruised and battered long before the not-so-playful battle play ended.

CHAPTER EIGHTEEN

Shaking his head in disbelief at what he'd just witnessed, the king entered the great hall unsurprised to see Thor seated by the high chair drinking a goblet of cider as he studied the pieces on the board in front of him. While chess was a favorite, the Golden Wolf had developed a passion for latrunculin during his mercenary days in the East.

David suspected the game helped him develop his talent for military strategy in the early days. Now, he just enjoyed winning at a game few were as intimately familiar with. However, he had managed to best his Wolf a time or two. He was confident he would likely beat him again this time. If Thor didn't feel the same he wouldn't be studying the board so intently.

"I believe I have won this time," David sat in his chair and accepted the goblet of cider from a page. "And I fear there is naught you can do about it."

"I fear you are right." Thor agreed as he sat back in his chair. "That doesn't mean I accept defeat without exhausting all the possibilities."

"You wouldn't be who you are if you did." The king studied his goblet still finding it difficult to accept he finally had the coveted set in his possession. The man sitting to his right was largely responsible for that happening whether he knew it or not. "If you want to know, and even if you don't, Lady Zan is in the training yard with de Montluzan. I suspect he is putting her through her paces. Or, more likely, she is putting him through his."

"I doubt that." There was no way a tiny woman like that could best a seasoned warrior. What the king suggested was preposterous at best an outright lie at worst. "I suspect they play at fighting instead."

"You can suspect anything you want." The king set his goblet aside. "However, you would be wrong. In my desire not to have you swayed in any way, I have deliberately told you little of your wife and ordered the court to do the same. I have begun to doubt the wisdom of that choice."

"Why?" Thor squinted at one of the pieces on the board, or more appropriately one of his "dogs" in the "city". "Because I doubt the woman is skilled with a sword?"

"Yes," David nodded. "And because you are wrong."

"In what way?" Against his better judgment, his interest was piqued by his words. "While I have known women to lead their men into battle, with one or two exceptions, none were true warriors. They just did what they had to do."

"While you are right, Alexandria is one of those exceptions." David moved the latrunculin board out of Thor's line of vision. "She was training with her father and brothers almost from the time she could walk. While Ian tried to shield her, as soon as she felt skilled enough to hold her own, your wife joined her father on the field of battle without his knowledge. Aimee can tell you more. I suspect you shared more with her than either of you ever shared with me. If you still doubt my word, go to the training field and see the truth for yourself."

Nodding, Thor rose to his feet ignoring the king's low laugh as he headed for the front door of the keep. Exiting the castle, he took a right at the stables and looped back through Oswald's garden. Stopping at the bench to the left of the fountain, he settled on the familiar perch. He'd discovered a while back that he could observe the training yard without being seen from this vantage point.

He frequently watched his men train as he was now watching two uninvited combatants spar in the otherwise deserted space. While they wielded blunted practice swords, both warriors did so with impressive skill. Although the smaller combatant would tire quicker than her larger opponent, she had a quick, efficient style that made lethal use of her speed and dexterity.

Whatever he'd expected, it wasn't this. A well-trained warrior of above-average size and physical strength, de Montluzan should be toying with his much smaller opponent as he would a squire in training. Nothing could be farther from the truth. This was intense sparring with neither side holding back.

Quick and agile, Alexandria of Drummond was no unskilled weakling playing at being a warrior. She would be deadly with a sharpened blade.

As it was, both warriors would bear the cuts and bruises of a hard-fought battle when the practice ended. He'd hazard a guess the lady of Drummond wouldn't move quite so fast on the morrow.

Observing a rapidly tiring Alexandria of Drummond make a foolish misstep, Thor was surprised when de Montluzan trapped her against his body before he dropped a kiss on her lips. Seeing her break free of his arms, Thor strained to hear her words as she pressed her hand against her mouth in undisguised shock.

"You mustn't do such a thing." Alexandria shook her head in denial. "I have a husband and you have a wife." She took a step back. "Don't." She pressed her fingers against his lips. "This isn't what you want and we both know it." They both knew it was, but she refused to let him say it. Once out, such words could never be taken back. "This is a trying time for both of us. You're breaking under the stress of Reina's illness and I'm fighting to win my husband back. While this is difficult for both of us, betraying our mates won't make either of those situations better."

"Zan." Lionel kissed the back of her hand.

"No." She shook her head. "While I fear Thor won't care what I do, you will not hurt my cousin that way."

"You are right." Lionel released her hand and took a step back. "I won't."

It was but a moment of weakness they would both regret and he knew it. However, if Reina's health continued to fail and the Wolf continued to mistreat his wife as he was, all bets were off. If, and when, they were both free, he refused to step aside this time. He'd done that once. He wouldn't do it again. He doubted Alexandria would ask him to. Laughing softly, he shook his head slightly, patted her shoulder, and slowly left the training field.

Watching him leave, Alexandria silently chastised herself for her foolishness. She should have known better. She and Lionel were both under tremendous pressure from many directions. The last thing they should have done was engage in battle play. A good way to expend excess physical energy, sparring stirred the blood and ignited the passions.

She wasn't surprised Lionel overstepped the bounds. Or that she let him. The vulnerable part of her wanted to lean into his kiss. The warrior in her knew to do so was trouble. Replacing the blunted swords in the rack, she stopped to stretch before heading for the keep. Right now she needed nothing so much as an hour or two of solitude and a long, hot bath. She reeked of sweat, blood, and horse flesh in the most unpleasant ways.

Watching his wife leave, Thor wasn't sure how he felt about the event he'd witnessed. It wasn't as though he cared about the woman. He didn't know her. Truthfully, he'd spared her scarcely a thought until he'd watched her ride into the bailey earlier today. He'd thought of little else since.

Though he'd walked away without a word at their introduction, he'd been struck by her calm demeanor. It was as though she'd expected his response. Rising to his feet, Thor silently admitted the situation was perplexing. Not only that but he was equally disturbed that he cared that a woman he couldn't remember was kissed by a man he remembered but didn't know. None of that made sense. Dragging his hand through his hair, he needed to find Aimee. If he couldn't, Rosalynd would do.

CHAPTER NINETEEN

Knocking, Thor waited patiently for Aimee to unlock the chamber door. He'd been here once before only to have his knocks go unanswered. He'd then looked for her in the great hall and the sewing room among that gaggle of gossiping hens. Not that he expected to find her there. He hadn't.

He'd then gone to the formal gardens instead and learned he'd just missed her from the gardener weeding the plants. Shaking his head in defeat, he decided to try her chamber one last time. She may have returned to rest before dinner. If he got no answer this time, he would go to the blacksmith's shop to see if his dagger was repaired. Perhaps he could catch her at dinner.

"I expected you to drop by earlier." From Aimee's loosely tied robe, it appeared the gardener was right. She'd returned to her room to rest. "When you never came, I went for a walk and ended up in the Queen's Garden."

Thor snorted softly as he walked through the open door. Queen's Garden indeed. The name was ludicrous. Maud had never set foot in this keep much less those gardens. The castle wasn't in David's possession while his queen lived. However, a queen of Henry I might be a different matter and the source of the title.

He wouldn't be surprised if Matilda of Scotland and Adeliza of Louvain sat on one of those elegantly carved benches reading a letter or doing needlework in the warm sunshine. While the keep was under his king's control at the present, he doubted it would remain so indefinitely. That wasn't the way of things. Keeps were taken and keeps were lost in the continuous cycle of war.

"I would have come earlier if I could." Thor watched Aimee perch on the edge of her mattress before settling in the chair across from her. "I was otherwise occupied."

"Is that what you call it?" Aimee's scoff was intimately familiar. "I've heard you were watching your wife trounce her guard dog at swordplay."

"While I wouldn't go that far, the woman held her own." Impressively so. "They will both be bruised and battered on the morrow."

"De Montluzan wished for a battering of a different kind," Aimee spoke quietly. "Or a kiss wouldn't have passed between them before the sparring was done."

Thor started at her words. "How do you know about that?"

"Do you think you were the only voyeur watching those two?" Aimee laughed softly as she rose to pour two goblets of ale from the pitcher Thor had failed to notice sitting on a flat-topped clothes trunk. "The king watched them from the battlements. He wished to see what might transpire between them while emotions ran high. Lionel's move wasn't unexpected. Your wife's refusal was."

Taking the goblet from Aimee, Thor wasn't sure what to think. He was confused at the time. He still was.

"Why would he think such a thing?" There was much he didn't know that put him at a disadvantage. "You have said she loves me."

"She does." Aimee smiled softly. "But that wouldn't necessarily stop Alexandria from accepting comfort from another after being thoroughly humiliated by you. I did. With you." She gently reminded him. "The difference between me and your wife is that Gilliard rejected me privately while your rejection was painfully public for many to see including your current bedmates."

Taking a sip of ale, Thor realized he hadn't considered his wife's perspective. All he knew at that moment was that the woman was nothing as he expected and what she was made him very uncomfortable. Silently walking away was as much an act of self-preservation as an act of rejection. In truth, his discomfort was all that mattered. He'd barely spared a thought for the Drummond wench or her feelings.

"Perhaps." Thor remained noncommittal. "Perhaps it was an act of self-preservation."

"Perhaps." Aimee shook her head over the top of her goblet. "Perhaps I have never seen the mighty Golden Wolf run from a woman." She set her goblet aside. "No, that isn't quite true. You ran the first time Alexandria came to court intent on trapping you in her web."

"You jest." Thor refused to accept her words. "I wouldn't run from a child."

"No, you wouldn't." Aimee agreed. "But you ran from the lust that child made you feel."

"While the king vowed you are trustworthy, I have begun to doubt his judgment." Thor stared her down. "There is no way I was consumed by lust for that woman."

"There is no way you weren't." Aimee corrected him. "No, not for the woman you met today, but for the woman you once saw in her."

"You speak foolishness." Thor drained his glass and set it aside. "The woman I once saw in her? What does that mean?"

"You knew Lady Zan came to court with a purpose, and being the vigilant Wolf, you were determined to discover her intent without ever realizing what that was until it was too late."

"Again, you make no sense." Thor rose to his feet. "Since I have learned nothing of value to me, I have things I must do. I will see you in the hall at the king's table."

"Sit down." Thor's left brow rose at her tone. "You have learned much you refuse to accept. Some things will never change." Like his unwillingness to hear the truth about the women in his life. "There is still much for you to learn."

"Like what?" The thin line of his lips was the only indication the Golden Wolf was done with talking. "Some foolishness like I came to love that woman in time?"

"You did." Aimee rolled her eyes at the look on his face. "But that is a discussion for another day."

"What if I don't wish to talk about it?" Thor sat back down and crossed his foot over his knee. "I vowed I would never love a woman. That is one thing I didn't forget."

"You did, as you vowed you would never marry again." Aimee laughed softly. "You did that as well, my friend."

Watching the woman tighten the sash around her waist before making herself comfortable on a pile of pillows, Thor knew instinctively that few in his life were offered the liberties she was taking. He knew as well that she always had, she always would, and he would let her.

It wasn't just the king's word that made him trust her as much as he did, it was the knowing he felt deep in his soul. While he remembered only bits and pieces of their friendship and interactions over the years, what he did recall supported a relationship of deep intimacy. One borne of years of familiarity, comfort, and trust.

"I believe you." Thor refilled his glass before sitting on the mattress beside her. "I have heard that truth from too many quarters to disbelieve it."

"Then you must listen to me before you do something you will regret the rest of your life." Aimee rested her hand on his arm. "I know Rosalynd and Caryn have filled your head with lies. Forget everything they have said. Both have ulterior motives behind every honeyed word they speak. Unlike them, I have nothing to gain but the happiness of my dearest friend."

"I know you are right, but it is hard to discount everything I have heard." Thor gazed down at her. "When some of it is true."

"Like what?" Aimee laughed at the thoughts in her head. "That your wife is a most unusual woman in appearance and deed?"

"That." Thor agreed. "Among other things."

"Like what?" She could only imagine. "That you were never faithful to any of your wives? That loyalty to one woman isn't in your nature? All lies. It was your loyalty to your marriage bed that almost cost the life of your wife and your unborn son and daughter."

"I don't recall the event you speak of." There was still a lot of his life he didn't recall. Perhaps more he would never remember. "When did that happen?"

"It isn't just the woman you don't recall is it?" Her suspicions were confirmed with every word he said. "You have forgotten your life at Drummond as well."

"I have." Thor reluctantly admitted. "I remember much of my childhood and my life in Normandy. I remember my father's murder and avenging his death. I remember Henry and every day I spent with my stepfather's kin. I remember my life as a mercenary and coming to David's court. I am intimately familiar with my royal duties and my first two wives. I know Brigetta died in childbirth and Julia broke her neck falling from her horse.

I have vague memories of you and I know we were close. I don't remember anything to do with that woman or my life with her." His tone was frustrated. "The king refuses to answer my questions..."

"And has forbidden the rest of us from doing the same." Aimee finished for him. "However, he has recently lifted that prohibition from me."

"Yes." Thor agreed. "He claims you are better informed than him because I shared things with you that I shared with no one else."

Save his mate perhaps.

"The king is right." Aimee reached out to hold his hand. "We shared things we dare not share with others including the king."

"Like what?" This day was becoming more uncomfortable with every passing hour. "How my loyalty to my marriage bed almost cost Alexandria of Drummond her life?"

"Perhaps, however, the story's details are best coming from your wife," Aimee absently rubbed his hand. "But I will repeat what you told me the next time I saw you at court."

"Please do." This would be interesting to hear. "My wife wasn't with me at the time?"

"She was not," Aimee confirmed. "Lady Zan was still recovering from her fall and the birth of your twins."

"Twins?" Thor digested her words. "What of my daughter?"

"You know about Bridget?" Someone had talked more than she should. "Your daughter died when Drummond fell to James MacLaren, but that is a story for another time."

One better shared by his wife who had witnessed the scene. She knew only his pain-filled confessions. Nothing more.

"Then tell me of these twins." While he'd been told much of his bride, most of which was likely untrue, he'd learned nothing of the offspring he shared with her. "The king mentioned children, but he never mentioned twins."

"You and Lady Zan have three children." Aimee had no doubts they would have more if the opportunity presented itself. "Your firstborn is Siward Thorsson by Joanna the Weaver..."

"My firstborn with Lady Zan is by another woman?" He knew of no highborn lady who would claim their husband's bastard as their own. "That makes no sense." He was saying that a lot lately.

"She is a better woman than I am." Aimee laughed softly. "If you doubt me, try to take that child from her arms. You'll regret it. She is as likely to slit your throat as look at you if you dared."

Thor quirked a brow at her.

"You will do well not to underestimate your wife." Aimee's tone was serious. "She is a woman like no other. Alexandria of Drummond will do what must be done for the good of her people and her family. As much as you believe otherwise, she was a worthy mate to the Golden Wolf. You said so yourself many times over."

"So you say." He would mull her words later, right now he was more interested in Siward Thorsson. "What of this child?"

"He is her sweet bairn." Aimee shook her head. "He was from the moment she delivered him and brought him to you when Joanna died soon after birthing your son. While she hated you for a few weeks, she never held your son's birth against him."

"What does that have to do with the rest of the story?" Thor studied their conjoined hands. "Or is there any connection at all?"

"There is a connection all right." Aimee scoffed. "If that fluffy-headed light skirt hadn't tried to seduce you when your wife kicked you out of her bed, the fall would never have happened at all."

"What do you mean?" Thor snorted. "Kicked me out of our bed?"

"Your wife gladly went when the midwife summoned her to a difficult delivery in the middle of the night." Aimee confided. "While a difficult patient, Zan wasn't angry until she held the babe in her hands and saw her husband's amber eyes staring back at her. Unfortunately, she couldn't stop your leman from bleeding out despite her best efforts. However, she did try. Joanna dying wasn't what she wanted. I think she knew even then that it would be better for your marriage had Siward remained with his mother and her betrothed."

He had no memory of this woman or her betrothed. More importantly, he had no memory of this child or his place within his supposed family.

"However, that didn't happen, and before she died, Joanna confirmed the child was yours and crowed about how she'd given you the firstborn son your wife had yet to conceive. When Joanna's betrothed abandoned the boy after her death to return to Flanders, Alexandria had little choice but to bring your son home to you."

Aimee paused to let him absorb her words.

"From what you said, she could accept Siward, but she couldn't accept that you knew your leman carried your child and you hadn't told her. I can't imagine how she felt discovering the truth in such a painful way. It didn't help matters when you shared your plan to send the child to Normandy before she ever discovered his existence."

Thor's raised hand halted her speech. "I what?"

"Planned to send the child to foster in Normandy before your wife knew he existed. It seems Joanna had agreed to your scheme for a price. Of course that was before her betrothal to the Flemish wool merchant."

Thor shook his head. "You are enjoying this."

"Far from it." Aimee forced him to look at her. "I'm ensuring you finally hear the truth as you told it to me. Your head has been filled with enough lies by immoral harpies with ulterior motives."

Thor rested his hand in hers in a gesture of trust. "Then continue with these truths."

"Fostering your son in Normandy was the last thing Alexandria wanted. She knew your son would likely return later to cause trouble for your family. She believed raising Siward as one of your own was best for everyone, so she took your son into her care. While it took weeks to work your way back into your wife's good graces, it didn't take long for your son to worm his way into your heart."

"How do you know all of this?" Thor shrugged. "Surely your Lady Zan didn't tell you."

"Your Lady Zan, and of course she didn't." Aimee laughed. "I've already told you that you did...Every torrid detail."

"Torrid details?" Thor stared at the ceiling for a moment before glancing in her direction. "Do I want to know?"

"Probably not, but you should anyway." Aimee patted his hand. "Your lady wife was quite the feisty one from what you said. She threw a dagger at you when you tried to sweet talk her into overlooking your by-blow. She wasn't interested in forgiveness, so it didn't work. Your wife threw you out on your ear. From what you said, you spent weeks in a dressing chamber deliberately upsetting your lady by drowning your sorrows in copious amounts of ale poured from her favorite rock crystal pitcher. The one her father brought from the Holy Land for her."

While he wanted to deny her claim, he couldn't. He'd had dreams of an elegantly carved rock crystal pitcher with a silver gazelle spout and a matching rock crystal goblet off and on. He'd dismissed the images as resurfacing memories of mementos he'd brought back from Constantinople.

No doubt he had quite the collection buried in his coffers at Ruthven. Knowing that he hadn't given the dreams a second thought. Now that he knew the pitcher wasn't his, he realized this was likely the first and only memory he had of a former life peopled by characters he didn't know but was currently meeting.

"I see." Thor turned his attention back to his narrator. "What of the fluffy-headed light skirt? Where does she fit in?"

"That was Lisle, one of your wife's companions." Aimee snorted at the thought the alley cat could be anyone's companion. "Once it became known the lord and lady of the manor weren't getting along, she lay in wait for the perfect opportunity to offer her services."

"Which came well into the night on one of those occasions when I'd been drowning my sorrows in ale?" Thor stated the obvious. "What happened next?"

"What do you think?" Aimee waited for his answer. "I'm curious to hear."

"I don't know." Thor's response was honest. "If it was now, I'd take her up on her offer. From what you have said, I likely sent her away."

"You did." Aimee smiled. "I think you hoped knowing you acted honorably would send your wife running back into your arms." And his bed. "It didn't work. Even though Alexandria's chamber was next door and she heard every word, she still couldn't bear to look at you."

"Then how did we get past the anger?" From everything he'd heard, the situation wasn't promising. "There wouldn't be twins if we hadn't."

"You are right." Aimee laughed at the picture in her head. "Lionel finally convinced you to end the feud. Your men were losing confidence in a leader who couldn't control his wife even if that woman was Alexandria of Drummond. Like you, her reputation preceded her."

"What did I do?" She was dragging this out much too long. "Burst into her room and demand a reconciliation?"

"Something like that." Aimee shook her head. "You burst into the sewing room, threw your wife over your shoulder, and carried her to your chamber. While we have a good idea what happened next, no one knows the lurid details and neither of you was telling. Both of you entered that room spitting mad and exited it united again. You must ask Lady Zan to complete the story as only she can."

"I will." Thor nodded. "One day. In the meantime, continue with what you were saying."

"You made up and all was well between you until Drummond fell to her enemies." Aimee slid off the bed and refilled their glasses. "While you and Lionel were at court on royal business, an enemy within the gates betrayed your home and opened the gates to the MacLarens in the middle of the night. Lady Reina managed to escape before Drummond was completely overrun and made her way here. Once you learned what had happened, you set about doing what you do best."

"Ensuring Drummond fell to her rightful owner." He wouldn't do anything else regardless of his feelings for his wife and family. "What happened next?"

"You killed James MacLaren and most of his men before you were done." Aimee took a sip of ale. "Then you learned your wife had been imprisoned in an oubliette for most of the months it took you to free Drummond."

Glancing at her pale face, Thor felt a sense of dread in the pit of his stomach.

"I don't want to hear this do I?" Nothing about an oubliette was ever good unless you were the one controlling it and that wasn't the case here. "And you don't want to say it."

"I don't." Aimee agreed. "But you need to hear it. When you and Lionel brought her out of the oubliette, Lady Zan was more dead than alive. Not only was she very ill, but she was far gone with child as well."

"One I never knew she carried." Dread clenched at his innards at the expected nod. "And one never meant to be."

"Yes." Aimee nodded. "Your son was stillborn a few hours later."

"I see." Thor wasn't unaffected by her words. "How did I feel about that?"

"You were devastated." He was gaunt and gray when she'd seen him next in that way that hinted at deep sorrows. "Moreso by what your wife was going through than by your loss."

"You make it sound like I loved the woman." He still couldn't get his mind around that idea. "I don't believe that."

"You did." Aimee struggled with his inability to accept the truth. "I know you don't believe me, but you did. Eventually, life resumed at Drummond and you settled in as the lord of the manor." He'd also become the king's sworn man, but she'd been forbidden to share that information. "The next time I saw you at court, you were a different man. Handsome and content. My dearest friend again. That was when I learned Alexandria was with child again and you learned I was the same."

She'd given birth to her son six months later.

"What did your husband think?" From Aimee's soft laugh, he was likely knocked on his arse. "Is that when Gilliard realized what a fool he was?"

One of the memories that had resurfaced about this woman was the knowledge they'd become friends over the infidelities of their spouses. Lovers had come later. When the bed sport finally ended, deep trust remained.

"Perhaps." Aimee laughed softly. "I believe it was when Gilliard finally realized Jehanne was more habit than anything more and ended their relationship."

"Then he was a wise man." While he didn't need a wife and family, Gilliard FitzAlan was cut from a different cloth. "I am glad you are happy. You deserve it after those years of misery."

"You deserve it, too." Aimee's voice was quiet. "And you had it before this took it away." She touched the scar on his head. "My friend, as unbelievable as the truth sounds, you were happier than I have ever seen you in your new life. When you weren't performing your duties for the king, you remained at Drummond enjoying your son and watching your wife's belly grow. The only fly in the ointment of your content was Lisle."

"Lisle?"

"The fluffy-headed light skirt you rebuffed that night in your chamber." Thor thought a moment before nodding for her to continue. "She couldn't stand the thought that any man refused her oft-used wares much less the mighty Golden Wolf. She foolishly believed you were one of those men who wouldn't find your heavily pregnant wife appealing even after a long absence." She couldn't have been more wrong even if Thor didn't remember. "While she should have gone after you, she went after your wife instead."

"Do I want to know what you mean by that?" His hackles were already rising. "More importantly, do I need to know?"

"Yes." Her nod underscored the seriousness of her response. "You want to know and you need to."

"Fine." He patted her hand. "Continue."

"From what you shared with me, you returned from your rounds to discover your wife had blossomed while you were gone. Alexandria feared you would reject her when you returned. Largely because Lisle preyed on her insecurities with her changing body. You didn't, but Lisle didn't know that." Aimee made a moue of distaste at that thought. "She waited until Alexandria left your chamber before sneaking in to offer herself in your wife's stead. Unfortunately, Zan returned while you were throwing Lisle out of your room and misinterpreted the situation. She attacked Lisle and stormed off.

Although you tried to reason with her, she refused to listen. She decided instead to go downstairs to join everyone in the hall. Still smarting from her lady's attack and angry that you'd rebuffed her a second time, Lisle shoved her lady down the stairs before you could stop her. However, you managed to stop Alexandria's fall before she hit the bottom."

"Not again." Where did that come from? "I don't know why I said that."

"Because that's what you said at the time." If Aimee was surprised by his words, she didn't show it. "Everyone heard you."

"What happened next?"

"While Alexandria received a head wound, you stopped her fall before she was seriously injured." Aimee gripped his hand. "However, you couldn't stop her from going into labor a few weeks early. I know there was some kind of complication, but your son and daughter were born strong and healthy." She could only share what she knew. "It took your wife a while to recover from the ordeal, but all was well when she did."

"What of this Lisle?" Thor swirled his goblet. "I believe I have seen her at court recently."

"You have." Aimee nodded. "You wed her to Guy de Lusagne."

"Guy of the Purple Face." Or Guy au Visage Violet as he was known in Normandy. "He is a friend. Why would I offer him such a woman?"

"Because he wanted her." Aimee laughed at the confusion on his face. "Poor Guy. He fell hopelessly in love with the unlovable. A vile creature who couldn't see past his face to the wonderful man underneath in the beginning only to fall madly in love with him on the day they wed. Again, that is a story for another day."

"There seems to be a lot of stories for another day you do not wish to share." Thor set his goblet aside. "Why is that?"

"Why do you think?" Aimee's gaze was intent.

"Because some things are better coming from my wife." The word wasn't quite as hard to say as it had been earlier. "Perhaps you are right."

"I know I'm right." Aimee kissed his hand. "I'm always right."

"Perhaps." In this instance, he believed she was. "I will speak with my wife at some point and hear our story from her lips. More importantly, I will know the truth of her words when I compare them with yours. If they don't match, I will know she is lying. That won't bode well for our alliance. Even should she speak only truth it may not change what lies between us."

"You don't know what lies between you." Aimee gently reminded him. "Don't do anything foolish until you do."

"I will take that under advisement." Thor agreed. "I will leave you to get ready for the evening meal. From the commotion I hear below us, that isn't long in coming."

"No, it isn't." Aimee rose to her feet. "The king will expect you by his side."

"Yes, he will." And his wife would likely be seated at his other side whether he wished it or not. "I won't claim to look forward to this evening. I don't. It can be nothing but trouble."

"Perhaps." Aimee opened her clothes trunk. "Or perhaps it will end some trouble instead."

"Perhaps." Thor rested his hand briefly on her shoulder. "We shall see."

Drawing a sapphire and gold patterned silk bliaut from her trunk, Aimee watched him walk out the door feeling their conversation had done little to advance Lady Zan's cause. However, she took great comfort in the fact she'd done nothing to harm it either.

This was the most usual situation she'd ever navigated and the most difficult as well. Righting her marriage was much less trying. She'd had but to tell Gilliard she carried his child to make everything right between them. Lightly shrugging, she decided she'd done the best she could with the time she had. Now, she must get dressed and below as quickly as possible. It was past time she joined the revelers in the great hall for the king's splendid feast that would end with music, dance, and fabulous storytelling.

CHAPTER TWENTY

Looking around her chamber, Alexandria wished Anna was here to guide her through this latest nightmare. She needed nothing so much as a healthy dose of her maid's irreverent wisdom to set her feet on the right path. While the pain of her absence had dulled with time, it was in these moments of indecision she still felt her friend's loss the most. As hard as Reina tried, she lacked Anna's sharp wit and impudent ways. Almost too genteel there were lines her cousin would never cross. While a worthy lady's maid, she lacked Anna's bossy ways.

Glancing at the vibrantly patterned crimson and gold silk bliaut Reina had selected before she left to dress for the evening meal, Alexandria opened a small velvet bag and removed the gold torque and matching bracelet Thor commissioned for her not long before he'd disappeared. Laying the jewelry on the bed beside her gown she fingered the ruby inset dragon terminals before removing the dangling ruby earrings from the pouch. While not sure wearing the set was a wise idea, she didn't believe it would hurt.

Standing back to study her ensemble, Alexandria admitted she didn't need help dressing. She did need the moral support she wasn't getting. Opening the lid to her clothes trunk again, she lifted the ornate cosmetics box she kept at the royal keep from within its depths. While she rarely bothered tinting her cheeks and lips anymore, she wanted to look her best tonight.

She was up against a court beauty with several marks in her favor. For one thing, she was blonde and willowy just as her husband preferred. For another, it was rumored she would soon be installed at Ruthven as her husband's official leman. Of all his recent actions, this was the one she found most objectionable.

Lifting the hand mirror from the box, Alexandria set it aside before placing each small stone vial and application tool on the table. In no time she'd skillfully applied kohl to her eyes and lashes, darkened pale eyebrows with vasmeh, applied rouge to her cheeks, and tinted her lips.

Satisfied with her handiwork, she pulled her bliaut over her head and fastened the tabs. Slipping into gold silk slippers, she leaned over to pull her hair into the same topknot and high ponytail she'd worn when she arrived in the bailey. Sliding the neck ring and bracelet in place, she slipped the earrings through her lobes before studying herself in the mirror. Hearing the knock on her chamber door, she decided there was nothing more she could do.

Answering the knock, she stepped aside to allow Reina to enter. She looked fresh and pretty in her sapphire silk bliaut. In truth, she looked healthier than she had in months. Contrary to being detrimental to her health as she'd feared, getting out had done her a world of good. Perhaps that was due to nothing so much as escaping the oppressive sorrow that permeated Drummond since Caturex returned without his rider.

"You look wonderful." Alexandria kissed both of her cheeks. "Where is Lionel?"

"Down below." Reina studied her cousin from the top of her head to the tips of her bejeweled toes. "He wanted to get the lay of the land before I joined him." While they wouldn't be at the high table with Alexandria, they would be seated one or two tables back. "I wish we could be closer to you, but I doubt you will need our support. I also doubt that the Wolf will be able to keep his eyes off you. I doubt any man will. You'll make that overused bit of nothing look like what she is."

"I pray you are right." Alexandria fingered the torque around her neck. "I'm not sure wearing this is a good idea."

"Why not?" Reina pulled her hand away. "It's the last thing your husband gave you and it looks like what it is. A love token from a Norseman."

"But is that sentiment even appropriate?" Alexandria shook her head. "We both know he doesn't love me anymore."

"We both know he doesn't know you." Reina rested her hand on her cousin's arm. "Don't let what you hear get you down. Hold your head high knowing you are Thor's wife, not Rosalynd. You have the right to be in his bed and by his side, not her, and in time that is where you will be again. Thor is not as indifferent to you as it seems. The more you stand out, the more intrigued he becomes."

"You are right." Alexandria nodded. "However, we both know Thor doesn't feel that way right now."

"No, he doesn't." Reina agreed. "Not yet, but he will."

"I wish I had your faith." Alexandria straightened the sapphire necklace Reina wore.

She was still confident her cousin remained clueless that the necklace had once belonged to her mother. As far as Reina was concerned, Lionel had her betrothal gift commissioned just for her. The truth was far different. Lady Donata had given the necklace to Lady Elise to keep for her daughter when she knew she was dying. Deciding she was old enough, Lord Ian had given the necklace to Lionel to give to Reina when he permitted them to wed.

"You don't need my faith." Reina smiled softly knowing her cousin didn't know she knew the truth of the necklace she wore. Lionel had told her not long after their marriage. "Perseverance is all you need."

"I hope you're right." Grabbing her key, she opened the door. "While I'm not looking forward to this night, we'd best get below before Godfather sends Lionel to fetch us."

"Then let's do this thing." Stepping into the corridor, Reina watched Alexandria lock the door behind them and drop the key in her pocket. "When you feel like you can't take it anymore, Lionel and I will be out there waiting to lift our glasses to you."

"I'll take you up on that." She followed her cousin down the stairs.

As much as she wished Lionel and Reina could join her at the high table, that wasn't possible. While they might be more lax at Drummond, the same couldn't be said for court. The social hierarchy would be strictly enforced. For all she knew she might not end up at the high table either although Thor certainly would.

She couldn't think of anything better than blending in at a lower table. Nor worse than the thought of sitting at the king's table with her husband and his mistress for all to witness her shame. Just contemplating the thought made her queasy.

However, there wasn't anything she could do about the rules. If the evening meal progressed as usual, she would be seated near, if not beside, the king. Thor would likely be seated on David's other side with Rosalynd clinging to him like a limpet.

If not that way, then he would be seated by her with his mistress on his other side. While painful either way, having Thor seated beside her would be intolerable. Hopefully, her godfather would have the wisdom to see that. Then again, the king might have more important guests and the seating order might be far different. All she knew for certain was that she and Thor would be seated above the salt. So would Lady Rosalynd, thanks to her position in Thor's bed more than to her father's noble rank. Even if she wished things were different.

"Hello, my dear." The king stepped from the shadows to loop his arm through hers. "I thought I would escort you inside. Since we have no special guests this evening, you will sit on my right and Reina will sit between you and Lionel. Thor will sit to my left and his guest will sit by him."

Nodding, Alexandria appreciated that he was trying to make things bearable. Bending the rules even. While none of this would stop her from seeing and hearing what went on between Thor and his mistress, the king would serve as a buffer between her and Lady Rosalynd. Murmuring her thanks, she allowed herself to be led to her chair. Taking her seat, she turned to the young page materializing at her side. No matter how her companions tried to make it seem otherwise, this was a night she'd wish to end long before it finally did.

WATCHING THE SCARLET-clad woman rise to her feet after beating the king at a challenging game of chess, Thor studied the heavy gold torque around her neck. It looked like something Orm Snake-Tooth would craft. If it was, he'd commissioned the piece for his wife. While her coffers were likely filled with many beautiful pieces of jewelry, he doubted the lady of Drummond had the wherewithal to commission jewels from the trickiest goldsmith in Normandy.

Studying the exquisitely carved finials, the ruby-eyed dragons weren't necessarily Norse if the thick gold neck ring was. They were more homage to his wife's Celtic ancestry. Shaking his head, Thor decided he was slightly taken aback by what he was seeing. If he was another man he would think such a gift was born of affection, but he wasn't.

He was the Golden Wolf. He'd likely commissioned the piece to reinforce the fact he was a wealthy, powerful man with the resources to bestow such useless baubles on his wife. Yes, that was it. It had to be.

"My lord, thank you for inviting me to join you here." Alexandria curtsied as she prepared to take her leave. "And thank you for a most challenging game."

"You are welcome, my dear." David patted her hand. "While I would enjoy another game, I know it has been a trying day." He nodded at her soft response of agreement. Between the long ride here and the hours spent watching Rosalynd hang all over her husband, it couldn't be any less. "I also suspect you shall have an unexpected guest before the night ends." He studied the tall blonde observing them over her shoulder.

"Perhaps." Curtseying again, Alexandria headed for the stairs unaware of the amber eyes following her every move. "Either way, tomorrow is another day."

Weaving her way through the merrymakers dancing, joking, and playing games, she stopped by a lower table to speak briefly to Reina and Lionel unsurprised they were deep in conversation. They'd never lacked for things to talk about. That they enjoyed each other's company was one of the strong points of their marriage.

Letting the couple know she was retiring she slipped out of the great hall and headed for the stairs. Lifting her skirts, she raced up the steps before taking the familiar corridor to the left when she arrived on the landing. In a matter of moments she'd unlocked the door and stepped inside the small chamber she'd always considered her home away from home.

Leaning against the door, Alexandria took a deep breath and whispered a few choice words. While she'd pleaded exhaustion, she wasn't. The truth was much simpler than that. She couldn't take another moment in the great hall without acting beneath her dignity.

If she watched another woman practicing her feminine wiles on her husband, she'd rip her hair out by the roots. She couldn't stop herself. Perhaps she would feel differently if those women hadn't known the Golden Wolf was married. They not only knew he was, but they knew they were in the presence of his wife. That was why she'd decided all bets were off and she'd best retire before she did something she would regret.

Walking over to the clothes chest, she lifted the lid. Unfastening the tabs of her bliaut, she stepped out of the garment. Lifting the dress before shaking it out, she carefully folded the gown and tucked it away in her clothes chest along with her slippers. Picking at her chemise, she wasn't quite ready to slide under the covers so there was no reason to get naked. Added to the fact she wasn't sleepy; the chill wasn't off the room yet. Grabbing a vibrantly colored woolen robe, she closed the lid.

Shrugging into the garment, Alexandria looked around the familiar chamber recalling the night that started it all. Given this latest turn of events, her memories were surreal. A lot had changed since then. More than she'd ever believe possible. Both for the good and the bad.

If she doubted that was true, the Thor she met earlier proved it. That he'd taken one look at her and walked away was incomprehensible. It was obvious that the man wasn't her husband. He wasn't even the man who'd claimed her in this room. He was *the* Golden Wolf, not *her* Golden Wolf. The feared and revered warrior of lore.

Her heart shattered, there was no time to despair. Not when her people and her lands needed her. Expecting Reina, she turned at the whisper of her chamber door opening. 'Speak of the devil,' roared through her head.

"What are you doing here?" She'd meant to lock the door behind her. She just hadn't gotten around to it yet. No, the truth was that she'd grown lax knowing she had little to fear in the royal keep now that the MacLaren was gone. "I didn't expect to see you so soon."

Eventually, yes, their paths would cross. She'd be a fool not to know that. Court wasn't that big and her husband was an important man. He spent as much time in the king's presence as she did. To think they wouldn't run into each other many times before she left was unrealistic.

"Aimee urged me to speak to you." Thor reluctantly admitted as he locked the door behind him. "She convinced me that I would regret letting you leave without doing so."

"I see." Alexandria huffed softly. "Your mistress persuaded you to converse with your wife."

"My friend." Thor corrected. "You must know we haven't been lovers in years."

Not since Gilliard FitzAlan realized what a fool he was for neglecting the beautiful young wife who adored him. Once that truth permeated his thick skull, he hadn't strayed again. Neither had his wife. Their simpering ways and growing family were testimony to a mutual change of heart.

He'd never seen a more doting husband or a more adoring wife. It turned his stomach. It was fortunate for the couple that FitzAlan was known to be more of a silvery-tongued court lizard than a skilled warrior. He wouldn't survive the battle. However, he had his uses as a diplomat, and if he didn't miss his guess, as a spy as well.

"I do." From what she knew of Gilliard FitzAlan, Thor wouldn't get anywhere near his wife if the other man feared being cuckolded by the Wolf. It was obvious that he had no qualms from that direction. "That's good to know."

"I suppose it is." Thor looked around the chamber he'd wandered through but had yet to truly see. "So this is where it started?" The small room had a surprisingly homey feel despite the things he knew. "In this room?"

"Where what started?" Alexandria's soft snort was dismissive. "You and me?"

"Yes." Thor agreed. "That."

"Yes, and no." Preferring to remain standing, she gestured to the only chair in the room. "This is where our relationship was first consummated, but I suspect the moment I arrived in the bailey is when we truly began."

"Meaning?" Thor leaned back in the chair and waited expectantly. "I fear that idea is beyond me."

"Is it?" Alexandria's laugh was more strident than she'd intended. "Then what I mean is you were more intrigued by the woman in men's clothing mastering a massive fawn destrier that day than you cared to admit."

Snort reverberating through the room, Thor knew no cross-dressing, sword-toting female with obnoxiously red hair and a milkmaid's bosom would ever catch his eye. However, her wealth, titles, and property may have although that twist likely happened later. After he'd learned her identity.

"Just as you're intrigued now. Deny the truth if you wish, but we both know better. You wouldn't be here now if you weren't."

"Perhaps." He would concur she was somewhat captivating for her strangeness alone. "Perhaps not."

"I'm sure you've heard the story of how we came together by now." If her godfather hadn't told him then someone had. The most likely culprit was Lady Aimee. His good friend if nothing more. "Of what happened that night."

"Perhaps." Thor evaded. "Perhaps the king felt your story better coming from you."

"Perhaps." Alexandria agreed. "But it's our story; not mine."

"Perhaps." Thor stared her down. "I will be the judge of that."

"Will you?" Alexandria stared back. "You truly do not know?"

"I do not." Thor walked over to sit on her bed knowing the intimacy of his action would unsettle her far more than occupying the sole chair in the room. "When I asked yet again, your godfather reminded me that he wasn't in the room to witness events better explained by the other party who was."

Alexandria choked on her laugh. That sounded like their king. Beneath his saintly exterior beat the heart of an unrepentant male. While her godfather was familiar with every sordid detail she'd deigned to share, he'd chosen not to divulge what he knew.

She doubted there was anything nefarious behind his actions. He likely believed her sharing what passed between them that night might serve to bring them closer together. While she doubted he was right, she was willing to try.

"Had he been things would have ended far differently." Walking over to lean against the window seal, she watched Thor watching her as he made himself comfortable on her bed. "Do you remember anything at all?"

"Nothing." Save the briefest flashes of burnished ivory skin and sanguine locks flickering in a dying flame as two bodies came together on a fur-covered mattress more comfortable than it should have been. "Nothing at all."

Watching amber eyes close briefly before opening again, Alex knew he was lying. He remembered something. She didn't know what. Most likely their most intimate moments if the sweat on his brow was anything to go by.

"I see." She had less to work with than she thought. "Then let's start at the beginning."

"What beginning?" Thor crossed his arms behind his head. "The one that says you came to court hoping to catch my interest?" He had his current mistress to thank for that information since the king was less forthcoming. "I have heard as well that you were less than successful in your quest."

"Who shared that?" Her mocking snort spoke volumes. "Lady Rosalynd Rosy Cheeks or the Trollop of Tewkesbury Tower?"

Thor resisted the urge to laugh at her caustic, but apt, description of Lady Caryn. The woman had passed briefly through his bed before he'd caught her enthusiastically swiving the royal stable master in a back stall. Needless to say, their liaison ended soon after. As for the rosy cheeks comment, he wasn't sure whether that referred to Rosalynd's arse or her face both of which were deliciously tinted after an enthusiastic romp. He didn't care.

No, he did care. It was more truthful to admit he didn't want to dwell too deeply on from whence, and from whom that nickname may have come. He still wasn't positive making Rosalynd official was a wise move although he'd all but done so already. He wouldn't have wasted precious time negotiating with her fool of a father if he hadn't.

"Neither, it was the same friend who urged me to speak with you before I did anything." There was no reason to lie. "Aimee has done everything in her power to return me to the wife she insists I once cared deeply for no matter that I don't believe her."

Alexandria recoiled at the verbal punch in the gut. While she doubted he'd meant his words so viscerally, they took her breath away. It was one thing to know Thor bore her no affection in her head. It was another for him to admit it.

"She is right." Alexandria closed her eyes against the memory of the arrestingly feline dark-haired beauty greeting Thor in nothing but bare skin and raven locks. "I failed miserably and returned to my chamber to lick my wounds in private since I'd given Anna the night off." She ignored the hiked brow. "She had friends to visit and I had other plans."

She'd hoped a certain warrior would play lady's maid when it was time to prepare for bed. However, nothing had gone to plan.

"Are you always that generous with your servants?" Every lady he knew was notoriously demanding of her attendants' time. "Or was it a fluke?"

"My servants are my people." Alexandria gently reminded him. "They are family, too."

"Anna was Lord Ian's leman." Thor laid a card she didn't know he had on the table. "I suspect she had more freedom than most to do as she pleased."

"Anna was my maid long before my father took her to his bed." Alexandria corrected him. "While things may have been different with another woman, they weren't with her. She was content with the life she had, and happy she was taken into the lord's household when her parents died within two days of each other from a fever.

No one was surprised when Anna caught my father's eye, or when she returned his affections. My father would have married her were the MacLarens not breathing down our necks. We children would have welcomed the marriage. As things were, Anna and Reina were my dearest friends."

"Your cousin." He laid another card on the table she wasn't surprised he had. The Golden Wolf was nothing if not thorough.

"Yes, my cousin." Alexandria agreed. "I wallowed in my failure for a while, then I went to bed. It was a long day."

"Where was I," Thor picked at the covers. "While you wallowed?"

"Embracing a naked Aimee FitzAlan the last I saw of you." Alexandria shrugged.

"I wasn't sure you would admit to following me," Thor smirked at the image in his head. "I probably wouldn't."

"You would be hard to miss," Alexandria stated the obvious. "Do you remember me following you, or did Lady Aimee fill in the missing pieces?"

"I was told." Thor looked her straight in the eyes. "I remember nothing of that night."

'Or any other night in your company' remained unsaid.

"While I remember everything." Alexandria sat on the window sill facing him overjoyed that not only was a fire burning in the hearth but the shutters were already closed when she'd retired for the night. "Including the look on your face when you took me."

Thor fluffed the pillows behind him as he settled in more intent on comfort than disconcerting his antagonist. There was plenty of time for that later. He would enjoy every second.

"I had such high hopes for that night." Alexandria laughed at the understatement. "I wore my best chemise and bliaut and dabbed a touch of color on my cheeks and lips despite Anna's disapproval. I was determined to make you admit the attraction I knew was there."

"You were determined to seduce me to your bed knowing your godfather would try to force my hand if you did." Thor snorted openly at that thought. "Better women than you have tried that trick and failed."

Biting her tongue, Alexandria let the insult slide. Were her husband in his right mind, he would never say such a thing. She knew it and he knew it somewhere deep inside. She was sure of that. If the faint glimmer of interest she saw in his amber gaze was any indication, he wasn't as immune to her charms as he claimed.

"Perhaps." She nodded. "But while that may be true, I got what I wanted in the end even if it took longer than planned."

"I suppose you did." But she wouldn't get it again if he had anything to say about it and he did. "However, that doesn't mean you will succeed this time."

"No, it doesn't," Alexandria spoke brave words she was far from feeling. "But it doesn't mean I won't either."

"Perhaps." He began to see what may have initially intrigued him more and more with every passing moment he spent in her company. "Why don't you tell me about that night."

"I can do that." Alexandria untied her sash and slid out of her robe before she wriggled into a more comfortable position on the window sill. Setting the garment on the floor beside her, she decided the room had heated up faster than expected. "As you already know, I failed miserably at even getting you to dance with me much less anything more so I returned to my room. Alone. I locked my door and undressed before slipping under the covers. The last thing I remember is planning my next move while watching the flames dying in the fireplace. I must have fallen asleep without realizing it..."

"I believe that is the way of things." Thor laughed softly at the ridiculous statement. "I also believe there was more to the evening than you simply slipping away in defeat to your lonely bed."

"Perhaps." Alexandria nodded. "Alright, I followed you to your room and saw Aimee FitzAlan greet you wearing nothing but a curtain of wonderous hair. I knew I couldn't compete so I returned to my room to lick my wounds."

"You did more than that." The careful way he studied her made Alexandria want to squirm. "From what I have been told you lingered where you shouldn't hoping to see God only knows what before you scampered away like a mouse."

"I see your friend has been sharing things better left unsaid." Alexandria rose to her feet. "I will admit to being curious about the nature of your relationship."

"You were curious about far more than the nature of our relationship as that was readily apparent," Thor stated bluntly. "However, from what Aimee tells me, you were sorely disappointed that night. She was more interested in talking about her husband and, according to her, I was more interested in you."

"Perhaps." Alexandria remained noncommittal. "I can't speak to what happened in Lady FitzAlan's chamber after I left."

"I can." Thor rose to his feet. "While I don't remember that particular night, I remember Aimee. We were always friends first and lovers second. There was many a night we did nothing but talk and that night was one of them."

"That's good to know." Alexandria watched him walk towards her. "There was always something sordid about believing you left her bed and came to mine."

"Again, from what I have been told, coming to your bed was never my intent." That it shouldn't have mattered if he had bedded his favorite mistress remained unsaid. "I'm under the impression I was headed downstairs when something drew me to your room."

"I screamed;" Alexandria admitted. "You burst through the door."

"I see." Thor turned to glance at the door, not surprised to see visible signs of past repairs. "And what did I find once I stepped inside?"

"James MacLaren trying to rape me in my bed." Eventually to become their bed, though that wasn't yet true. "Had you arrived a moment later, he would have succeeded in his plan."

Thor digested her words. While he suspected the king knew of this event, David had failed to share the information with him. Likely for a lot of different reasons. Not the least of which was that something so heinous should never have happened in the royal keep. He doubted the attack was even known outside of him, the king, and a handful of his wife's closest associates. If that night ended as he suspected, James MacLaren would be the last person wanting the truth to come out.

"I see." He didn't. "Why wasn't your door locked?"

"Godfather assured me the MacLaren would not be at court during my visit," Alexandria shrugged. "And I've already told you that my door was locked. I suspect one of James MacLaren's spies sent word that I was at court and slipped him a spare key. This was a storage room until I claimed it so I'm sure keys have been lost, forgotten, or stolen over the years."

"You are right." Thor agreed. "It wouldn't be hard for the wrong person to get their hands on your key."

While she wouldn't have believed anyone brazen enough to take such a risk at the royal keep she now knew she was wrong.

"What happened in here?" Thor looked around the chamber deciding what he was seeing in the moment wasn't all that different from what he'd seen that night. Not if he imagined the fire slowly fading to glimmering coals that cast creepy shadows on the walls. It *was* the same small space with nowhere to run and nowhere to hide. "You fell asleep, then what?"

"I fell asleep with my hand under my pillow gripping," Alexandria reached inside her robe to pull the bejeweled dagger from within its folds. "This."

Gazing at the weapon Thor laughed softly. The woman was full of surprises. While a pretty trinket, the blade was as lethal as it was beguiling. He'd seen similar on his stint in Constantinople.

"The sound of rushes crushing under someone's weight must have awakened me." She took a deep breath. "When I heard a slight dragging sound I knew I wasn't alone, so I eased my dagger from beneath my pillow but I never got to use it...Jamie must have suspected I would be armed because he knocked my weapon out of my hand when I tried to stab him..." Alexandria fought to control her emotions. "I assume he arrived after dark and scurried about like the rat he was...It wouldn't be hard to slip past the court while everyone was seeing and being seen, especially if he hid beneath a mantle."

Thor couldn't deny the truth of her words. It was a useful ploy he and his men often used successfully. Why wouldn't other men use it as well?

"So the MacLaren attacked you in your chamber." While he'd heard words to that effect, no one knew what truly happened behind closed doors.

Alexandria nodded. "When I fought back, he knocked me senseless and crawled on top of me." Gathering her thoughts, she looked anywhere but at Thor. "He would have raped me if you hadn't heard my scream and burst through the door."

"Again, I just happened to be walking by in time to intercede?" That was too convenient to believe if he hadn't heard it before. "Surely there is a better explanation than that."

"You know as well as I that the corridor outside my room is a shortcut from your lover's room to the stairs." Alexandria stared him down not liking his choice of words. "I imagine your only intent was to get to a goblet of ale and the evening's entertainment as quickly as possible. I know as well, had you not interfered, Drummond would belong to Jamie MacLaren and I would be long dead."

It was no secret the only interest the MacLaren had in her other than possessing her lands and title was the legitimate heir or two she could give him. Once that was done, she was expendable. He would no longer need a wife. Not when her possessions were already his. Had events turned out differently, her whole family would be dead and there would be nothing the king could have done to prevent it.

"What happened after?" He could well imagine his reaction if what she said was true. "I have been told I threatened to gut the sniveling roach on more than one occasion." Thor briefly closed his eyes. "I imagine I did the same this time, but I don't know why."

"I am sure you were given many possibilities." Alexandria watched his eyes flicker open. "Now you have heard the truth."

"I believe I have." Thor nodded. "What happened after I burst through the door?" If he even did such a thing when all he had was her and Aimee's word for it.

"You tore the MacLaren off of me, threw him against the wall, offered to gut him if he came sniffing around my skirts again, and tossed him in the corridor." Alexandria ticked off each thing as though having the Golden Wolf offer to disembowel someone was an everyday occurrence. Then again, she suspected it wasn't that uncommon either. "Once he slithered into the darkness like the shadow crawler he was, you turned your attention to me."

While her words could have a sensual slant, he suspected they weren't meant that way. If he knew himself, and he did, he'd immediately been seized with the need for damage control. Word getting out would be the last thing he wanted to happen.

A noblewoman almost getting taken against her will in the royal keep wouldn't have gone over well with David's friends. It would have given valuable ammunition to his enemies instead. Knowing himself as he did, he would have done everything he could to silence the king's goddaughter short of harming her.

"I'm assuming you don't mean that the way it sounded." Thor quirked a brow at her. "I suspect my first course of action was to pressure you to keep quiet about what almost happened. I suspect my second course of action was to reassure you that you were safe for the rest of your stay. That I vowed to make sure of that."

"Something like that." Alexandria agreed. "But your third course of action is what you refuse to acknowledge or contemplate."

"What do you mean?" Thor ran a hand through his hair. "My third course of action? My last action would have been to ensure the MacLaren had left the premises and the gates were locked behind him. Once that was done I would have met with the king to apprise him of that bastard's latest transgression. Then I would have rooted out his accomplices and ensured their banishment from court as well."

While he refused to contemplate why he felt so strongly about a man he'd killed a lifetime ago, he wished he could revive the MacLaren and slaughter him all over again. As much as he wished he could say otherwise, he knew his feelings had to do with more than just what he'd been told about the fall of Drummond but he wasn't going there. He wasn't an emotional man and some things were better left buried even if Aimee and his wife felt differently.

"While I'm sure you did all of that eventually," Alexandria was amused some things never changed. "That wasn't your third course of action."

"Oh?" The quirked brow said it all.

While her husband didn't remember her, much less love her, his flesh still responded readily to memories he didn't know he had. She expected nothing less. His body had always responded to hers. Even when he didn't want it to.

Besides, the mighty Thor left his mark on his possessions. His wife was nothing if not a possession-at least in this man's eyes. Her husband felt differently. However, her husband wasn't the man she was dealing with. Yet, a man was still a man and her Golden Wolf lay hidden within the depths of those unholy amber eyes. She knew that in her soul.

"This was." Alexandria rested her hand on his chest feeling muscles tense beneath her palm. Pulling his head down to hers, she pressed her lips against his expecting him to resist. Surprised to feel him draw her closer, she allowed him to deepen the kiss. Eventually pulling away, she laughed softly yet again. "That was your third course of action, and this was mine."

Untying the ribbon to her chemise, she allowed the garment to flow over every curve as it gradually pooled around her feet reminiscent of a silken sheet on a different night. Taking a deep breath to steady her nerves, she allowed Thor to study her naked form. While not fashionably angular, she was slender and toned with womanly curves few men could ignore. That included the one standing before her. It was apparent by the dilation of his pupils and the quickening of his breath that he wasn't immune to her charms as much as he might wish to be.

Stepping out of the puddle of fabric, she walked over to her husband. Lifting the hem of his tunic, she pulled it over his head. As she'd expected, Thor didn't resist her overture. He lifted his arms to help her instead. If the situation weren't painfully sucking her heart from her chest, she'd laugh at how easily he'd fallen under her spell.

This was a scenario she'd never imagined nor one she'd ever wished to experience. Even on that first night, his touch wasn't as devoid of emotion as she knew this encounter would be. He'd desired her of his own accord with a passion he'd never wanted to feel back then.

This night was different and they both knew it. While she could toy with him much as he'd toyed with her, they both knew why he'd appeared in her doorway this eve. It had nothing to do with getting reacquainted. Not in any meaningful way. The act was merely reasserting ownership over what belonged to him, whether he truly wished it or not.

He was reclaiming her body, titles, and lands in the most primitive way possible and they both knew it. Perhaps it even meant claiming his heirs if he'd thought that far ahead. Both the sons he'd already fathered and the ones yet to come. While that was the way of their world two could play that game.

She'd let Thor believe he'd accomplished his goals while that belief was in the best interests of protecting her body, titles, people, and lands. When their alliance no longer benefited everything she held dear, she would repudiate that pretense and make alternate plans. Her godfather would help her.

Once her marriage was dissolved, she would wait for the man who truly loved her. Everyone knew it was only a matter of time before he was free again. Having experienced real love, she would settle for nothing less under these circumstances. Even if that meant the Wolf no longer populated her life or bed.

Watching Thor back up to sit on the bed, she stepped naked between his thighs. Lifting her hands she closed her eyes and ran her palms over his torso and arms noting every new scar marring his skin. Opening her eyes, she studied new welts and puckered ridges with practiced hands.

While Lionel said he'd not been injured in the skirmish, he'd taken a hell of a beating somewhere between there and here. Probably more than one. Most likely after he'd fallen in the ambush. If he'd truly fallen at all? From the positioning of the scars it was far more likely he'd fought through his last conscious breath.

While she'd yet to learn exactly what happened, she refused to believe the random whispers she overheard. When the time was right, she would hear the truth from the only man still living to share the events of that day. In the interim, they had more important things to do that were far less traumatic for both of them.

Though none of their men had fallen in battle, they were scattered over the battlefield when the truce was called. That made it likely her sources were somewhat accurate. She knew Thor remained behind to witness the final agreements. If he'd done as Lionel said he vowed, he would have traveled part of the way with a neighboring party. There was nothing unusual about that.

Warriors from differing locals often traveled together for protection and to reinforce alliances and camaraderie. That most of the party fell to enemy swords wasn't all that uncommon either. Nor was the reality the rest had died in an enemy dungeon. Those were common occurrences. She couldn't deny that Drummond housed her fair share of enemies below ground over the years.

"This alone should have killed you." She kissed the puckered skin near his temple. "Or this." Her lips brushed the scar on his neck. "And this is why nothing is as it should be." She ran her hands through his hair feeling the jagged tear so similar, and yet so different from the injury that had claimed her father on the battlefield.

Shaking her head, there was no reason to ask if his injuries were ever treated. The truth was in the scarring. It was a miraculous testimony to Thor's physical strength that he'd survived the infections that ravaged his body. A miracle but not that surprising. The Wolf was a preternaturally strong man.

"Perhaps," Thor grunted as she straddled his lap before leaning over to caress the wicked scar running diagonally across his abdomen from chest to groin. "But they didn't." As for the scar on his scalp, he had nothing to say because, in his opinion, everything was as it should be.

Catching his eyes, Alexandria wasn't surprised when Thor buried his face in her shoulder. Some part of him remembered her and what they had. If that weren't true she wouldn't be mounting him as she was. This man would never allow a leman to dominate him. He would never lie back so just any woman could have her wicked way with him body and soul. Staring into amber eyes, she smiled and moved her hips in the way that always drove him wild.

Watching his eyes slowly drift closed, she wasn't surprised by the conflict on his face. The Golden Wolf refused to be bested by any woman. He always had. He always would. Or so he'd believed until he met Alexandria of Drummond. However, this man didn't know that or their history, but he would learn. It shouldn't take long to disavow him of his fallacies. Once she'd learned his intimate secrets she'd brought her Wolf to heel. What she'd done once, she would do again.

The only fly in the ointment, the same was true for the Wolf. He'd brought her to her knees without even trying and she'd gladly let him. More importantly, she'd willingly walked beside him and he'd let her. No matter where their path led.

She'd even fought with him the one time a neighboring lord sought to claim Ruthven for his own. Childless, the upstart had lost his life and his legacy for his trouble. With the king's blessing, Thor claimed de Clercy's properties as his own. He'd remarried his child bride to a loyal vassal and ensured no one would try that move again. One she helped him select. Neither they nor the happy widow had regretted that choice in the years since.

Looking into Thor's dilated pupils and hearing his breath quicken, Alexandria decided it didn't hurt that they'd connected physically from the start. Love and trust came later. Feeling strong fingers bite into her arms, she laughed softly as Thor flipped her over to assume the dominant position before the sound died in her throat.

Were it another time and place, her heart would overflow knowing she could drive her Wolf to such rabid passion...But those days were long gone...There was nothing of love or adoration in their frenzied coupling...Just lupine lust and her hemorrhaging heart.

CHAPTER TWENTY-ONE

Carefully sliding from beneath the arm resting across her body, Alexandria rose to her feet. Freshening up, she dressed in a clean chemise and simple bliaut from her clothes trunk. Brushing her hair, she quickly wove vibrant tresses into a fat braid to flow freely down her back. She didn't have time for the elaborate coils, braids, and twists she favored at home. Nor did she have flowers or ribbons to weave through her locks to give the illusion that all was well with her world. Nothing could be farther from the truth. She refused to pretend it was.

At the moment she was more intent on escaping the room where her husband lay sprawled across her bed pretending to be dead to the world than she was in impressing anyone. While she knew it was a lie, Thor's pretense gave her the reprieve she didn't request but desperately needed. Although they'd spent the night grappling for dominance and mindlessly coupling, she knew nothing had changed.

If anything they'd grown further apart. Unless she missed the mark, her husband would spend tonight in the bed of his paramour trying to wipe the memories of their encounter from his mind. Unfortunately, she didn't have that option. Unlike her husband, she remembered their marriage and took her vows seriously.

Making her way out the door, Alexandria headed for the great hall preoccupied with her memories. Lying beneath the rutting beast pounding so ruthlessly into her body with such finesse, she understood why the women of court lined up for the opportunity to share the Golden Wolf's bed. He approached bed sport with the same enthusiasm he embraced a battlefield.

While she would think him a magnificent lover under different circumstances, her *husband's* performance was lacking.

Senses drowning in erotic sensation, her heart shattered into a million bloody shards realizing there was no love in Thor's skillful dance. Only the slaking of carnal appetites to the pleasure of both parties. Nothing more, nothing less. The only emotion in their copulation was the certainty her lover intended to complete his erotic quest the conqueror the Golden Wolf was always meant to be.

Refusing to shed the tears burning her eyelids, she'd willed herself to feel the same detachment her husband felt and revel in the experience instead. She'd succeeded to a certain degree. It was only after Thor was spent and quietly snoring in her ear that she'd finally given into silent tears of despair.

Making her way to the great hall, Alexandria grabbed a roll, tore it open, and stuffed a thick slice of juicy roasted venison slathered in garlicky mustard sauce between the halves. Taking a delicate bite she filled her cup with aleberry and headed for the door.

While the king and court had broken the fast a while ago, a small spread was always left out for the guards ending their shifts and the warriors returning from early morning battle play. Men who appreciated the simplicity of thick slices of crusty bread, hearty rolls, slabs of cheese, and meat washed down with generous pitchers of mead or ale.

Forget the wine and posturing of the aristocrats gorging on the fat of the king's table. Prepare a raspberry mint sauce or a hearty mustard sauce to enhance the flavor and they were satisfied. As much as Bertie would hate to hear it, she felt the same. Simple was better.

Deciding to stroll over the grounds to get reacquainted with a keep she hadn't visited in a while; Alexandria set her ale on a ledge and wiped her hands together to banish crumbs and grease. Draining her cup, she tucked it into her pocket glad she'd grabbed the vessel on her way out of her room. Laughing softly, she could imagine Anna's outrage that her lady took such pleasure in drinking from her peasant's cup.

Besides the convenience of fitting neatly into her pocket, the cup reminded her of the dear friend she'd lost a lifetime ago. Just as watching the king drink from one of her father's bejeweled goblets reminded her of the brave warrior he'd once been. Fortunately, she didn't need a trinket to remind her of Thor for that warrior still lived and breathed.

"How are you, my dear?" The king's hand resting on her shoulder halted Alexandria's forward progress. "We haven't had a chance to talk."

Oh, they'd talked alright. They just hadn't *talked*.

"How do you think?" Alexandria shook her head. "That man isn't my husband."

All she needed to keep her head straight was the knowledge that Thor had left another woman's bed to come to hers. She hadn't been sure when he first arrived in her room, but she'd grown certain she was right as the evening wore on. While she'd ignored the cloying lavender scent still clinging to his skin to seize the opportunity that might never come again, the reality of what she'd done turned her stomach in the light of day.

"No, he isn't." David agreed. "But the man you made of him is still deep inside."

"Perhaps." Alexandria huffed softly. "Perhaps not...I don't know."

"You have given up?" The king took a step back to look at her. "That's not your way."

"No, it isn't," She agreed. "But it's been recently pounded home that failure is possible no matter what I do."

"That is always true with anything worth doing." David reminded her. "How do you think I feel every time I go to war?"

"That failure is a possibility." Alexandria's laugh was raw with pain. "Rest assured, I have not given up and I won't until he gives me no other choice."

"Good." David nodded. "If the day comes when you cannot bear Thor's actions, I will see you freed to wed another. You have my promise. If necessary I will call in favors long overdue to accomplish that end."

He had already initiated correspondence with the Archbishop about the matter. If the time came when he needed to get that ball rolling, his ally would know his goddaughter had done everything in her power to bring her husband home. He was confident if anyone could get the claim of consanguinity through the appropriate channels his friend would. That it wasn't true didn't matter. Only getting the approval of the necessary church authorities did. He was prepared to be quite generous to ensure his end was achieved if it came to that.

"Thank you." Alexandria smiled. "If that day comes, I will take you up on it."

"But for now, you will fight to rediscover what you have lost," David smiled back. "And I will help you."

"Aye." Alexandria sounded braver than she felt. "I need all the help I can get."

"You may get badly hurt before you are done." David's face was serious. "Are you prepared for that?"

"Are you ever prepared for your husband to stop loving you?" Alexandria answered honestly. "Ever prepared to watch him woo and bed other women? Ever prepared to know he just spent himself within another before he came to you?"

David winced at her words. He'd hoped to shield her from such knowledge, but he knew better. Few secrets remained secret at court. Least of all infidelities. Not when so many waited in the wings to share every indiscretion with his goddaughter out of the goodness of their hearts. Right, there was nothing good about their motivations or intent. The king laughed at that thought. The only thing in those blue-blooded hussies' hearts was the hope they'd get their chance to tup the Wolf while his broken-hearted bride looked on.

"Surely you didn't think I was that blind?" Alexandria scoffed at the thought. "That isn't possible. He reeked of lavender without the fresh scratches across his back I suspect were inflicted mainly for my benefit." She laughed at the lengths some women would go to claim another's mate. "As for getting hurt, that has already happened more than once. What are a few more lacerations?"

"More than you can take?" David patted her hand.

"Nay," Alexandria admitted. "I must persevere for my people and my bairns." And though she refused to admit it, for herself as well. This stranger was her husband. As much as it hurt at the moment, she still loved the man he used to be. She would come to love the man he was. "We both know I won't walk away without trying. I can't, as much as I want to."

It wasn't her way to surrender without a fight. She never had. She never would. It wasn't in her nature.

"I do know." He expected nothing less. "However, don't destroy yourself in the process. That is more than anyone should ask you to do." He squeezed her hand. "If it helps, I believe you will win in the end."

"So do I." As long as she remained strong. "If I can hold on that long."

Knowing hers wasn't the only bed Thor shared was slowly killing her. While she wanted to react to the truth she knew, she wouldn't. She couldn't. No matter how deeply the pain cut. To throw a tantrum or attack his other lovers would only drive Thor away. She knew that as well. He must come to her of his own accord when he was ready. She refused to contemplate the possibility that may never happen. It was too soon to claim defeat.

—⁂—

WATCHING THE WOMAN leave through slitted eyes, Thor knew she wasn't fooled by his ploy. Alexandria appreciated the reprieve as much as he did. There was a reason he never remained with his bedmates once they were done. A quick departure avoided the awkward conversations that eventually came though they shouldn't have. He made it clear that he lingered but a season from the start. He couldn't stay for several reasons.

For one, he never wanted to stay. For another, he was a married man. It mattered little that knowledge did nothing to curtail his extramarital activities. For a third, he would never wed again if he could. Lastly, he lived by his code of honor. He never promised what he wouldn't give.

Rising from the bed, Thor washed up before donning his clothes. Looking around the chamber, he wasn't surprised everything was in its place. Even his clothing had been neatly draped over the back of a chair. Against his will, he appreciated the woman's neatness. The small chamber would grow untidy quickly if she weren't.

Deciding he'd waited long enough for his bedmate to make her escape, he headed for the stairs and the great hall. On his way to the practice field, he'd swing by the kitchen to visit with Cook and do any heavy lifting she needed to have done.

It was a game established long ago when he was but a young cub visiting the royal keep with Prince Henry and it was a game they still played today.

Everyone knew her Wolfie always paid Cook a morning visit when he was at court and she always prepped him a drawstring bag of goodies.

If he was lucky, there would be an apple fritter or two as well as fresh oatcakes, some Crowdie cheese, and several rashers of bacon to tempt his palate. If there happened to be a flask of hard apple cider included, he wasn't telling anyone. That Cook felt good deeds should never go unrewarded had played in his favor for many years.

Nodding to the king in passing, Thor saw that his suspicion was right. Alexandria of Drummond was nowhere in sight. While a pleasurable romp to see what he was missing and fill uncomfortable holes in his memory was one thing, anything more was another. One tumble was as far as it went.

He still had no desire to acknowledge his marriage or share his wife's bed tonight. He had more important places to be. If some insignificant part of him rebelled at that idea it was easily ignored. He wouldn't give the woman any reason to believe they were reconciling. That would be deceitful to both of them.

As soon as his wife's visit ended, Lady Rosalynd would be installed at Ruthven as his official mistress. In time, perhaps she'd become more. Young and nubile, she had a generous dowry, a pretty face, and a lissome form to recommend her.

Admittedly, her dowry wasn't as generous as Drummond but, as he'd already said, he didn't need more wealth, power, or property. He had more than enough as it was. Even without his wife's properties should life come to that. It was more important to him that his partner was tolerable both in and out of bed. While his wife was an exceptional lover, she was far from tolerable in any other way.

CHAPTER TWENTY-TWO

Walking out on the battlement, Reina ignored the soldiers milling about. She was used to sweaty, smelly men underfoot. The only difference was that there were more of them at a royal keep. Some things never changed. Given where they were, she was surprised her cousin managed to find a quiet corner away from everyone.

Then again, she shouldn't be. Alexandria had found a small, cluttered chamber to lay claim to soon after her presentation at court a decade ago. Or, more likely, the king's steward had found and prepared the room for his goddaughter before her arrival. The how didn't matter. That she had a private space did. Looking around to ensure they were alone; Reina silently approached her cousin.

"Alex?" She rested her hand on her cousin's shoulder. "What is wrong?"

"Nothing." Alexandria's smile didn't reach her eyes. "Everything." The words poured out of her. "I don't know this man."

"Your husband could say the same." He didn't know his wife. "While Thor would be right, you are wrong." Ignoring her cousin's indignation, she refused to hold her tongue. "Whether you see it or not, this is the man you wed and the man you forced to love you. What you did once, you can do again."

"I don't know." She wasn't sure she wanted to try. "I'm not that woman anymore."

Her life was different now. She was no longer the warrior maid fighting a madman for survival. She was a grown woman with a household to run and bairns to raise. While no longer her savior, the Golden Wolf had become her port in a storm. The one stable thing in a life filled with uncertainties. Now all of that was gone.

"Aren't you?" Reina challenged. "You're wrong about that."

"I'm not," Alexandria shook her head. "If I were he wouldn't go from my bed to hers."

"The blonde hussy?" Reina snorted again. "Rosalynd is but a comely bit of naught. An absent-minded bed warmer. Not a woman of substance. You are Thor's wife and a celebrated healer and warrior in your own right. Your husband isn't a foolish man. He will come to his senses in time."

"Perhaps." Alexandria blinked against the emotional pain. "But I'm not sure I can endure as long as that takes."

"Then you have heard." It wasn't a question. "He will soon tire of Rosalynd. Or more likely, like the others, she will spread her legs for another. Being the partner of the Sheriff of Lothian isn't easy. Ruthven, like Drummond, is isolated when one is used to the excitement of court. If that isn't bad enough your bed gets lonely when the Wolf is away as he frequently is. You know that."

Everyone did. They'd watched their lady silently pine for the Wolf's return every time he departed on the king's business. They watched their joyful reunion when he finally returned and knew the Golden Wolf was as anxious to return to his wife as she was to have him home.

"When your husband learns of her transgressions, he will send her packing. Thor will not tolerate being cuckolded by his mistress."

Or claim any bastards that were not his. He'd traveled that road before with both of his wives before her cousin. Don't even get her started on the taverner's daughter. Not unless it was to say they were all blessed Siward was free of that mess. That he now lived where he was truly loved.

"There is no guarantee that will happen." Alexandria shook her head. "Thor is a very desirable man. Why would she risk losing everything she would gain as his mistress?"

Or, more importantly, as his wife should their marriage dissolve and Thor forsake his promise to never wed again.

"Because she is a spoiled, promiscuous strumpet whose reputation precedes her." Reina shrugged. "Her proclivity for infidelity is well known."

"I see." Alexandria rolled her eyes. "I won't ask where you got your information." She had her suspicions.

"Then I won't tell you from the king." Reina nodded once. "You mustn't lose hope. Your godfather says Rosie's eye is already flicking to and fro searching for her next target. It seems her ambitions are loftier than the Sheriff of Lothian."

"Like a prince?" Alexandria's laugh was more mocking than pity. "That will never happen."

"No, it won't." Reina agreed. "But there are less lofty goals than the king or his son that are higher on the pecking order."

"Perhaps." Rosalynd had yet to realize that while there were wealthier men with more impressive titles in the land, no one was more powerful than the Sheriff of Lothian. He was the right hand of the king for a reason. David knew his Wolf was content to serve him with unwavering loyalty. "Let's pray you are right. That is the only way I will win this battle. I fear the woman that I am cannot compete with the willowy perfection of Fair Rosalynd."

"Keep telling yourself that and you will lose." Reina resisted the urge to shake her cousin. "I repeat, what you have done once, you can do again."

"I will try," Alexandria repeated. "That is all I can promise and all I can do."

"No one has asked for anything more." Looping her arm through her cousin's, Reina led her back inside. "I do believe I hear goblets of wine and a chess game calling our names. What say you?"

"That you shall be Lady Rosalynd's forces," Alexandria's tone was mirthful. "And I shall be the lady of Drummond."

"Why do I have to be Rosalynd of the Rosie Cheeks?" Reina stopped on the landing. "Why not you?"

"Because I'm the better player," Alexandria reminded her. "And I always win."

"You're right." Reina nodded. "You'll win this time too although I'm getting better."

"Yes, you are." Alexandria agreed. "When the day comes that you can beat me, I'll play Rosey Rosalind. Until then, we mustn't let her win."

"No, we mustn't." Reina led her cousin into the great hall to the bench containing the chess game they'd abandoned late last night. "It appears our game is still as we left it."

Nodding, Alexandria watched her cousin study the board before making a surprisingly good move grateful for the opportunity to leave her woes behind for a while.

CHAPTER TWENTY-THREE

Exiting the sewing room, Rosalynd caught sight of a golden-haired giant heading in the opposite direction. While her first instinct was to cry out, something held her back. The only reason he would take that corridor was to visit *her* chamber. Well, she knew something he didn't. *She* wasn't in there.

Lady Alexandria was puttering around in the gardens with Oswald. She'd seen them from the window as she'd left the sewing room a few moments earlier. That red-haired shrew and shriveled magus were crawling around in the dirt harvesting garlic, leeks, and parsnips. How undignified...No wonder Lord Thor found his wife so strange...Well, he needn't worry she'd do such a thing once they were married. She wouldn't. Ever. Under any circumstances.

Falling behind Thor, she followed him to his wife's chamber. Seeing him knock on the door without success, she wasn't surprised when he didn't take no for an answer and pulled a key from his pocket. Briefly wondering what iniquity he expected to find, Rosalynd stepped up to the doorway and looked inside. While comfortable, the chamber was neither as large nor as opulent as she expected the king's goddaughter to inhabit. Nothing like she would demand when the time came.

It was a modest room with a fireplace and several brightly colored tapestries covering the walls instead. A beautiful pelt covered the large bed and three substantial trunks rested against the walls. A single chair and a cloth-covered table were set to one side almost as an afterthought. Someone had placed a vase of roses from the king's garden on the table and left a bowl of apples on one of the clothes trunks. Watching Thor hesitate briefly before walking to the window, Rosalynd closed the door before scampering across the room to wrap her arms around her lover's waist.

"She is in the far garden." Abs tightened beneath her palms as her hands drifted ever lower. "I saw your wife and the healer digging roots when I left the sewing room." Expertly stroking his length, she wasn't surprised to feel her Wolf respond to her ministrations. "We should have just long enough to finish what we've started before her return."

"Do we?" Turning, Thor lifted Rosalyn against the wall and ruched her skirts around her waist. "Then perhaps we'd best get to it."

Reaching up to pull her gown over her head, Rosalynd closed her eyes and threw her head back enticing Thor to bury his face in small, pert breasts. By far her wealthiest and most skillful lover, he wasn't her only lover. While she hadn't ruled out the thought of wedding her Wolf, the voice in her head constantly said she could do better.

Meeting him thrust for thrust in the way that ignited Thor's passions, Rosalynd glanced towards the door not surprised to see her lover's wife standing in the open doorway. Catching Alexandria's eye, she moaned loudly as she urged Thor to go faster and deeper.

Confident her tonics worked, there was no reason to interrupt her pleasure. If they failed, there were other means to rid her body of unwanted consequences. She had used them before. While there was a time and a place to produce offspring, this wasn't it. She wasn't even sure her Wolf was the man for her.

However, she would use what he offered to climb the social ladder. In the interim, while she was waiting to arrive where she hoped to be, she would enjoy what her lusty lover offered.

"Oh, my lord," Rosalyn stretched her arms over her head proffering pert breasts as she felt him harden within her again. "Surely you are tired?"

"Is that what you think?" He wasn't an inexperienced pup to spend himself once and be done. Hearing her laugh as she adjusted her position, they both knew better. "I thought not."

Casting a look of victory over her lover's shoulder, Rosalynd watched her rival silently close the door behind her. Whatever Thor's intent in coming to this room, she'd stopped him in his tracks. Not only that, but she'd also proven no place was sacred to either of them. It became more apparent with each passing day that she had the power in this relationship. While the Golden Wolf had yet to learn this, she knew. Now his wife did, too.

Laughing softly, Rosalynd ignored Thor's puzzled look as she expertly directed his attention back to what they were doing. The quicker they were both completely engrossed in the carnal the better. The last thing she needed was her lover asking questions better left unasked.

———— ◦⟨⟩◦ ————

HEARING UNUSUAL SOUNDS from within her chamber, Alexandria gently pushed the door open before stepping back in shock. Covering her mouth, she couldn't believe she saw her husband's bare arse clenching and unclenching as he took his mistress against her chamber wall. Torn between kicking the door off its hinges and running screaming down the hall, she decided to do neither. That evil gleam in the witch's eyes meant Rosalynd was aware of her presence and she'd meant her to find them exactly where they were.

Deciding not to give her the pleasure of seeing her distress, Alexandria silently closed the door and headed for the stairs. The best thing she could do was find a quiet place to purge the vision of Rosalynd's alabaster thighs wrapped around her husband's waist as he emptied himself within her against her bedchamber wall.

Pressing her hand against her mouth, Alexandria prayed no one saw her as she ran down the corridor and out on the battlements. She silently prayed the woman was taking one of Oswald's tonics to prevent conception as well. The last thing she needed was another bastard son to muddy the waters more than they already were. Unlike Joanna, Rosalynd wouldn't conveniently die and disappear from their lives.

Finding a deserted expanse of battlement, Alexandria leaned on the wall and closed her eyes. Reliving the vision in her head, she recalled opening the oiled door and noting the insipidly pink floral fabric piled on her floor. Hearing a soft moan she'd raised her eyes to the last sight she ever expected to see. One where her husband had Lady Rosalynd impaled against the wall tupping her like there was no tomorrow. Seeing the glint in those evil blue eyes, she'd been instantly aware that while her adversary saw her distress, her husband hadn't.

Wiping her face with her hands, Alexandria was surprised to find her palm wet. She didn't realize she was crying. In truth, she didn't know why she was crying if she was crying at all. No, that wasn't true. She was mourning the death of the life she once knew. Much too brief, her life since the fall of Drummond had been wonderful beyond belief.

While far from perfect or trouble-free it was genuinely happy. She'd awakened every morning to find herself engulfed in her husband's arms and retired most nights the same way. If they happened to share a round or two of enthusiastic lovemaking in between, that was even better.

More important than their bed sport was how effortlessly they'd managed their lands between them. While Thor reveled in working the fields side-by-side with their villagers between royal duties and rounds, she'd overseen their keep with the same intimate attention to detail.

In the evenings they'd enjoyed entertaining their guests and playing with their children. They'd even gone to court on occasion to visit her godfather for a few days leaving their children and their keep in Lionel and Reina's capable hands. Unfortunately, it seemed all of that camaraderie was gone. Her husband preferred cavorting with his harlot to spending time with his wife.

Resting her hand on her stomach, Alexandria prayed none of the times she'd lain with Thor had taken root in her belly. The last thing she needed was to conceive a child at a time like this. She didn't even know if she and Thor would still be wed this time next year. She didn't know if she would care if they were. This last blow was too painful. She wasn't sure she could stomach it. She was fighting a strong desire to heave her disgust across the battlement floor as it was.

Taking a deep, calming breath she headed for the deserted staircase that led to Oswald's garden. Grabbing a basket from a stack in passing, Alexandria studied the layout of the plants noting where each herb was located. While most healing gardens were laid out in the same familiar pattern, they weren't exactly alike. Oswald's garden was different from most. He grew plants others didn't even know existed. That made her job more difficult. All she wanted was some fragrant cuttings to spread about her room giving an earthy, grassy scent.

Removing her shears from her pocket, Alexandria headed for the mint. After cutting several sprigs she moved onto the Sweet Annie. If she ran into tougher stems, she had a dagger sheathed at her thigh she could discretely grab. However, she doubted she would need the blade. Oswald's plants were still young and tender. Clipping Clarey sage and coneflower, she moved on to dill, oregano, and peppermint. Snipping a few more herbs she stopped to study the plants in her basket.

Overwhelmed by the day's events, she halted and shut her eyes. She needed to pull herself together. The last thing she wanted was to appear undone at the evening meal. She refused to let Rosalynd see how upset she was by her actions. She was stronger than that. She was a warrior in her own right. It would take more than some selfish snip to upend her world.

"Alex," She turned at the sound of Reina's voice. "What is wrong?"

"Why would you think aught is wrong?" Alexandria's laugh was caustic. "To hear you tell it, naught could be wrong with the world now that we know Thor lives."

How much longer that would be true was in question. She had a fleeting desire to kill him herself for this latest insult. It was an urge she wouldn't act on, but she was slightly surprised at the depth of her bitterness.

"Because you have stood there with a basket on your arm staring at the same spot for God knows how long." She'd spotted her cousin in the herb garden from a third-story window. Alex had yet to move in the time it had taken her to get from there to here. "You were standing in this same spot when I left the sewing room."

Weary of court, she'd escaped to the familiar room hoping to gather useful gossip while she helped with the mending and needlework. Who knew what she would learn from a gaggle of loose lips and flapping tongues? She'd had little fear of Lady Rosalynd or any of the younger women being present.

Most were away on an impromptu hunt arranged by Prince Henry. However, she was surprised to learn Thor's lover had left a few minutes before her arrival. She'd kept her shock to herself that the girl had turned down an opportunity to be in the prince's company. Maybe she was wrong about Rosalynd hoping to graze in greener pastures.

"I see." Alexandria set her basket on a bench. "You saw me and decided I needed company."

"Something like that." Reina agreed. "It is clear something is wrong."

"Something has been wrong since Thor didn't come home." Alexandria spoke softly. "We both know that.

"It has," Reina nodded. "But this is something new."

"Aye." Alexandria squared her shoulders. "I can't do this anymore."

"Do what?" Reina asked what she didn't want to know.

"Lie with a man who does not care." Her cousin stated bluntly. "I am nothing but the sanctioned receptacle for his lust."

"Oh." This wasn't good. "Have you told your husband how you feel?"

"Why?" Alexandria couldn't reconcile this indifferent man with the adoring husband she'd once known. "He can't make himself care." She shook her head. "Or make himself value me or the bairns."

Despite how she felt, that was too much to ask.

"He doesn't remember you or your babes." Reina reminded her. "He doesn't remember who he was or the life he led. You are fortunate you have stirred his loins. It is too soon to ask for anything more."

Reina shook her head remembering a similar conversation from long ago. It had taken a while for the truth to penetrate her cousin's brain back then, too. Alex failed to see how fortunate she was that Thor had broken yet another promise to himself. They both knew he'd never intended to share her bed after that one encounter, but he hadn't been able to stay away entirely.

"Perhaps." Alexandria agreed. "It's bad enough not being sure I can still do this, but it's worse not knowing if I wish to anymore."

"Why do you feel this way?" That wasn't what she expected to hear. "Have you stopped loving Thor?"

Alexandria contemplated her words as she recalled vivid images of Thor swiving Rosalynd against her chamber wall.

"Perhaps," She admitted. "Lord Thor, but not my husband."

She would never stop loving her husband. She couldn't.

"Thor is your husband." Reina reminded her. "Not the vision in your head."

"Oh, no." Alexandria shook her head. "He is not the same man."

"Oh, no, yourself." Reina stared her down. "We have had these words before. He is the same. You were just too desperate to see or care." Or too passionately in love with the Golden Wolf living in her head to see the real man. "Thor wanted nothing to do with you before. Even after you lay together." He'd known she was trouble from the start. She'd heard him utter those exact words with her two ears. "You made him change his mind. You can do the same again."

"I guess I was." Alexandria nodded. "I had to save Drummond at any cost."

She had to save her people, herself, and any future children she might bear.

"As you must again." Reina didn't mince words. Their lands and people were vulnerable as long as the Wolf was indifferent. While the shadow of his presence would hold challengers at bay for a while, an unknown warrior would ride from the trees to challenge his dominance one day. "It is but a matter of time before Drummond is attacked. You must make him love you again before all is lost."

"I don't think I can." Alexandria swiped a tear. "I don't know how."

"You do it the same way you did the first time." Reina longed to yell, "Snap out of it!" but didn't. "Be the strong, independent woman Thor fell in love with."

"What if she doesn't exist anymore?" That fear had grown the more she'd come to rely on her husband. "What if I've let her die since I didn't need her anymore?"

"Do you run Drummond and oversee your villages while your husband is away on royal duties as you did for your father before him?" Reina stared her down. "Did you not lead one of four search parties in the hunt for your husband?" Alexandria nodded. "I thought so. However, the real question you must answer is can you lead your people without Thor standing by your side?"

"What do you think?" Alexandria felt her hackles rise. "I did it before; I will do it again."

"Then you are still the same strong, independent woman you have always been." Reina rested her hand on her cousin's arm. "Don't let that empty-headed bed warmer distract you from your purpose."

"That is hard to do," Alexandria's voice was but a whisper "When he reeks of attar of lavender and sweat when he slides between my sheets and when I just saw him bare-arsed tupping that bitch against my bedroom wall."

Reina winced at her words momentarily taken aback by her cousin's visceral pain.

"I'm so sorry," She grappled for the right words to say. Finding none, she bluntly stated what was on her mind. "However, were he satisfied by their encounters; he wouldn't come to you."

While her cousin didn't yet see what was obvious to her, Thor was beginning to realize something was missing from his life. If all went as it should, he would soon discover that something was his wife. Alexandria had but to hang on until that day came.

"Perhaps he wouldn't." Alexandria agreed. "Perhaps I would prefer that he didn't."

"You would prefer he sought solace and satisfaction with another?" Reina knew that wasn't true either. "Or perhaps you would prefer he remain where he is? With Lady Rosalynd?"

"You know better." Alexandria reluctantly admitted. "I just wish it didn't hurt so bad."

"So do I." Reina's smile was weak. "But we both know the physical connection between you is your strongest weapon. If you wish to win, bury your emotions and do what must be done."

"That is easy for you to say." Alexandria snapped. "You didn't walk in on him swiving his mistress against the wall in your bedchamber."

"Is it?" While she winced at her remark, Reina's expression said they both knew otherwise. "Easy?"

"I am sorry." Her remark had been thoughtless at best, and cruel at worst. "Lionel would never stray from your marriage bed."

"You are right and I know he loves me." Reina rested her hand on her cousin's arm. "But do you think knowing that makes it easier to accept in the wee hours of the morn that another woman took residence in his heart years ago or that she still lives there despite his love for me?"

Alexandria flinched from the raw pain in her eyes. They both knew she would change things if she could. She couldn't. She had tried. But that didn't change the reality that *she* was the other woman of which her cousin spoke.

While she had never lifted a sword or commanded a destrier, they both knew who the stronger woman was. To love a man with all one's heart while knowing you had but a piece of his would destroy a lesser woman. It would have destroyed her. No, Zan silently corrected herself, it would destroy her now if she let it. If Reina could endure such a dreadful wound of the heart, so could she.

"Then I suppose if you endure, I will too." Alexandria nodded. "However, with every passing day, I believe the time is nearing for our return to Drummond. We have been gone too long and my heart aches to hold my bairns."

"You may be right." Reina nodded. "But you must stay strong and do your best to prove to your husband who is the better woman. He will remember that when Rosalynd falters."

"That sounds like good advice." Alexandria contemplated her words. "I will join you inside in a while. I need time to lick my wounds in peace."

"Then I will wait for your return." Reina nodded again before turning to go inside. "Just remember I have already told you all is not lost. Lady Rosalynd will stray. When that happens, there will be no turning back. Thor will be done."

"Perhaps." Alexandria nodded. "In the meantime, the best I can do is return to my room and erase the nauseating scent of another woman with fragrant herbs and a generous sprinkle of perfume."

Her vial of frankincense, cinnamon, and sweet rush topped with anise and coriander should do the job nicely. The spicey perfume would eradicate the cloying scent of lavender as thoroughly as it wouldn't eradicate the equally unpleasant vision from her mind.

"Why don't I do that for you?" Reina offered. "I know where you keep everything."

"Thank you." Alexandria agreed. "Here are the keys you'll need."

She handed her key ring to her cousin.

"I'll put the herbs in water and sprinkle your room with perfume." Her cousin had a small collection of ewers and jars packed away that would serve nicely as makeshift vases. "By the time you return, today will be a bad memory."

"I doubt I'd go that far, but things will have improved somewhat." Alexandria laughed softly "I can see that happening."

But not the other.

"Okay." Reina agreed. "I can too."

Watching her cousin leave, Alexandria shook her head. She appeared to have rallied from her last bad spell. She didn't know what she would do without Reina. Losing Anna was bad enough. Losing her cousin would be worse. She would be all alone in an unfamiliar reality.

However, that wouldn't always be true. Lionel would anchor her once an appropriate period of mourning had passed, but that wasn't the scenario she wanted. Reina *deserved* her happily ever after as badly as she *wanted* hers even if both futures were more than slightly dented.

Taking a seat on a bench, Alexandria decided to bask in the warm sunshine and enjoy the peace around her. It would be time to return to her chamber to dress for the evening meal long before she was ready. Mercifully, by that time, Reina would have eradicated all signs of Thor's encounter from her room. She would hopefully have laid out an ensemble for her to wear as well. With any luck, it would be the vivid yellow-red and gold silk bliaut she'd yet to wear minus the veil. While it was unseemly for a married woman to run about with her hair uncovered, she'd never observed such foolishness before. She wouldn't start now.

Closing her eyes, Alexandria was surprised when she opened them to glance at the sundial a while later that more time had passed than she thought. She must have fallen asleep which wasn't surprising considering she hadn't been sleeping well lately. While not a major issue if she hurried, there wouldn't be much time to waste in selecting her ensemble. Rising to her feet, she made her way to her room thankful she didn't run into anyone in the corridor. Like her, everyone was busily getting ready to join the king in the great hall for the evening meal and entertainment.

Slipping into her room, Alexandria locked the door behind her. Reina had done an excellent job of restoring her room to order. The spicey Eastern scent blended well with the woodsy scent of the herbs and flowers spaced about the room in ewers and jugs without overpowering her.

Opening her trunk, she found the vibrant yellow-red and gold silk bliaut she wished to wear along with the matching slippers and deeper yellow-red bejeweled girdle. Quickly touching up her face, she slipped into her bliaut and fastened the tabs. Sliding into her slippers, she fastened the girdle around her waist. Combing her hair, she braided her front locks and twisted them into an intricate circle on the top of her head leaving the rest of her hair to flow free. Glancing in the mirror, she decided she was presentable. Forget a veil. She didn't wear one at home; she refused to wear one here. Hearing a knock on her door, she wasn't surprised when Reina poked her head around.

"Are you ready to go down?"

"I think so." Alexandria nodded. "Where is Lionel?"

"Waiting for us in the hall." Reina stepped into the room and studied her cousin. "You look very regal which isn't a bad thing. It seems all three of us will be seated at the high table for the evening meal."

This was only the second time that had happened since their arrival.

Alexandria snorted softly at her cousin's exuberance. "How exciting for you."

"It is." Reina nodded. "If all goes well, you will be seated by the king and I will be seated by you."

Alexandria snorted softly again. "With Lionel on your other side like good little guard dogs."

"Perhaps, but it is foolish to think tonight won't be more difficult than other nights." Cinching Alexandria's girdle a little tighter, it was easy to see her cousin had lost weight she didn't need to lose since coming to court. "We both know Rosalynd will use every trick to get under your skin and you will be forced to take it. If you lose your composure, she wins."

Alexandria pondered her words for a moment. "You are right. While I can act, I mustn't react. We both know all eyes will be on us this night." It was too much to hope Rosalynd hadn't crowed her victory all over the royal keep.

Stepping forward to loop her arm through her cousin's, Reina waited for her to grab her mantle and lock the door. Stopping, she hugged Alexandria reassuringly before leading her towards the stairs. She didn't envy any of them this evening. It would take all her mental and emotional strength for her cousin to make it through. But, knowing Zan, she would do just that.

Hesitating at the bottom of the stairs, Alexandria took a deep breath knowing all eyes would be on them as they entered the great hall. From the sound of music bleeding into the hall, the entertainment was well underway.

CHAPTER TWENTY-FOUR

Taking one last look around the great hall, Alexandria's gaze rested briefly on the dancing couple. She easily recalled the day she'd taught her husband to dance a sprightly country jig against his better judgment. They had been celebrating their recent union with the people of Drummond. In the years since Thor had learned other dances and proved adept at complicated footwork despite his size. He was currently participating in a carole with a giggling Rosalynd by his side. Watching them laughing and ogling each other as the line dance progressed, she turned to leave the hall.

She had no reason to stay where she wasn't needed. The king was having an animated discussion with a visiting monk most likely over the fermentation processes of herbal wines while Reina and Lionel were playing chess. As usual, the hall was a raucous place filled with activity. Deciding it was time to go, she left the hall and headed for the exit. It would be time to return for dinner when the music began to die down. Until then, she could amble as she pleased.

Making her way to the garden, Alexandria was glad the moon was full and the night sky filled with stars. While she had grabbed a small cresset lamp to light her way from a niche in the corridor, the plants and flowers looked ethereal bathed in silvery beams of moonlight. Breathing deeply, she savored the scent of night-blooming flowers. While it was a cool evening, her mantle kept her warm enough to enjoy a relaxing walk in the crisp night air. Hearing a crunch on the path behind her, she turned to observe her husband behind her.

"Were you following me?" While a nice thought, she doubted it. He hadn't spared her a second thought when she entered the hall. He was too busy basking in Lady Rosalynd's company. Seeing that, the last place she expected him to be was here confronting her in the garden. "You must know I can take care of myself."

"I wasn't following you." Thor shook his head. "I come out here when my head hurts." A not uncommon occurrence since his head injury. "Something about this place seems to ease the pain."

While it was most likely just the quiet; he might be inhaling some aroma that eased his misery. She didn't know. Reaching into her pocket, she removed a small vial.

"Rub this on your temples before bed." She dropped the stoppered vial in his hand. "It's just peppermint oil. I believe it will help."

While she had popped the vial in her pocket for personal use, she could get another from Oswald tomorrow. The pinched look on his face suggested Thor needed the relief more than she did right now. Considering the tensions of the night, she was surprisingly headache free.

"Thank you." Thor nodded. "I'll do that."

"Good." Alexandria sat on a bench. "I believe it will help."

Sitting on the bench beside her, Thor popped the cork from the vial, poured a few drops of the pungent oil on his fingertips, and rubbed it into his temples. Closing his eyes, he breathed in the scent as he felt the tension gradually recede. Opening his eyes, he turned to look at his wife wondering why he suddenly felt as though she had something important to say.

"What is on your mind?" Hopefully not the fact it had been nearly a week since he'd last shared her bed. He'd meant what he promised when he'd told himself he wouldn't share her bed any longer. It was time he moved on. To that end, he was taking Rosalynd to Ruthven before the week was out. "Since I am here, you might as well speak."

"I saw you with Lady Rosalynd in my chamber earlier today," Alexandria spoke quietly. "Why were you there? I presume not to end up doing what you did. Even you wouldn't be that thoughtless intentionally."

"You are right." He didn't feel obligated to apologize for witnessing in the flesh what she knew was occurring behind closed doors anyway. As for the chamber being hers, the room was as much his. Truthfully, more so. Everything she possessed became his on the day they married. While that might not remain so if the marriage was dissolved, it was true at this moment.

"I don't know what I had in mind when I went to your room. I believe I just wanted to talk about things I still don't know. Nothing particularly that important."

"That's good to know." Somehow, his words didn't ring true. "I would hate to think I missed out on anything that mattered while you were otherwise occupied." Thor nodded since there wasn't much he could say. "Now that we've gotten that out of the way, Reina and I are leaving the day after the morrow. Drummond has been under the protection of others and I have been away from the bairns for far too long."

Thor nodded again. "I see."

"You could always come with us." Alexandria made the one suggestion she knew he wouldn't accept.

"I can't," Thor spoke quietly. "I must leave on my rounds in a few days."

Alexandria nodded, not bothering to call out the lie. If he wanted to pretend he hadn't returned from his rounds many weeks ago, so be it. She wouldn't contradict him. It wasn't in her best interest to lay all of her cards on the table yet. She suspected the only rounds he would be going on was one to familiarize Lady Rosalynd with her new home. If she didn't miss her guess, the other woman would be installed as the unofficial lady of Ruthven about the time she resumed her role as the official lady of Drummond.

"While I'm sorry to hear that," Alexandria rose to her feet. "It doesn't surprise me." She nodded once. "However, it is late, and I must go. There is much to do before we leave."

For one thing, she had to make it through tonight's meal. For another, she needed to sort through her clothes trunk for old bliauts to take back home. While she could have done that at any time, she had more important things to do. It was easier to just add the new bliauts she'd brought from home to the trunk and worry about the rest later. For another, she had to inform her guards, her cousin, and her godfather they were leaving soon. That would be far less pleasant than playing dress-up.

"Then I will bid you good night."

Not how he expected the evening to play out, but not that surprising either. He didn't expect anyone to be in the garden in the first place. Especially his wife. He'd merely been seeking a few moments of peace and solitude in hopes the pounding in his head would ease.

"Good night."

Sitting back on the bench, he watched her disappear into the night without a backward glance. While he should be glad she was leaving without a fight, some part of him was reluctant to see her go. While he had no intentions of resuming their marriage, there were still questions she had yet to answer and gaps yet to be filled in. Perhaps that was why he already felt this ambiguous sense of loss deep in his soul.

CHAPTER TWENTY-FIVE

Knocking, Reina didn't wait for a response before she pushed the door open with her hip. Stopping in her tracks, she was surprised to see Zan carefully stuffing an embroidered bliaut in a leather bag. It was clear that she was going through her clothes trunk deciding what to take back to Drummond. This wasn't entirely unexpected since she'd brought three or four new bliauts to leave behind with her.

"Alex?" Reina sat the small tray she'd brought with her on the table. "We missed you in the hall when we broke the fast...I thought you might be hungry so I brought you a tray."

"I'm sorry." Alexandria closed the lid on her clothes trunk. "I overslept and I wasn't all that hungry." However, that may have changed over the last couple of hours. A nibble of cheese, a chunk of chicken, and a slice of crusty bread wasn't amiss. "Thank you."

"You're welcome." Reina sat on the edge of the bed. "What are you doing?"

"Packing." Alexandria bit back the sharp response on the tip of her tongue. "We leave on the morrow."

"With or without Thor?" Reina knew the answer without asking.

"What do you think?" Alexandria looked her cousin in the eye. "His rounds start before the month is out."

"His what?" Reina drew back in disbelief. "Who told you that?"

"He did." She absently folded a linen chemise.

"When?" Not in the great hall at dinner.

Zan rolled her eyes. "Last night in Oswald's garden when I asked him to return with us."

171

"Seriously" Reina rose to her feet, wiped her hands on her hips, and walked over to gaze out the window. "What a liar, and not a very good one at that."

Alexandria walked over to stand by her cousin. "I guess not."

"I know not." Reina reached into her pocket and tossed a plum at her husband in the bailey below. "Everyone knows his rounds were over before we arrived." Reina waved at her laughing husband down below. "Surely he didn't think you would believe that lie? I hope you called him on it."

"I didn't," Alexandria admitted. "I told him to do what he needed to do and I would do what I must do. That my people and my children need me, and Drummond has been in Bertie and Adela's hands long enough. It is past time we go home."

"What of your marriage?" Reina sat on the window seal. "Are you sure leaving is right?"

"No," Alexandria admitted. "I'm not, but I know I can't remain at court while he installs his mistress at Ruthven."

"I suppose not." The smug looks of pity and empathy would be unbearable.

"I have not given up," Alexandria reassured her. "However, I won't accept less than I had, and I won't continue to share my husband with another woman while praying he will come around in time. That he will eventually realize that what he is doing is wrong." She shook her head in disgust. "Nor will I remain here until my belly swells despite my best efforts to ensure that doesn't happen. I will not be the Sheriff of Lothian's broodmare."

"Thor may never come around." Reina reminded her. "Even you do not believe his memories will return. That he will ever remember how he felt about you and the bairns. His head wound was too bad."

"The torture was too bad." Alexandria snapped. "He fought so hard not to betray his family to his enemies that he forgot we existed instead."

"You don't know that." While that explanation was comforting, Thor's head wound was in an area of the skull known to cause memory loss. "And I've heard nothing more than the head injury affected his memory."

"You wouldn't hear any of what I said." Alexandria sat on the edge of her bed. "Godfather kept it secret."

"But he told you?" Reina sat beside her. "Then it's time to share what you know."

"I can do that." Alexandria grabbed her hand. "As you know, the king has added several men as large as Thor and Lionel to his army since the Wolf and I wed. Most of them are fair-haired like Thor although de Brescy and Gabaldon are dark like Lionel. Because of this, Thor doesn't stand out as much unless he wears something that identifies him as the Golden Wolf. Since this was a simple sneaky land grab, he dressed plainly and rode a different mount to disguise his presence."

Reina nodded knowing every word was true. Lionel and Thor had elected to dress plainly and ride different mounts than they usually rode to make them harder to pick out in the fray. Both were more cautious now that they had families to return home to than they might have been in years gone by. While no less lethal, their wives appreciated their efforts to return to the women who loved them.

"Godfather spent many hours talking with Thor while he was healing." Alexandria laughed softly. "Hours I could have spent with him had I known my husband lived."

"You know why your godfather didn't send for you." While she understood her cousin's point of view, she thought the king was right. "No one knew if Thor would live or how he would be after healing."

He could have become a raving lunatic. It was known to happen. Her cousin's presence could have made that worse.

"He forbade Lionel to tell me the truth even after they knew he would live." Alexandria shook her head. "While I understand why he did it, that doesn't mean I like it or believe it was the right course of action. I don't know. Maybe Godfather was right. Maybe my presence would have made things worse for Thor while he healed. Maybe Godfather was wrong. Maybe Thor would have accepted me more readily in the early days before the likes of Rosalynd got their claws into him. We'll never know, will we?"

"No, we won't." Reina agreed. "So, why don't we trust the right thing was done and move on?"

"I will try." Even if she didn't feel that way. "It does no good to resent what is already done. All I can do is return home and pray, in time, that my marriage will change for the better."

"That sounds reasonable." Reina nodded. "There's nothing more to be done here."

"No, there isn't." Alexandria turned to go inside knowing her cousin would follow. "I have done all I can do."

During her conversations with her godfather, she'd learned Thor's captors didn't know his identity. Even worse, he couldn't tell them if he'd wanted to. No matter the torture. They had, however, recognized he was a lord worthy of ransom from his size and weaponry, so they'd bided their time hoping to discover his identity while they prayed King Stephen never learned of their treachery. He would not be pleased they'd broken the truce.

While a chance they were willing to take, they didn't care if their captives died along the way. Every dead man was one less warrior to come against them when their king crossed the border into England again. However, one captive had wrecked their plans by escaping before his identity was learned or he was slaughtered inadvertently or deliberately. Whichever came first. By the time Thor made his way back to Scotland and the king, his memories had returned. All save the memories of his wife and family.

However, Thor knew who and what he was when he stood before his king. He remembered his life before Drummond, and he remembered his life since. In time, the healers realized the brief years in between were likely gone forever. While David was grateful to have his Sheriff back; he was clueless about how to deal with this man he did not know.

When his vassal had physically recovered from his injuries, he reluctantly informed him of his forgotten wife and family. Thor refused to believe he had wed a third time until a fiery redhead finally proved otherwise. Even then, it hadn't felt real. It still didn't. Her husband felt as though she belonged to another life and another man. Again, he had told her so. As for their children, they were meaningless in his universe. He felt no connection to what he didn't know. While the healer in her had seen this before and understood where Thor was coming from, the wife in her lamented the loss of her husband.

Dismissing her thoughts, Alexandria turned to Reina. "I don't have much left to do in here. While I'm finishing up, why don't you let Lionel know everyone needs to be ready to leave in the morning and join me in Oswald's storage chamber? We have permission to take what we need from his stores. It seems this was a good year and he has more medicinal herbs than he can use."

Reina nodded. "You'll be okay while I'm gone?"

"Why wouldn't I be?" She'd had all night to come to terms with situations she couldn't change.

"Then I'll see you in the storeroom." She wrinkled her nose at the thought of all those competing scents. While the storeroom at Drummond was pleasantly fragranced, Oswald had a collection of plants that weren't necessarily a joy to smell.

"Sounds good." Alexandria smiled softly as she puttered about setting her chamber to rights. "I'm going to finish my meal and head over to Oswald's after I return this plate to the kitchen. I'll see you when you get there."

Alexandria laughed as Reina skittered out of the room more excited by the prospect of spending a few minutes with Lionel than she was in spending time with her. If she didn't miss her guess it would be a while before her cousin joined her. When she did there would likely be a piece or two of hay still entwined in her rich brown curls.

CHAPTER TWENTY-SIX

Standing on the battlement, Thor watched the commotion below. The pack animals had been loaded and brought to the bailey a while ago. His wife's party would exit the keep any time now. Making a sound of disgust, he wasn't surprised to see his prediction play out before his eyes.

The dark-haired woman being lifted onto the sleek red mare was Reina, while the fiery-haired figure attired in a black tunic, hose, and boots swinging into Loki's saddle was his bride. However, the sword strapped to her side wasn't hers. Selene was his. She must have taken her from the weapon's chest in their chamber.

A fine sword he'd commissioned in Constantinople years ago, she would give Avenger a run for his money. Made of Damascus steel, the silver grip was decorated with crescent moons while the pommel was a stylized griffin's head with flashing ruby eyes. He would instantly recognize the blade by its size, shape, and pommel anywhere. Laughing softly, he shook his head at her audacity before watching the group exit through the open gates.

"I recall you doing this once before." Thor didn't turn at the sound of a man's voice behind him. "You refused to admit you wanted her then as well."

"I don't recall such an event." Thor glanced at the king now standing beside him. "But I am sure you will tell me."

He would not lie. He didn't need to. David knew he would do as he pleased where his marriage was concerned. Nothing he said would change that. Marriage was a necessary evil. Love and fidelity were not. Both were exceptions, not the rule, in the relationships around him.

While it was true that he had partaken of his wife's wares off and on, another would occupy his bed tonight. He was no different than so many other men. A wife was for birthing heirs. His mistresses and lovers were strictly for pleasure.

"Alexandria spent a fortnight at court trying to catch your eye back then and failed miserably." David chuckled at the thought anyone could ignore his goddaughter. "Or so she thought."

She would have quaked in her boots had she known how wrong she was. He'd observed the unholy lust in the Norseman's eyes with a godfather's dismay. He'd then vowed to ensure the lady of Drummond suffered no dishonor at the Wolf's hands. Even if he had to force his hand. Fortunately, his goddaughter had done that instead.

"She is a striking woman." Thor conceded. "Though not to my tastes."

"It was not her looks that tempted you." David shook his head. He now realized how much Alexandria had changed Thor now that he was confronted with the man he used to know. "It was her fire and her spirit that caught your interest although her physical attributes grew on you with time."

"I will take your word for it." While his loins were not unaffected by the woman; he would never choose her over the more appealing morsel now occupying his bed. Womanly bits were womanly bits, and an attractive bedwarmer was just that. A bedwarmer. If he happened to wed her, that meant only that he would spill his seed willingly. "However, we both know a woman is a woman when it comes to slaking one's needs."

"I had forgotten this side of you." He didn't like it in the past. He liked it even less now. "Forgotten how much your wife and family changed you."

"Weakened me." Thor stared out over the countryside. "I have not, and will not, ever love a woman although you believe otherwise."

"But you did." David corrected. "Very much. That is what got you in this mess in the first place. Your desire to protect your loved ones. However, despite your beliefs to the contrary, you were never weakened. I have never seen you stronger than when you were standing by Zan's side. Loving my daughter made you a better man and a more powerful warrior."

"Your what?" Thor glanced in David's direction. "I am sure I never knew that."

He wouldn't have forgotten it if he had. No matter what was done to him. Wedding a king's daughter, even one born on the wrong side of the blanket, changed the dynamics of relationships. It wouldn't with him but it could have and they both knew it.

"No one does." While he hadn't meant to say those words, he didn't regret his slip of the tongue. "Not even my daughter. I won't take her father and her family from her. It is enough that I know and her mother knew. Now that you do, too, I expect you to take that knowledge to the grave."

"No wonder you wished me to wed the girl." Thor was amused that he'd never realized the truth before now. "No wonder you refused to let the MacLaren win even though you could not challenge him directly."

"I let you win instead." David reminded him. "However, I fear you are on the verge of losing everything you have won."

"That will not happen." He protected his lands and titles. "You know that."

"I don't refer to lands or titles." David leaned on the edge of the wall. "I refer to your wife and family. You are a fool if you think my child will not find comfort in another's arms. She will fight for you as long as she can; but if you continue to mistreat her as you have, she will seek love and protection elsewhere in time. Hear my words and hear them well, I will not stop or censor Alexandria for finding comfort in the arms of another. But you should know one thing, when that happens you will be lost in a way you have never been before."

Thor snorted at the thought he'd be lost over any woman. That would never happen. He'd wed twice before. Neither had impacted his life or his ways greatly either through their lives or their deaths. He couldn't see his third marriage being any different especially now that he'd met the woman involved.

"If you do not believe me, ask yourself why none of your lovers have conceived when your wife gave you three bairns in as many years. It would have been four had the MacLarens not killed your firstborn son." He conveniently chose to forget Joanna. She was long dead, and more importantly, was now little more than a name to Thor. "Believe me, I know it's not for the lack of trying on their part. It's your unwillingness to cooperate that foils their plans.

As for Alexandria, you feel differently. Some buried part of you still remembers what you choose to forget. Were she not using her healer's arts, I have no doubts she would already carry my grandchild within her. However,

I'm equally sure she will do everything in her power not to conceive as long as you bed others."

"You speak nonsense." Thor scoffed. "I don't wish for children with any of my mistresses." He took appropriate steps to ensure that didn't happen. "A wife is a different matter. She must give me heirs. That is her sole duty."

"Really?" David shook his head. "You didn't feel that way when you were in your right mind. You didn't feel that way when you feared you would lose her birthing your twins. You swore never to touch her again more than once. I heard that declaration from your lips."

Thor snorted; the very idea was preposterous. He'd said no such thing. He was sure of it.

"I do not believe you feel the way you claim about your wife or your children now. If I am wrong you need to rethink your feelings before you lose everything. Your wife's cousin is not strong." David spoke quietly. "She never has been. While she looks fine, I don't believe Reina will survive another two or three winters.

If my words are true her husband won't be content to stand in the shadows while you mistreat his lady." The king doodled in the dust on the railing. "He will make his move and Alexandria will not turn him away. She will accept the love he offers. That they once cared deeply for each other is no secret. That they could easily love again is known as well. That you disdain your marriage is no secret either."

Nor was his lack of true affection for his wife, but David wouldn't go there. He stared his Wolf down instead.

"I seem to remember this Lionel saying something to that effect a lifetime ago," Thor smirked at the memory. "No, I believe the threat had more to do with dealing with him if I hurt his wife's cousin. I do not believe I was pleased by his words at the time. Now, they are meaningless."

Images of that encounter flashed through his head eliciting an unpleasant jolt in his gut. He knew with a certainty that he hadn't felt about anything else that he would have gladly hurt the man had common sense not halted his hand. He'd decided de Montluzan's intimate familiarity with Drummond and her lands would prove more valuable than the temporary satisfaction he would get from punishing him for his impertinence instead.

"Then so be it." David shook his head. "Live your life as you must, and my daughter will live as she must."

While he knew Lionel would not step out of line while Reina lived, others would before too long. David was sure of it. His daughter and her lands were too vulnerable and valuable to leave undefended. Someone would try to take what was not his. That was the way of the warrior and they both knew it.

"Thor, if you pursue this course, I will petition to dissolve your union," David spoke softly. "Once that is done, I will strip you of Alexandria's coffers, lands, and titles. If you do not want the woman they belong to you don't want her dowry either. Besides, we both know you have more than enough of both without Drummond and all she has to offer. You have said so often enough."

"Do what you feel you must." Thor shrugged lightly. "And I will do the same."

David watched him turn on his heel and enter the keep leaving his liege staring over the moors shaking his head. The man was an obstinate fool. In this if not other ways. He would come to regret both his words and his actions if things didn't change. The king was sure of it. He knew his daughter. She would endure Thor's mistreatment only so long. Once she felt she'd suffered enough heartache she would walk away with his blessing.

CHAPTER TWENTY-SEVEN

Staring over the great hall lost in thought, Thor contemplated the weeks since Rosalynd moved to Ruthven. While he'd enjoyed acquainting his mistress with his keep and lands, things hadn't gone as smoothly as he wanted. While not openly hostile or disrespectful, there was a certain distance in his servants that didn't feel right. While nothing he could put his finger on, he suspected their feelings had something to do with his wife. Or perhaps their attitude was due to Rosalynd assuming a lady of the manor demeanor from the start. He didn't know.

He did know the weeks had passed faster than expected in some respects but not in others. He enjoyed the time he spent with his mistress, but it wasn't the same at Ruthven as it had been at court. For one thing, his lover was far more demanding of his time than she had been and far more demanding of his servants. He was seeing sides of her that he'd never seen before. Ones he wasn't sure he liked.

While it was true his wife's dowry meant little to him, he was conflicted about the rest. A part of him wasn't ready to turn his back on the family he had yet to meet. Or sever all ties to the life he'd left behind. A man of action, he wasn't used to questioning his decisions as he was now. Setting his emotions aside, he finally admitted more was at play than just the wound to his head.

Were that not so he would have recovered memories of his wife and family as he'd gradually recovered others. He hadn't. Not a single one. Perhaps Aimee was right. Perhaps he couldn't recall that chapter of his life because he didn't want to. If true, there was a reason. One he doubted had anything to do with hating his wife or his former life. That wasn't possible.

Not from what he'd been told by the people he trusted. Nor from what he'd felt since meeting the woman.

Rising to his feet, Thor exited the hall and headed for the battlements unaware that his king watched his every move. If David had a hint of the thoughts going through his head, he kept them to himself. He would know the truth of it soon enough. Besides, it was a crisp, moonlit night perfect for contemplation.

Taking the steps three at a time, the warrior soon found himself standing in the same deserted spot where he'd witnessed his wife's departure several months ago. While he didn't want to accept the idea, he had started to believe that Aimee and the king were right. That he'd forgotten his wife and family because he cared too much.

While every part of him rebelled against such self-betrayal, he couldn't dismiss the thought out of hand. Whether he wanted to accept it or not. If they were right, continuing as he was would cost far more than wealth, titles, and property. Though that mattered little to the man he was now, did he wish to lose everything he once valued? That he might come to value again? Probably not.

Contemplating his life, he felt a growing curiosity about the seed of his loins. Did his sons take after their sire or their dam? Were they fair-haired giants like him or fiery-haired rebels like their mother? Would his daughter grow into a willowy, golden-haired beauty like his first wife or would she be a diminutive firebrand like her mother? He didn't know, but somewhere deep inside he longed to.

As for his wife, she wasn't insufferable. He'd enjoyed the brief time he'd spent with her. Both in and out of bed. She'd approached his inquiries with honesty even when her answers showed one or the other of them less than favorably. He respected that, as he respected the fact she was confident in herself and her place in the world to a degree usually found in much older women. From the little he knew, there was a reason for that.

She, like him, endured a difficult upbringing due to circumstances beyond her control. All of that aside, he found her self-sufficiency compelling. He briefly wondered if that was what drew him to her the first time around. He suspected that was part of it and David had all but confirmed the idea.

That she was both warm and welcoming while able to hold her own against her detractors set her apart. He knew few women possessing such attributes and he could see how such a rare flower would be captivating. Especially to a man like him. As much as he wanted to walk away, he couldn't. He would always wonder what might have been if he did.

Sitting on a bench, he recalled the last conversation he'd had with Alexandria of Drummond. He hadn't been completely honest with her when he claimed not to know why he'd gone to her chamber that day. He'd wanted to talk. Find out more about their lands and their people. While he knew he'd been to Drummond a few times, Lord Ian usually dealt directly with the king. He'd rarely been to the estate before he'd married its lady. Maybe that was why he couldn't conjure an image in his mind. Or maybe, like his wife and family, he'd wiped all memories of the keep from his mind.

At first, he'd wanted answers to the questions roiling in his mind. Then Rosalynd appeared. While he could have sent her away and pursued his original intent, her agenda was far more gratifying. Added to that, the voice in his head reminded him there was no logical reason to pursue the answers he sought. Why should he? He was leaving that life behind in favor of a new life with the woman so expertly turning his attention to more pleasurable pursuits.

Though he hadn't meant for his wife to walk in on them, he didn't care that she had. He'd meant that as well when he'd said it. She knew his relationship with the other woman was carnal. He'd never hidden the truth from her. However, he didn't expect her to leave the way she had either. Most wives ignored their husband's infidelities. Then again, many wives were as guilty as their mates of straying so they had no room to talk. Alexandria of Drummond was different. She had yet to take another to her bed.

Rising to his feet, Thor walked over to stare at the sundial in the middle of the garden. He briefly recalled watching his wife do the same before she'd resumed cutting fresh herbs for whatever concoction she was distilling with Oswald's help. Snorting softly, he decided that shouldn't surprise him. She'd spent as much time with the healer as she spent with him. Maybe more. However, that was likely his fault for not seeking her out.

Hearing a sound above him, Thor glanced in the direction of the battlements. The king was lurking in the shadows watching him. That didn't surprise him either. His liege noticed everything so he wouldn't have missed his departure from the great hall. Curiosity piqued; David had discretely followed to see where he was going. Once that was determined, the king would think nothing of going upstairs to the battlements where he could observe his quarry without being observed.

Used to walking about the grounds at night, Thor ignored the king as he contemplated leaving on the morrow. His business concluded there was no reason to remain here beyond seeing and being seen. Both were a waste of time in his opinion. Besides, the king and the court would move to another keep soon and his men would appreciate returning to Ruthven and their regular lives sooner rather than later. They hadn't been excited about returning to court so soon anyway, but he'd needed to meet briefly with the king over a minor discrepancy he'd found in the records of a royal burgh.

While he doubted anything would come of it, David needed to know what he'd uncovered so he'd returned to court to inform him. That was why they worked so well together. He never took anything for granted when conducting the king's business and the king never took him or his service for granted either. Thor wished he could say the same about others in his life, but he couldn't. He was beginning to see that now.

WALKING THROUGH THE front doors of Ruthven, Thor wasn't surprised the corridors were deserted. He'd deliberately arrived home when the hall was being prepared for the evening meal, his men were manning the walls or sparring, and the other inhabitants were resting or going about their duties as they always did. Rosalynd's ladies were in the sewing room or outside basking in the afternoon sun doing what empty-headed girls did at this time of day.

As for Rosie herself, she was likely in their chamber going through her jewelry chest or napping. That was where he hoped she was. If all was as he believed, he'd gently awaken her and prove how happy he was to see her. Afterward, he'd order a bath brought to their room. Once he'd washed the grime and the scents of his journey from his skin, they could get reacquainted as a man and his mistress should after a three-week separation.

Taking the steps two at a time, Thor arrived at his chamber and pushed against the door. When it didn't give he wondered who Rosalynd had locked their door against. It wasn't him since she didn't know he was returning early. There hadn't been time to notify her. As it was, he'd wanted to surprise her instead.

Hopefully, this was but a careless mistake. If he got word anyone was frightening her, there would be hell to pay. His people would soon learn why. Rosalynd was to become their new lady once his marriage was officially dissolved. Laying his reservations to rest on that final walk through the gardens, he'd decided contemplations were done. His old life was over. His new one had already begun.

He'd quietly informed the king of his intent to make his mistress his wife while they watched an archery contest earlier this morning. Whether he liked it or not. He didn't want David surprised when he requested an end to his marriage. Nor did he want Alexandria bewildered when their children were declared illegitimate. All necessary if he wanted his children with Rosalynd to inherit his wealth and titles. While he knew she would be hurt, that was the way it was.

Reaching into the pouch at his waist to remove his key, Thor knew he would pay whatever it cost to obtain that divorce. He would willingly surrender Drummond and everything that came with her to bury his past and build a new life with Rosalynd. He would gladly finance a small chapel if that would help pave the way to the future. All he had to do was get Lord Ailred's consent to the betrothal and his life could start over again.

Turning the key in the lock, Thor quietly pushed the door open and stepped inside. If Rosalynd was dozing, he didn't want to startle her. He'd much rather kiss her awake before sliding between the sheets to get reacquainted as they'd done so many times before. Removing the key from the lock and silently closing the door behind him, Thor turned to the bed. Loudly clearing his throat, he wasn't surprised when his mistress suddenly froze at the unexpected sound behind her.

"While I realize I'm a few days early," Thor studied the sight before him. "This isn't the welcome I anticipated. Carry on. I expect both of you in the great hall as soon as you've finished."

Ignoring Rosalynd's shocked pleas, he turned and walked out of the room closing the door behind him. Laughing unpleasantly at his stupidity, Thor decided he now knew how his wife felt. He didn't like it. However, he had no one to blame but himself. The king and Aimee had tried to warn him and he'd heard whispers at court. Whispers he'd discounted as ruthless back-biting from the competition.

Rosie wasn't the first comely woman hoping to become his mistress, nor was she the first to audition for a place in his life. She was simply the one he'd found the most appealing. Lovely to gaze upon, reasonably intelligent, aristocratic, and not too needy, she was also willing to turn a blind eye to the time he spent with his wife.

Unlike so many women, Rosalynd understood his actions were influenced by their king. David had demanded he attempt to get to know his goddaughter whether he wished it or not. She knew as well that if his marriage fell through as expected, she stood a good chance of becoming the fourth wife of the Sheriff of Lothian. He'd believed that was what she wanted. He thought that was what they both wanted.

Now, he knew one of them was wrong. Oh, Rosie, wanted to be his wife. That hadn't changed. She expected marrying him to catapult her a few rungs up the social ladder and closer to the power she coveted. Perhaps she'd even expected to be widowed sooner rather than later. Everyone knew the life of a fighting man could be cut conveniently short in battle.

However, there were three major problems with her plan. The first was his refusal to die anytime soon to make her a wealthy widow pursued by powerful men.

The second was that while he chose to be known as the Sheriff of Lothian, he was far more than a mere shire reeve. He possessed titles he rarely used along with the overflowing coffers and lands that went with them that few knew about. While his mistress never fully realized who shared her bed, there weren't many men in Scotland with loftier titles than his. Most were already married.

The third, and fatal, flaw in Rosalynd's plan was that he'd demanded she not break faith with him. Unfortunately for both of them, it appeared she couldn't stop spreading her legs for other men. She was no different than his first two wives in that respect. Against his will, he realized that while the monogamy issue was a mark against his current bedmate, it was a mark in his wife's favor.

Entering the hall, Thor motioned for a servant to bring him a goblet and a pitcher of hard cider. Assuming his seat at the high table, he watched as the glass was filled in front of him. Taking a hearty gulp, he calmed his roiling thoughts.

It wouldn't do to appear addled when Rosalynd and Lord Anselm appeared. Shaking his head, he wondered what the nobleman was doing at Ruthven. Had he come to see him and, finding him not in residence, succumbed to Rosie's charms instead? Or was he one of the rumored lovers he'd heard whispers about? He didn't know. He only knew what he'd just witnessed in his bed.

Looking up at the sound of cracking rushes, Thor stared at the dark-haired man a few years younger and much smaller than him, and the fair-haired woman standing beside him. That they weren't touching in any way didn't diminish they'd done far more than touch a short while ago. Wrinkling his nose, Thor drained his glass. From how the couple reeked, the romp he'd interrupted was far from their first of the day...Far from their first of the last several days...Making a disgusted sound, Thor fixed the man with a glare.

"While I could kill you, and I likely would if this woman meant more to me," Thor raised his hand at Rosalynd's open mouth. "I won't. She isn't worth the aggravation of explaining my actions to my king."

Casually refilling his glass, Thor turned his attention back to Anselm.

"However, at this point, you are not welcome in my home nor will you ever be. The best thing you can do is get on your horse and ride as far from this place as possible before I change my mind. As for Lady Rosalynd, she won't be harmed unless you consider being sent back home detrimental to her health. I don't."

Watching the lord wisely exit with a curt nod, Thor turned his attention to his mistress.

"There was but one rule to stay in my good graces." He shook his head. "You couldn't keep it. I was a fool for thinking you could. I shouldn't have discounted the whispers I heard at court as malicious slander, but I did.

It didn't seem possible you were witless enough to destroy everything you worked so hard to get."

"Forgive me, my lord." Coming to stand behind him, Rosalynd wrapped her arms around Thor's neck. "It was but a foolish mistake."

"One of many, if the rumors are true, as I now believe they are." Thor closed his eyes briefly against the images flooding his mind before opening them again. "Take your hands off me, and gaze on what you have lost."

Reaching into his pouch, Thor pulled the opulent sapphire and ruby necklace from his pocket and laid it on the table.

"Don't touch it." He gently slapped her fingers away. "I don't believe my wife has a necklace like this. It was meant to be my betrothal gift."

"Forgive me." Rosalynd gazed enraptured at the long gold chain inset with large cabochons of rubies and emeralds. "And it still can be."

"No, it can't." Thor stuffed the necklace back in the pouch at his waist. "I've walked this road before with two other women; I won't walk it again. Pack your belongings and have your ladies do the same. Take only what was yours before you came and what I've given you. You will leave tomorrow after breaking the fast. How and when you choose to tell your ladies of your disgrace is up to you as long as you are gone at the appointed time."

"No, my lord." Rosalynd squeezed him a little tighter. "You do not mean what you say."

"I mean every word." He despised the feel of her arms around him. "Take your arms from around me, return upstairs, and pack your trunks. Again, take only what is yours and what I have given you. My room and my trunks will be inspected before you take your leave." He wouldn't put it past Rosalynd to have wormed her way into his coffers. Hopefully, she hadn't, but she wouldn't get away with it if she had. "We are done."

"No," Rosalynd shook her head as the enormity of her loss sank in. "My lord, we aren't."

"Yes." Thor rose to his feet. "We are." Rosalynd stepped back fist against her mouth as though to hold back tears. "Your father will receive just compensation along with an explanation of why you have returned home so abruptly. I expect his written response in return. There will be less opportunity for misunderstanding that way."

Halting a passing servant, Thor ordered his bed stripped and a bath brought to the master's solar along with a dinner tray and a pitcher of ale once his bath was cleared away. While he'd looked forward to holding court in his hall with Rosalynd by his side a few short hours ago, he no longer felt the same. A quiet evening spent in solitude held far more appeal.

"Remove your belongings from my chamber. Once my bed and bath are prepared, it will be too late for you to get anything. " He drained his goblet before rising to his feet. "Once my bath has been cleared away and my evening meal arrives, my door will be locked for the night. I expect you and your ladies gone before I come down to break my fast."

As soon as the words left his mouth, he knew that wasn't exactly how things would play out either. He would be down to break the fast at the usual time and he would take particular pleasure in watching Rosalynd and her party leave. While he made it sound like he would keep her belongings, he wouldn't. Anything she left behind would be sent behind her.

"My lord." Rosalynd reached out to him yet again. "My lord, please."

"Your only lord is your father now." Thor easily avoided her touch as she sank to her knees in the rushes. "Where is Nicholas?" Nodding at the servant's response, the Wolf walked away without a backward glance leaving his mistress wailing in defeat. "Send him to me when he returns."

While he would write the letter to Ailred de Rouen, Nicholas and a coterie of his men would escort the ladies home. He knew he could trust the warrior to deliver his letter to Rosalynd's father and return de Rouen's response seal unbroken. He knew as well that Nick would give him an honest assessment of the situation. If he believed there would be unexpected consequences to his actions, his man would state his concerns and he would listen. However, all of that was future endeavors. In the present, he was going upstairs to bathe, eat, and think things through.

CHAPTER TWENTY-EIGHT

Arriving at his chamber door, Thor resisted the urge to beat his head against the door. Dealing with the fairer sex was more trouble than they were worth. Stepping inside, he was pleased to see the steaming tub and several bars of soap displayed on fluffy towels. Locking the door behind him, he removed his belt and pulled his tunic over his head. While his valet would normally assist him tonight he preferred to be alone to lick his wounds.

Grabbing the bars of soap, he whiffed each one before deciding on a crisp rosemary mint fragrance that felt hauntingly familiar. Shaking his head, he'd never used this soap before but there was a first time for everything. The rough block was likely left behind on some visit by his wife a lifetime ago as were several of the other strangely scented bars he'd been offered.

Shaking his head at his ridiculous thoughts, Thor removed his braies, slid beneath the hot water, and grabbed a cloth. Lathering the rag, he set the soap aside before scrubbing the grime from his skin. Lifting the washcloth to his nose, he decided the fragrance of rosemary with underlying notes of mint was more pleasing than he'd initially thought.

Leaning his head back on the tub's edge, his eyes closed in defeat. Why bother? He'd never had good luck with his wives or mistresses. Opening his eyes Thor admitted, that while that might be true, he'd never swear off women. He would try to choose his lovers more wisely instead.

He thought he'd done that with Rosalynd. She knew he had a wife and family when she entered his life. Truthfully, she knew it before he did. Of all the women passing through his bed, she was the only one who understood she was entering a delicate situation that couldn't be forced. As the king's servant, he could only defy the hand that fed him so much. He'd known she wanted more but believed her when she said she would wait. He'd thought her patience was due to her affection for him and the life they would have together. He was wrong. She'd betrayed him instead.

Ignoring that he'd done the same to Rosalynd, albeit with her knowledge, Thor contemplated his next move. He could have his pick of the women vying to take her place if he wanted. He didn't. None of them truly caught his interest. They hadn't in the past. They still didn't. Sinking beneath the water only to bob up again, he poured a fragrant oil from a stoppered flask that he suspected was left behind by his long-suffering wife.

Working the cleansing oil through his locks, Thor realized there was more to Alexandria of Drummond than he thought if she could afford to make Castille soaps and hair cleanser from imported olive oil. While familiar with both from his travels, he knew few nobles who could afford such luxuries. No, he knew few who were willing to pay for such luxuries. Costly wines, spices, and sweeteners were more relevant to them than overpriced bathing supplies.

Personally, Thor begged to differ. Silently railing at his stupidity, he wondered why he'd ever considered wedding Rosalyn in the first place. It was clear that smelling sweet and clean was not a high priority with the woman. She wouldn't reek of days-old fornication if it were. Something told him that his wife likely held a similar approach to cleanliness as he did or he wouldn't have several different soaps at his disposal.

Swiftly rinsing his hair and body from the buckets of clean water warmed on the hearth, Thor exited the tub and grabbed a warm cloth. Drying his body, he wrapped his hair in the large sheet before sliding into a pair of loose trousers he found in his clothes trunk. While he usually preferred sleeping naked, his bath still had to be cleared, and his dinner tray served so it was best he wore some semblance of clothing for a while longer. Expecting the knock on the door, he opened it and watched the servants quickly clear the tub and buckets away before two of Mara's servers suddenly appeared with his dinner tray and a pitcher of ale.

Watching them set their burdens on the table before disappearing as quietly as they'd come, Thor locked the door and poured a goblet of ale. Sitting in one of the two chairs, he wondered who was responsible for this arrangement. Likely his wife since nothing had changed in this room since he brought Rosalynd to her new home. However, the party responsible for the coziness of the room hadn't mattered as much as the fact that he and his lover enjoyed putting it to good use did.

Glancing at the half-empty tray, Thor shook his head. He should be far more displeased by his lover's betrayal. He wasn't and it didn't feel right. If anything he was more relieved than devastated. His pride was dinged but he wasn't the first person this happened to. Infidelity was rampant in his circles. Besides, he found comfort in knowing Rosalynd's mistake would affect her life far more than it affected his.

Setting his half-eaten tray outside his door, Thor checked through his trunks to ensure nothing was missing. Fortunately, nothing was. He would do the same with Rob and the main coffers in the morning. While he doubted he would find anything amiss, it was better to be safe than sorry, especially with someone as duplicitous as Rosalyn. The woman had lived at Ruthven for several weeks unsupervised.

If she was sharing his bed with other men while he was away, what else was she doing that he should know about? Nothing he wouldn't hear about soon enough he was sure. Removing the necklace from the pouch, he locked the gems in a small coffer before carrying the pitcher and his goblet of ale to his bed. Leaning back, he decided his pillows were fluffed just as he liked them.

Setting his goblet on the floor, Thor closed his eyes as he contemplated his next move. Managing his private life was more trying than planning a military campaign had ever been. For one thing, he knew everything there was to know about warfare. He wasn't considered a military genius for nothing.

However, relationships and women were another thing. It appeared he knew next to nothing about them. At least not the ones worthy of his time and energy. Maybe he should listen to Aimee and the king. Maybe he should give his marriage a try.

Deciding to evaluate the situation much as he would plan for battle, Thor contemplated Alexandria of Drummond. While the woman wasn't a willowy blonde, she wasn't unappealing either. Just different. While reluctant to admit it, her looks had grown on him the longer they were intimate. Her personality wasn't all bad either.

For one thing, he admired her strength and her independence. She was dealing with a difficult situation far better than he'd expected. One he was almost solely responsible for causing. In making things easier for himself, he'd made things harder for his wife. He would admit that now although he hadn't felt that way before.

If that wasn't just cause to reconsider his recent actions, there were the children. His children. The children he claimed not to care about. While he'd been willing to see them declared illegitimate through lust-crazed eyes, he wasn't sure he could have gone through with it.

Not that he would have had a choice. Illegitimacy would have occurred automatically when his marriage to their mother was declared null and void. Perhaps he was fortunate fate interceded before he made the biggest mistake of his life. While he wasn't sure that was true, he suspected he would come to understand everything better as he worked through the tangled mess his life had become.

⸺ ⟲ ⸺

RISING BEFORE DAYBREAK, Thor went downstairs knowing he would find Rob in the kitchen with Mara. Unsurprised to discover he was right, Thor motioned for him to follow him to the storerooms. Letting the other man know what he was about, he quickly went through his coffers noting nothing was missing.

While he didn't think Rosalynd was secure enough in their relationship to consider what was his hers one never knew with women. He had only to think of his mother. A beauty beyond compare, the vile woman was a foul murderer in disguise. Satisfied everything was in order, Thor dismissed his seneschal before heading for the training field. He could get through several hard rounds of sparring with his men before he needed to oversee the departure of Rosalynd and her ladies. None were early risers.

Noting the warriors accompanying Nicholas on today's journey were already on the training field, Thor decided to join the fray. It had been a while since he'd enjoyed a vigorous workout with his men. He'd been at the royal keep reviewing records with the king for several weeks so he'd missed the familiar training. Drawing his sword, he fended off Herman's attack.

It would take more than an underhanded assault most warriors would never see coming to get the better of him. Thor laughed at the thought some believed he had eyes in the back of his head. Ridiculous. What he possessed was a sixth sense developed from utilizing many different styles of warfare in many countries over the years. When one understood his reputation was borne of experience, there was nothing mystical about his abilities. It made perfect sense that he would correctly anticipate another warrior's moves more often than not.

Two hours later Thor decided his men had put him through his paces as resoundingly as he'd put them through theirs. That didn't surprise him. Every man in this group was a good soldier. They were wasted here at Ruthven. However, they were loyal to a fault. They would go or stay where he sent them.

Wiping his sword, Thor inspected the pommel, tang, grip, and cross guard for damage. Satisfied the hilt was perfect, he turned his attention to the blade. Satisfied the edge was sharp, he inspected the groove running down the middle of the blade for cracks. Finding none, he finished cleaning the weapon.

Laying the sword aside, he inspected the round shield he'd used earlier. While he usually favored a variation of the kite shield for serious combat, he frequently trained with a round shield to stay agile and sharp. He'd discovered this wooden shield overlaid with leather and covered in concentric iron fittings surrounding the boss in Ruthven's armory when he'd first taken possession of the keep. Recognizing it was a fine specimen seeing little combat use, it quickly became one of his favorites. He still used it regularly in training years later. Finding no damage to the shield he set it aside and looked at the sun.

Slipping his tunic over his head, he grabbed his weaponry and headed for the keep. Rosalynd and her ladies should be mounting the waiting palfreys any minute. If she thought he'd changed his mind overnight, she had another think coming. If she thought he'd lost any sleep over her coming departure, she was wrong. All he cared about was seeing her back as she exited Ruthven as soon as possible.

When Nicholas returned with de Rouen's response he had other plans to make. Once he knew there would be no foolish retaliation over Rosalynd's nonexistent honor he would move on. Such action wouldn't be in the other man's best interests, but some men were ruled more by ego than common sense. He hoped Ailred was wiser than other men.

Rounding the corner, Thor saw that he was right. Nicholas and his men had rounded up Rosalynd and her ladies. The eight men were efficiently herding them, and the wagon carrying their trunks, out the front gates. Looking back, his ex-lover caught his eye. When he didn't respond to her silent plea, she pulled herself upright in her sidesaddle and turned away. Watching the gates close behind the last horse Thor headed for the hall. He was eagerly anticipating enjoying his breakfast in peace.

Stopping to speak to both nobles and servants in passing, Thor knew his breakfast would arrive shortly after, if not slightly before, he was seated in the high chair. He saw the page headed for the kitchen to alert Mara that he was walking down the hall. Like the royal cook, she knew he preferred hearty bread, eggs, and a few slices of lean meat to break the fast. A slice or two of cheese never went amiss, nor did a glass of her hard cider.

That Thor ate sparingly, but adequately to rebuild muscle, was one reason he'd recovered so quickly. That he'd never halted his daily training, except while bedridden, was another reason he was stronger than before his imprisonment. Taking his seat, the Wolf was pleased to see the great hall was all but empty. He could enjoy his meal in peace.

"My lord, warm bread, boiled eggs, fresh butter, and cheese," Rob set the plate on the table in front of his lord before taking the pitcher of hard cider from the page beside him. "Alfred will bring your fish as soon as it is done."

Thor nodded. While Rob was an exceptional Seneschal, he still enjoyed his forays into the kitchen to work beside his wife. Thanking the man he waited for him to leave before pouring a glass of ale. Sprinkling salt on his egg, he took a bite and chewed as he contemplated his next move. While he could return to the royal keep and throw himself into court life, the thought didn't sit well. What would he do while he was there? Audition his next mistress? That idea held even less appeal than remaining at Ruthven.

Besides knowing his presence wasn't needed here, Rosalynd's antics had left a bad taste in his mouth. This was the last place he wanted to be. Taking a sip of cider, Thor contemplated the possibilities swirling in his mind. Depending on de Rouen's response, he might ride over to Drummond. See what all the fuss was about. Who knew, he might decide to stay a while and discover what, if anything, he was missing.

Making a final effort to save his marriage before it was dissolved would please the king. What did he have to lose? Nothing but time. What did he have to gain? Continued royal favor. Watching perfectly cooked salmon fillets in a delicate green sauce set before him, Thor knew he would go to Drummond once he tied up loose ends here. The only thing he didn't know was what he would do when he got there.

CHAPTER TWENTY-NINE

Staring at the towering keep before him, the only familiarity Thor felt was a vague awareness he had been here in another life. He'd likely passed Drummond regularly on his rounds for years. Perhaps he'd gone inside a few times. That wouldn't be unusual. He'd been invited by their lord to enter many different castles over the years conducting the king's business.

He'd also brought many of those same lords to their knees by entering uninvited. That wasn't the case here. Drummond had never rebelled against her king. He knew all that from reading through the royal records hoping to understand happenings he didn't recall. Gazing at the sprawling edifice, he felt a sense of steadfast continuity as he contemplated the massive defensive walls before him. What he didn't feel was a sense of home.

Dismissing the sentiment, Thor motioned for his party to follow as he urged Wotan towards the massive gates of the exterior walls. Patting the beast, he was grateful to ride his favorite mount again. Like Avenger, he'd left the destrier behind when he'd joined that last skirmish. He'd been urged to ride a different mount and wield another sword. By following that advice he still had the legendary sword and his beloved mount to show for it.

While he didn't recall who'd dared suggest such a thing, he suspected their identity. If it was his wife, he was grateful to her. He was equally pleased both were returned to him when Alexandria visited the royal keep for the first time. Besides the fact they were his, she'd hoped the familiar objects would restore his memory. While he'd remembered his sword and his horse he didn't remember her.

Hailing the giant standing on the curtain wall, Thor watched the massive gates slowly open to allow him entrance. Riding into the bailey, he slid from Wotan's back. Ignoring his men, he studied the buildings around him. While he knew Drummond had fallen to the MacLarens, there were no visible reminders of the event. Whoever had overseen the repairs had done an excellent job.

As for doubting if he'd ever lived here, that was impossible to deny. Thor saw his mark on recent improvements made to the buildings and walls surrounding him. As much as the idea unsettled him, there were too many signs that he *did* consider this place home to be ignored. He would never invest the coin to make a keep near impregnable if he didn't. He wasn't a wasteful man. Or one given to extravagant displays of wealth and power. He had no need. Not when his name struck terror in the hearts of many.

Whatever his previous thoughts, he now knew he would be a fool to walk away from this place sight unseen. While it was true that he had more lands and titles than he needed, this keep was his crowning glory. He knew this deep in his bones. Everything he saw around him validated that impression.

Walking the grounds he noted the location of the stables, the dovecote, the beekeeping skeps, the extensive flower and herb gardens, the wells, the barracks, and the forge just as he'd noticed the remnants of an earlier motte and bailey tower rotting without the walls in passing. Glancing around him, he suspected other courtyards were woven around the buildings and a large training ground lay hidden somewhere deep within. He would discover each of their locations after he completed more pressing business. He refused to inhabit a place he didn't know like the back of his hand.

"Does Zan know you were coming?" Ignoring the giant, Thor didn't dignify his question with a response. "I thought not." Lionel turned to walk towards the keep. "I'll let her know you're here."

"Don't." Thor shook his head. "I'll let her know when I'm ready."

"Fair enough." Lionel nodded. "I'll get your men settled."

Snorting lightly at the expected silence, Lionel watched Thor head towards the entrance of the keep. He would be insulted if he didn't know the other warrior was a man of few words. The subtle nod he'd barely caught was thanks enough. While his lord's arrival today was unannounced, it wasn't entirely unexpected. Everyone knew it was only a matter of time before the king forced the Wolf's hand. Whether he walked away or chose to stay was the only mystery.

While the answer wasn't yet clear, Lionel suspected the Wolf would do the latter. Walking over to the mounted warriors, Lionel watched Thor's second-in-command dismount. Motioning for a stable hand, he spoke quietly to the fair-haired warrior before leaving him in Mac's capable hands. While the men were getting their mounts settled, he would alert Bertie to the fact they had a dozen new mouths to feed. As usual, the cook would take the news in stride. She was always prepared for such occurrences.

⁃⁃⁃⁃⁃⁃ ⟨⟨⟩⟩ ⁃⁃⁃⁃⁃⁃

THOR TOOK THE STAIRS two at a time after stopping to ask a passing servant where he would find her lady. While he didn't recognize the woman, she recognized him and welcomed him home. She then informed him that her lady was in the master's solar going through the clothes trunks as the morrow was laundry day.

Following the woman's directions, he found himself standing in front of a cracked door. His wife either expected someone or wanted to be available to her people if she was needed. That was as it should be. It was also something Rosalynd never was. Pushing against the handle, Thor wasn't surprised the door didn't squeak on the hinges.

From what he could see, everything around him was orderly and well-maintained. Entering the room, he studied the woman with her back to him before silently locking the door behind him. Walking up to wrap his arms around her middle, the gesture felt eerily right like he had done it hundreds of times before.

Turning slightly, Alexandria started at the feel of a large hand covering her belly as she was pulled against a masculine chest. Relaxing, she closed her eyes seeking to regain her composure. She would know that touch anywhere. While unexpected, the feel of his body against hers was not unwelcome. Expressing a breath, she wasn't sure she could say what needed to be said.

"Are you home to stay?" The words were shaky. "Or is this a brief stop on your imaginary rounds before you return to Ruthven and your mistress?"

"You know my rounds are done." Thor owned his lie. "As for returning to Ruthven, that remains to be seen."

"I see." Alexandria turned to face him. "Then why are you here?"

"To learn why I broke my oath and surrendered my freedom," Thor admitted. "I would not have done so for titles and land."

Or for a keep as fine as the one around him.

"No, you wouldn't." Alexandria agreed. "I could tell you, but you won't believe me." He would laugh in her face instead. "Besides, we both know the true reason you are here. My godfather issued you an ultimatum. Stop hurting me and attempt to rebuild our lives. Otherwise, our marriage will be dissolved and my properties and titles revoked."

When that happened, she would be free to move on with her life. Alexandria wasn't sure how she felt about that. Too much had happened too fast. Added to that, if she couldn't have Thor, she couldn't envision herself with anyone but Lionel and he was already taken.

She knew what was whispered behind their backs: that his lady wife wasn't long for this world. She believed differently. Ever the fighter, she would do everything she could to ensure Reina lived a long and prosperous life. She might consider giving Lionel what he always wanted if she proved wrong, but until then the man was off limits.

"That is true." Thor agreed. "It is also true that I am curious about the life I had."

And why everyone claimed he was a contented man.

"What of your mistress?" Alexandria continued to stare him down. "Is she still at Ruthven?"

"We have parted ways." It still rankled he'd discovered the mouse dallying with a rat while the cat was away. "I returned early from visiting the king to discover Rosalynd cavorting in my bed with a visiting noble. One who shouldn't have been in my home, much less my bed, while I was away."

"I see." He didn't need to say his mistress had summoned her lover when the truth was painfully obvious. "I hope you changed the sheets."

A sharp bark of laughter was his only response.

"We agreed there would be no others when she moved to Ruthven." While never explicitly stated, it was strongly implied that he would seek to end his marriage if things went well between them. "When Rosalynd broke faith with that promise, I ended our relationship and sent her home."

Fortunately, the letter he'd sent with Nicholas had been positively received and the bag of coins had gone a long way in soothing Ailred's injured pride as he'd known it would. While he could squash de Rouen like a bug, he wanted no trouble with the man. A feckless daughter wasn't worth breaching a worthy alliance. That wasn't in his best interest long term. From the letter he'd received in return, de Rouen felt much the same.

It didn't hurt that being his lover played in Rosalynd's favor. Two days after her return a high-ranking noble asked for her hand. That he was older, wealthy, and willing to indulge his young bride's every whim was a dream come true for father and daughter. The last he'd heard; Rosie was soon to be wed. He wished her every happiness.

"What of you?" Her tone was skeptical. "Did you break faith with your leman?"

"What do you think?" The quirked brow was intimidating, but she expected nothing less. She'd poked the wolf's honor. It was foolish to think he wouldn't snarl and snap. The Golden Wolf was nothing if not an honorable man. Or he had been. "Did I break faith with the fair Rosalynd?"

"No, I don't think you did." She answered honestly. "Not as you have broken faith with me."

"Aye, I have." Thor agreed. "More than once, but I don't believe your husband would have. However, we both know I am not him."

"Yes, we do." Alexandria agreed. "Nor do I think you ever will be."

"I suspect you are right." Thor agreed. "Perhaps I can be a better man."

"That is doubtful." Alexandria shook her head. "The Golden Wolf was bested by no man."

Thor rolled his eyes. "I believe the scars on my face and body prove otherwise."

"They speak of treachery and dishonor." Alexandria corrected. "The Golden Wolf ambushed no one as your captors did. He didn't have to. His word was his bond. If he made a promise, he kept it. If he declared your house would fall to his sword, your house fell."

"As your house has fallen." Thor watched her backstep. "More than once."

"Yes." Alexandria didn't feign ignorance. "As my house has fallen."

"Perhaps we can rebuild what was." He wasn't sure what he was offering. "Or perhaps we can start anew."

"Perhaps." So much had happened in the months since she'd learned he was alive. Painful, humiliating things that weren't easily forgiven or forgotten. "I don't know how we can, or where to start."

"We start with you telling me how our life began." There was much he didn't know. "You have told me what happened between us that night. You have shown me the pleasures we can find in each other. What you haven't shared is how we got from there to here. Though I have heard many whispers, none seem plausible to my ears."

"I see." Alexandria walked out on her balcony unsurprised when he followed. "These implausible whispers claim what? That I had you kidnapped from your leman's bed?"

"That I have not heard." He would have laughed the bearer of such tales into eternity. "However, I have heard that you bewitched me with your womanly wiles and your warrior ways."

"Really?" Alexandria made a rude sound. "Then again, that isn't entirely wrong either."

It was Thor's turn to make a rude noise. "Something tells me it is not entirely right either."

"It isn't." Alexandria agreed. "While it was a close-kept secret, you were kidnapped from your leman's bed and spirited to Drummond on my orders."

"The hell you say." That wasn't possible. "Who was this leman, and why would she betray me?"

The bigger question was how. He let down his guard around no one. Not even the women sharing his bed.

"You don't remember?" While she knew he had no memories of their life together, she never believed he could forget Joanna or the havoc she wrought in their lives. "She was your mistress for several years before we met."

"Be that as it may, I do not know the woman." Closing his eyes, he vaguely recalled tinkling laughter, a pliant body, and a sweetly pretty face. "Joanna."

"You remember her." That was one less thing she had to explain.

"No." Thor shook his head. "I recall only the name and a laughing brown-haired woman. Nothing more."

In truth, Aimee had mentioned Joanna the Weaver and their son. However, he'd never been told that he was taken from her bed. This was a tale he'd yet to hear. As far as he was concerned, that mistress could have been anyone until Joanna popped into his mind instead.

"I see." Alexandria shook her head. "Then I will tell you what I know." And what he'd shared of his life before Drummond. "Whatever you have heard, we had a good marriage despite your restlessness. We often talked much as we're doing now." Usually pillow talk, but he didn't need to know that now. "According to you, you had a favored tavern in Stirling where the innkeeper catered to your physical comforts and his daughter to your carnal needs. Joanna was a lovely, ambitious woman a few years older than me. When she caught your eye, she ended her betrothal with the local miller to become your mistress."

One of two at the time if she counted his friendship with Aimee FitzAlan. Again, Thor didn't need to know that either. Truthfully, he probably already did.

"I don't know how, or when, my father learned of your relationship. I do know my brother Crinan saw the two of you together in the tavern. He told my father what he'd seen and they worked out a desperate plan."

Thor listened intently not sure he believed a word she said.

"My brothers watched Joanna for a while. It didn't take long to learn her ambitions went far beyond running a tavern. When she was ripe for the picking, my father offered to fulfill her dreams in exchange for you. While Joanna never refused the offer or betrayed my family, she never said yes either. I believe she was waiting for you to make a better one."

"My vow never to wed again was no secret." Thor looked over the moors. "If she didn't know, I am sure I was honest to tell her from the start."

He always was. Even were he not, she knew he would never marry a tavern drudge. He was of noble blood and the Sheriff of Lothian. She was not.

"She did." Alexandria agreed. "But she hoped her loyalty would change your mind."

"Then she was a fool." Thor shook his head. "Sometimes I think all women are fools."

"Perhaps." Alexandria didn't disagree. "As men can be fools as well."

"I won't disagree." Thor nodded. "I assume I never made that offer."

"You did, just not the offer she wanted." Alexandria contemplated going back inside when she felt a heavy woolen mantle descend around her shoulders. "Thank you." She glanced at her husband out of the corner of her eye. "You gave Joanna the coveted shop on the corner along with everything she needed to become a successful weaver and merchant instead. What you didn't give her was your name."

"I see." The pieces were fitting together in ways he didn't anticipate. "Then you took advantage of her broken heart."

"Perhaps." Alexandria laughed softly. "Although I believe Joanna was more scheming than brokenhearted. She never hid her desires. From anyone. She was quite proud to share them with me as I'm sure she shared them with you."

"I'll take your word for it." Everything she said was a fresh revelation to him. "I don't remember any of these events."

"I know." Alexandria closed her eyes against the pain of knowing if he didn't remember Joanna, he didn't remember her as well. "That's why I'm repeating a story better left unsaid."

"You think I would harm you for what you have done?" While he didn't remember this woman, she was still his wife. He would never physically harm his lady. Even if he hurt her in other ways. "Since it appears I forgave you for your sins, harming you now is foolish."

"You mean considering who my father is." Alexandria cut to the chase confident the king had finally shared his darkest secret with his most trusted servant. Thor wouldn't be here now if he hadn't. "Oh, yes, I know the truth although he doesn't know I do. I'd like to keep it that way. Ian was my father in every way that mattered, and it serves no purpose for his people to think less of their king because he loved my mother."

"Did she feel the same?" Thor asked what he didn't know. "Your mother?"

"She did." Alexandria nodded. "But she loved my father, too."

In truth, she was torn between two men she loved equally in different ways. The king was the lover she couldn't have, and her father was the lover always by her side. While she didn't condone what her mother and godfather did, she understood they were star-crossed from the moment they set eyes on each other. To expect them never to fall in all the years they were thrown together was unrealistic. That they had only fallen twice was a miracle.

"So what of us?" Feeling her shiver beneath his mantle, Thor firmly ushered Alexandria back inside. "If Joanna wouldn't cooperate with your father, how did you win her trust?"

"I struck when the iron was hot," Alexandria reluctantly admitted. "And played on injured pride and greed."

"Meaning what?" Thor leaned against the wall. "That Joanna repaid my generosity with treachery?"

"Meaning my six brothers and my father were dead by the MacLaren's hand. My back was against the wall without any honorable options left." Her tone was unapologetic. "If we hadn't moved when we did, Drummond would have fallen to the MacLaren long before she did."

Her life and the life of her people would have been more hell than it already was. Everyone involved knew that, hence the decision they made.

"All right." Thor quirked a brow. "I don't know what you mean."

"Then my godfather has done an exceptional job of shielding you by royal command." His shrug wasn't unexpected. "I suppose he felt it best that you hear our secrets from me."

"I don't know." Thor's tone was frustrated. "Either no one knows our secrets or no one is willing to risk his wrath."

"Few know the truth," The ones who did were wise enough to keep their mouths shut. "We felt it safer to keep it that way."

"From what I am hearing," Thor closed the shutters before removing his mantle from her shoulders. "That sounds like a wise move."

"It was, and still is." Alexandria watched him drape his mantle across her chair as he'd done so many times in the past. "We will get to the fall of my home in due time. Now isn't the time. You need to hear how we truly came together before you learn how we fell apart."

"I will take…" Thor turned at the sound of the door opening behind him.

"I am sorry." Reina made to back out of the room. "I didn't know you had company."

"Stop." Alexandria halted her cousin's hasty exit. "You were in the nursery when Thor arrived."

"I was." Reina handed Alexandria her son. "Siward refuses to go down without his nightly kiss."

"It's okay.' Gazing at Thor, this moment was painfully reminiscent of that moment a lifetime ago. "My lord, I present your son, Siward Thorsson, compliments of Joanna the Weaver."

"Conceived before or after we wed?" Thor wasn't ready to embrace his son and she didn't expect him to.

"Before." Alexandria kissed her sleepy boy before handing him back to Reina. "Be a good boy, love." She dropped another kiss on his head. "I'll check on the bairns in a bit. After I explain to my husband how his son by the weaver ended up our precious bairn."

"That sounds like a good idea." Reina bobbed in Thor's direction before kissing Alexandria's cheek. "You owe me an explanation, too."

"I know, and you'll get one later. For now, I'd appreciate you sending up a pitcher of ale, a loaf of bread, and some cheese." Alexandria watched them leave before turning back to Thor. "Since we have only just begun, neither of us will make it down below in time for the evening meal."

However, the tray Bertie sent up would be laden with far more than a loaf of bread and a slab of cheese. If she didn't miss her guess, there would be several different meats to tuck between warm loaves and sauces to season them. She could forget the ale as well. Her cook would send up a generous pitcher of her famous mead instead.

"How did you end up..." Thor wasn't surprised when Alexandria cut him off.

"With your firstborn son?" She stopped to gather her thoughts. "It wasn't easy." She settled in her chair and draped Thor's mantle over her. While the room should be comfortable, she was surprisingly cold. "Since we knew about when you would come through town on your rounds, I paid Joanna to drug your ale and hide my men in an empty room at the tavern. You were taken from her bed that same night, but not before you got the job done."

"It wasn't the first time." There were snippets of a conversation playing through his head. "There were two others she didn't have."

"So I was told." Alexandria refused to hope this was more than some random memory he chose to recall. "You were brought here that night rather battered and bruised."

"I tried to escape." Thor laughed at the thought. "I suspect your men were equally battered and bruised."

"They were, but you were drugged and outnumbered." Alexandria shook her head. "I doubt you would have fallen had my tonic not weakened you so."

"What happened after I arrived?" He suspected he wouldn't like her answer. "How did you trick me into wedding you?"

"There was no trick." Alexandria rose from her seat. "I tended your wounds and informed you, since you broke our betrothal when I was a bald-pated babe, that we were wedding now."

"The hell you say." Thor's expression spoke volumes about what he was thinking. "There is no way that ploy would have worked."

"But it did." Alexandria brushed her palm over his chest. "You see, the night I was attacked by the MacLaren in the royal keep you took me in his stead."

Only four people still alive knew that fact and they weren't talking.

"You seduced me." Why wasn't he surprised? "And I let you."

"We seduced each other." Alexandria corrected. "Truthfully, we but acted on the attraction we'd fought since my arrival at the royal keep."

She still recalled those longing glances in her direction when he thought no one else was looking. She'd done much the same. Despite what he might believe, Jamie MacLaren had only accelerated what would have been eventually.

"You had never lain with a man?" Something told him this woman wasn't casual in her love affairs.

"I still haven't." Alexandria opened a small chest. "None save you."

"Then I took advantage of an evil situation." And acted dishonorably. "That doesn't sound like me."

"We both did." Alexandria absolved him of his blame. "You only took what was freely offered."

"I will take your word for it." He had done that a lot recently. "What happened when I awoke from this drugging?"

"You spoke the same words you just uttered and refused to wed with me," Alexandria stated honestly. "And I threatened to slit your throat."

Noting her demeanor, Thor suspected it wasn't an idle threat. She'd made a promise. Likely with her sword pressed against his throat. One she would have tried to carry through.

"I capitulated?" The snort was incredulous. "I think not."

"You think right." Alexandria smiled at her memories. "I was too desperate to see the truth before me, and too frightened to halt the path I was on. You could have walked out of Drummond and destroyed everything I held dear. No one would have stopped you."

"But I didn't." For some reason now long forgotten. "Did I?"

"No." Alexandria agreed. "You chose to stay." Likely due to what he stood to gain from their union. "We wed later that afternoon in Drummond Chapel." Despite a few bruises here and there, he'd been every inch the conquering Wolf that day. "I presented you as my new lord to our people later that night."

Never knowing his child was growing within Joanna's womb. Thor shook his head. The whole story smacked of madness from start to finish. However, he knew it was essentially true. Aimee and the king had both verified he married this woman. Not just them. He'd heard that truth from others including Rosalynd.

If she'd considered landing in his bed a major fait accompli, being installed at Ruthven as his sole mistress was an even bigger one. Now he knew why, even if he'd dismissed her self-satisfied crowing as unbecoming and envious. It seemed his affection for his bride was legendary to everyone but him.

"What happened after?" Thor studied her intently. "I can't imagine life was easy."

"Easier than you think." Alexandria huffed. "My people were grateful to have the Golden Wolf on our side."

"What about you?" She ignored the quirked brow. "Were you grateful to have the Golden Wolf on your side?"

"Aye, and the beast in my bed," Alexandria smirked at the sharply amused bark. "You seemed to feel the same."

"I'll take your word for it." Thor wasn't sure what to think of this woman who laughed when she shouldn't and shrugged off obstacles that would leave other women devastated. "I was content with this life?"

"Aye, from what I could see." Alexandria rose to her feet. "Content with your life and with me. If you must know, I didn't see much of you in the daylight hours. Training yourself and your men along with preparing for the MacLaren's attack occupied your days while I occupied your nights."

Thor nodded. Her explanation was logical and in keeping with the man he knew himself to be. Having sampled her wares at the royal keep, he was unsurprised she'd satisfied him in ways others didn't. If their past relationship was anything like their recent reunion, he would have shared their marital bed as often as possible.

From the whispers he'd heard in the great hall upon his arrival, his assessment was right. Everyone assumed he'd returned for just that reason. He missed his marital bed. Snorting softly, Thor decided that while that wasn't the whole truth, it wasn't a lie either. From what he'd seen of his wife's home so far, he'd likely remained loyal to their marriage out of self-preservation. No infidelities would have gone unnoticed in this place.

"Much of what I know of your life before Drummond," Alexandria continued her tale. "I learned through pillow talk."

"I see." That was unexpected. "What do you think you learned?"

"I don't think anything; I know." Alexandria addressed his challenge head-on. "I know you witnessed your father's murder at the hands of his closest friend. I know as well that your mother wed the man who killed him and they sent you to Normandy to train. That's where you met Prince Henry and where you became good friends. I know you were a mercenary for most of your life and I know you are a hard man. I know as well that my godfather trusts you above all men."

As she did, and always would.

"You learned all of that in bed?" He shook his head; pillow talk wasn't his way. "I doubt that."

She'd likely pulled the information from an overindulgent godfather who should have known better.

"Like you, I am not a liar." Looking anywhere but at him, Alexandria shook her head in disgust. "It took a while, but eventually you were glad to unburden yourself to a willing ear."

"Then I must have trusted you." Thor relented. "Some of what you have said could only have come from me."

Hanging his head, Thor decided the man he was had broken another sacred vow. The one that said he trusted no woman. And very few men for that matter. Even Aimee didn't know all of his darkest secrets.

"In time, you did." Alexandria agreed. "You shared all of that and much more"

"Again, I will take your word for it." That he didn't know what to think was written across his face.

"I believe I've said enough for now." Alexandria took pity on him. "You need time to contemplate what you have heard. Come, I have something to show you. It will take your mind off of this," She motioned all around her. "For the next few minutes."

Taking Thor by the hand, she led him from their chamber down the hall to the nursery. Watching her nursemaids silently scramble from the room, she led Thor over to the bed where Siward lay curled protectively around his younger siblings. There was no denying the boys had the look of their father about them and the girl had her mother's fiery hair. Nodding silently, Thor followed Alexandria out of the nursery noting the gentle smile she gave the nursemaids in passing. Turning slightly, he watched the two young women fuss over the bed before settling in their chairs to watch over their charges.

"Maidlin and Annas are dedicated protectors," Alexandria reassured him. "Our bairns are in good hands. The only reason Reina brought Siward to my room this evening is she likes to give the wee ones a good night kiss on her way to the hall after evening prayers. Sometimes your son gets fussy if I'm not there to tuck him in."

Thor nodded recalling the chapel was on the upper story of the gate tower. He didn't stop to ponder how he knew that. It seemed natural he would remember something of the place he'd called home for several years. Large swathes of his memory might be gone, but random bits and pieces still lurked in dark recesses waiting to be called into the light.

"I see." Thor walked over to gaze out the window. "I didn't expect twins."

"No one did." Alexandria laughed softly. "It was a miracle we survived."

"Were you expected to die?" His detached tone cut her heart in two. "Why?"

"Women die in childbirth every day." Alexandria reminded him. "Joanna did."

"Did she?" Thor's stare was blank. "Was I impacted by her death?"

"Not in the manner you think." Her laugh was ugly. "The night I brought Siward home was the night I moved into my childhood chamber for the next few months."

"I see." Alexandria snorted at the raised brow.

"You don't see anything." She answered the knock and opened the door to allow the servants to bring two heavily laden trays into the room. "Give Bertie my gratitude."

Nodding, the men did as they were told and silently left the room.

"I hope your favorites are still the same." Alexandria poured two glasses of milk fully aware a pitcher of Bertie's secret recipe mead awaited them on a separate tray. "Bertie will be disappointed if they're not."

"Bertie?" Thor slathered a generous dollop of mustard sauce over two slices of bread before adding a thick slab of roasted pork in between unaware that this was his favorite meal. Taking a bite, he savored the succulent flavors. "This meat is perfectly spiced."

"I'm sure it is." Alexandria set his ale beside him. "Ethelbertha, Bertie, our cook is very familiar with your likes and dislikes. She pandered shamefully to every one of them."

"I see." Thor studied the milk in his glass. "Do we not have wine?"

"Yes, we have wine." The best France had to offer. "However, your preference was always milk, ale, or mead with dinner.

"I see." Thor took a sip of ale instead. "It's not bad."

"I'll send for a carafe of wine." Alexandria rose to her feet. "It won't take but a moment."

"Don't bother." His raised hand halted her midstep. "It's more important you continue your story."

"Then there is mead if you'd prefer." Alexandria gestured to the other pitcher.

"After dinner." Thor took a sip of milk and decided it wasn't bad either. "I'm sure we'll both be ready for something stronger."

"Okay." She nodded. "You're probably right."

"How did you almost die in childbirth?" Thor made another sandwich with a generous slather of what he suspected would prove a raspberry mint sauce. "That's something I was never told."

Thor lied shamefully, but she didn't know that. Aimee and the king had told him enough to form an impression of the life he'd left behind.

"The first time?" Alexandria watched him eat. "Or the second."

"Both." He closed his eyes as the subtle spices exploded across his tongue. "It appears there is much I have been sheltered from."

"It's out of context, but the first time I almost died was when Drummond fell to the MacLarens." Alexandria turned to look at him. "Do you remember Bridget?"

"My daughter." Thor nodded. "I was told she died when the keep fell as did your friend Anna."

"Yes, that is true." As much as she didn't want to tell him, her husband had the right to know. "Both Anna and Bridget died at the MacLaren's hands. You'd brought Bridget here under the misguided hope we might turn her into a worthy wife for a lord. Perhaps we could have if she hadn't hated me so much for taking you away from her. But she did."

Hearing every word, he felt nothing but a detached degree of sorrow a life had ended so young. While a man of war, he wasn't without honor or compassion. He chose not to hurt women and children if he could help it. That wasn't always possible, but he tried and expected the same of his men.

"Bridget was a beautiful girl who could have probably wed any man she chose, but she was twisted. Spoiled and entitled in ways that weren't healthy." The girl was also a master of using her body to get what she wanted, but she wouldn't share that yet. "She opened the gates of Drummond to the MacLarens one night while you were away at court. She believed Jamie meant only to steal me away. She thought getting me out of the way would ensure she had you all to herself.

It didn't work out that way. The MacLarens poured through like demons from hell killing and maiming everyone in sight. When she protested that turn of events, James MacLaren slit her throat for her trouble. I watched him do it from this window powerless to stop it from happening ."

Thor set his sandwich aside having suddenly lost his appetite.

"My daughter betrayed everything she should have held dear?" He couldn't get his mind around that. "Her family and her home."

"Aye." There was no other answer. "And she paid for her sins with her life."

"Do you believe that?" Even at his most mercenary, he would never have done such a dishonorable thing. "Did I feel the same?"

"She was your daughter." Alexandria gently reminded him. "Though your wife's family raised her, you loved her. She was betrayed as much as we were. I was the only one Bridget meant any harm."

This woman was more forgiving than he was. While he felt little for this unknown daughter before he'd learned of her dishonorable ways, he felt even less now.

"She knew you carried my child." Even as he said the words, he prayed he was wrong. "Yes?"

"Aye." She wouldn't lie to him. "I believe so although I had shared my secret with none save you. I wanted you to be the first to know and I suspect she overheard us talking that day. Your daughter was more like you than either of you knew. She had a penchant for skulking about in places she shouldn't be spying on everyone."

"She doesn't sound like any child of mine." Thor wiped his hands on a towel. "My wife's family did not raise her well."

"You hoped we could change all of that." Alexandria shrugged. "Bridget was your daughter and you loved her despite who she was."

Speaking ill of the dead would accomplish nothing.

"If she knew of the child, she knew more than you would get hurt." Thor shook his head. "She didn't care. From what you have said, her willful actions cost the life of our unborn son or daughter."

He didn't stop to wonder why this suddenly mattered. Why a hot rage suddenly welled in the pit of his gut. He'd made it abundantly clear that he cared nothing for his wife or children over the past few months. Now, he was struggling to accept some part of him did care. Whether he wished to or not, he wouldn't feel this way if he didn't.

"Our son." Alexandria ignored his involuntary wince.

However this man thought he felt about his family, she knew better. Her Golden Wolf loved his cubs. Even the unborn. This man would too in time. Even if he never loved her again, he would come to adore their bairns. That part of him wasn't lost. She'd seen it in his eyes.

"I spent several months in an oubliette, so I was very ill by the time you freed me." He could learn how she'd ended up there later. Tonight was neither the time nor the place. "Our son was stillborn a few hours later."

She couldn't bring herself to say anything more and Thor didn't press her.

"The second time you almost died?" Thor asked. "It was when Sweyn and Maryse were born?"

He remembered the day he met the lovely silvery-haired lady and her overprotective husband. The sight of that raspberry birthmark had brought recollections of the times he and Guy de Lusagne fought side-by-side in the past. While he was pleased to have his memories of his old friend back something about his pretty bride raised his hackles. No one had bothered to tell him. He hadn't taken the time to ask. Now he wished he had.

"Aye." Alexandria nodded. "One of my lady's maids took your rejection to heart. She blamed me for thwarting her plans to steal you from me, so she pushed me down the stairs when you weren't looking in a fit of rage."

"Did I kill her?" While he knew he hadn't, the sudden surge of anger he still felt at her words meant he couldn't imagine how he felt when he cared. "That feels like something I would do."

"You tried." Alexandria's laugh was genuine. "But Lionel wouldn't let you."

"Then I should either thank or strangle him." As of now, he was undecided. "Who was this woman?"

"Lisle de Lusagne." She caught the recognition on his face and thought he may have already known that information. "The wife of Guy de Lusagne."

"I have met the man." Both met him and called him a friend. "I have met his wife as well."

"And realized she was wary of you for no just cause." Alexandria laughter. "While your hackles rose for no apparent reason."

Taken aback, Thor realized this woman still understood him better than he would believe possible given he was a different man.

"Yes." He agreed. "Although I suspect she would have just cause under different circumstances."

"Perhaps." Alexandria laughed softly. "Although the prospect of marrying Guy was torture for Lisle until the day they wed." Not just because of the man's disfigurement. "I'm afraid my maids tormented her daily with fairy tales of Guy's cruel treatment of his late wives and the punishments she could anticipate at his hands."

"I saw no signs of cruelty," Thor responded honestly. "They seemed most content for a married couple."

They were more the exception than the norm in his experience.

"There isn't any." Alexandria laughed softly. "Our friend Guy had fallen hopelessly in love with Lisle from afar and asked for her hand in marriage. We tried to warn him off, but he wouldn't listen. While you didn't want to saddle him with such a woman, Lisle's vanity rebelled against Guy's disfigurement.

Her distaste for Guy was undeniable as were her prayers that their betrothal would be broken as you'd broken ours so long ago. You decided Guy was a grown man capable of making his bed and lying in it. You decided as well that allowing the marriage was just punishment for Lisle.

They were married here at Drummond where we watched Lisle fall madly in love with her husband before the night was over. Against the odds, they've been happy ever since."

"With a child every year to show for it." Thor laughed remembering their smallest downy-haired chick crawling into the king's lap before anyone could stop him. David had taken it all in stride and showed the babe several pages in his illuminated manuscript before surrendering the boy to his horrified mother. "As we likely would have if things were different," Thor repeated what the king had said.

"Aye." Her husband was a virile man and she was a fecund woman. "Very likely."

Rising to his feet, Thor poured two goblets of mead and took a long draught. Settling back in his seat, he studied his wife for a few moments. She was much too young to have lived the life she had. As a result of much hardship, her eyes held a depth of wisdom and experience belonging to a much older woman. Watching her look away from his scrutiny, Thor wasn't surprised when she took a long draught of mead as well before setting the half-empty goblet aside. This conversation wasn't easy for either of them.

"Why have you put up with my treatment of you?" He finally asked. "Because of this?" He touched the scar on his head.

"Because I have no choice," Alexandria admitted. "Because I still have hope."

"Why have you not taken another to your bed?" As he had done many times remained unspoken. "You would have been well within your rights."

"Because I still have hope." Her tone conveyed that hope died a little more with every passing day. "Because the only man I would grant that honor is happily married to my cousin."

"De Montluzan." Thor sneered at the thought she had but to crook a finger in his direction and that valiant warrior would forget his happy marriage. "I have been told of his deep devotion."

"As you have been told of his love for Reina." Alexandria's response was sharp. "I would never presume on that affection nor would I hurt my cousin as you have hurt me."

Thor took her rebuke as it was meant and nodded. Perhaps this woman was as different from other women as she seemed. Time would tell.

"I won't apologize for my actions." There was no reason. "The man I am now isn't the man you knew."

"I know that." Probably better than anyone. "If I believed otherwise, our union would have been dissolved already." She drained her glass. "It still might be if we cannot work this out between us."

"If I will not remain faithful to our marriage bed," Thor stated what she wouldn't. "And stop seeking my pleasures elsewhere."

"Aye." Alexandria rose to her feet. "It is the one thing I will not countenance, and we both know dissolution will be done if I request it."

While rare, a suitable cause could and would be found. She was a powerful king's daughter even if that truth was known to only three people still living.

"Your godfather has said as much." Thor's laugh was ugly. "The church will find that convenient consanguineous relation even though the parties involved know such a relationship doesn't exit. The king will strip me of the properties and titles coming with our marriage only to bestow them on the next man to wed the heiress of Drummond. That was made very clear."

"Clear enough that you're taking actions to see that doesn't happen." Alexandria tossed her head in a way that conveyed what she thought of such empty power plays. "Again, I'm not sure whether to be flattered you think so highly of my dowry or insulted you think so little of me."

"Neither." Thor walked over to the window to stare over the moors before turning back to her. "I have more respect, titles, land, and coin than I need without Drummond or anything she has to offer. I am here because some part of me wants to understand this place and the life I once had. Everything I have heard has made me question what used to be."

Knowing he was faithful to one woman and content to live anywhere other than court intrigued him more than anything else. He had always preferred his bench in the great hall to a private chamber unless sharing a lover's bed.

"I see." Alexandria rose to her feet. "Then I accept your reasoning." She reached up to untie her chemise. "While you claim that nothing about me is to your liking," She casually shrugged out of the garment. "This is how our relationship began." She kicked the chemise aside. "And I suspect it is how it will begin again." She stared him down. "In two naked bodies coming together by the light of a flickering flame to the pleasure of both over and over again."

Nodding, Thor knew her words were true. Reaching down to grip the hem of his tunic, some part of him recalled doing this same thing in this same room many times in the past. He felt the phantom brush of this woman pressed beneath him in a mutual dance of ecstasy far different from their recent couplings. Feeling the stir in his loins, he took a step forward as he dropped his tunic to the floor. Whether it made sense or not, some part of him desired his wife in ways he'd never desired another woman.

It was a strange feeling, and not knowing the emotion behind the feeling unsettled him. This strong, curvaceous woman was nothing like the genteel, willowy lovers he gravitated towards. While slender, she was muscular and overblown. More solidly peasant than delicately aristocrat in build and mannerisms. She should have repulsed him, but she didn't. As much as he knew he hated his mother, he'd always been drawn to her physical and emotional doubles.

"Come." Alexandria pushed him down on the bed and straddled his lap. "This isn't anything you haven't done before."

Laughing, Thor shook his head. The woman so expertly sheathing him within her would never cease to surprise him. While she lacked courtly graces, there was something incredibly erotic in her bold honesty. Grunting with pleasure, he laid back on the mattress. While not a position he accepted with other women, it felt right with his wife. Familiar. As though it was something they had done many times in that life he no longer knew. While the familiarity of the moment should have comforted him, it disturbed him instead.

"The first time we made love like this was the night we wed." Alexandria stared him down. "You kissed this scar," She nodded at the vivid pink pucker marring her arm. "And acknowledged it was won in honor..."

"How?" Thor closed his eyes against the mindless pleasure nearly robbing him of speech.

"How what?" He hadn't changed as much as he believed. "Did I get the scar?"

She smiled at the feel of his hand caressing the puckered ridge.

"Yes." Thor laughed at the knowing look in her eyes. While part of him wanted to flip her over and show the wanton bit of baggage who was in control, he was curious to see how far she would take her little game. "How did you get the scar?"

"One of the MacLaren's men hacked me when I broke through the lines to catch my father before he slid from his mount after Jamie split his head like a turnip." Just as she'd expected, Thor caught his breath at her words and the look he cast her was even more feral than it had been. "Losing your memory hasn't affected you as much as you think. Strong, capable women still excite you. I still excite you even though you don't want me to."

"You are right." Thor flipped her over on her back. "You do, even though I don't want you to."

"Your feelings aside," Alexandria reached up to caress his face. "I'm glad you're finally home."

Ignoring her words, Thor refused to allow her touch to disrupt their sensual dance. Resisting the urge to laugh at the typical response to questions he didn't want to answer, Alexandria lost herself in the pleasure of his touch.

While she eagerly anticipated the day when they made love again, until that happened she would take as much mindless, animalistic pleasure as she could get. From what she'd seen so far, Reina was right. Her Golden Wolf did lurk somewhere deep within this stranger.

If what they believed was true, every intimate encounter between them brought him closer to the surface. One day he would shatter the cage that held him. Until that happened, or she came to believe it couldn't, she would endure whatever she must to bring Thor home again and enjoy every sensual moment along the way.

CHAPTER THIRTY

Rising, Alexandria grabbed her shift and pulled it over her head. Glancing over at her sleeping husband, she smiled softly thinking this was probably the best sleep he'd had in months. She knew from experience that Drummond was the only place he'd ever let himself truly rest and recover. If she didn't miss her guess, Thor would be surprised he trusted her, and this place, so much.

Easing out of her room she locked the door before slipping down the hall to look in on her children. Satisfied they were sleeping soundly, she smiled at their keepers and returned to her chamber. Opening the door she was confronted by a naked Thor staring out of the window.

"I heard you leave." He didn't bother to turn around. "I didn't like it, but I assumed you were checking on the children."

"I was." Walking to his side, Alexandria was amused some things never changed. "They're safely tucked in bed with their nurses watching over them."

As expected, both nursemaids were asleep since it was the middle of the night. But, also as expected, both had awakened before the door fully opened. Maidlin and Annas had been chosen to safeguard her bairns because they adored their charges and were incredibly light sleepers. They were also more than proficient with their swords which was incredibly rare in a woman.

"I didn't expect anything different." He knew better. "I know they are loved and protected."

Unlike him, their mother doted on them. He'd noticed from the start that this woman was devoted to her family and people. From the little he'd seen, everything about this place was well-run and well-maintained. He'd been told Drummond was prosperous, and from the villages he'd passed on the way, that appeared to be true.

Before he was done, he'd go over the books to ensure appearances weren't deceiving. He suspected they weren't. Something told him that his lady wife was well-versed in running her household and their lands. Something told him that she could balance the books and understood commerce as well as any man. Perhaps better. She likely spoke more than one language as well. He'd know the truth of all of that soon enough. But not now.

"They are." Alexandria agreed. "One child lost too soon is enough."

She didn't need to articulate that she would do almost anything to ensure that it never happened again. Turning slightly, Thor drew her in front of him and rested his palms lightly on her stomach. While he suspected Alexandria was doing everything in her power to prevent conception until their relationship was on better footing, he wouldn't mind if her infusions failed.

The thought of her rounding with his child wasn't as undesirable as he'd previously thought. In truth, he liked the idea more than he thought possible. He might even go so far as to say he wanted it to happen and wanted it soon. However, he wouldn't force his wishes on anyone. He was a patient man. Besides, were he honest, he wasn't convinced this was where he wanted to be.

"It is more than enough," Thor stated firmly. "When it should never have happened at all."

And it wouldn't have save for another misguided child. His. Briget's actions had caused the loss of her unborn brother. While he wished he could say that wasn't her intent, he couldn't. From what Alexandria said, his daughter meant her harm. Not only meant her harm but meant harm to the child she carried. If that was true, he couldn't excuse her actions.

While he didn't want to believe any child of his could act in such a way, he did. What made the situation worse, it was all his fault. Having little interest in his daughter as a younger man and even less to offer he'd left her upbringing to his late wife's family. That was his first mistake. His child was neither loved nor properly raised. However, he'd sought to rectify his earlier failings by providing Bridget the stability and affection his new life afforded them both.

While he'd learned he visited his daughter several times a year and generously financed her upkeep, he knew he was never intimately involved in her life until he'd brought her to Drummond. He must have believed the change would positively influence the girl or he wouldn't have done it. That was his second mistake.

All it had done was feed her jealous obsession with the father she'd never had. Shaking his head, Thor silently acknowledged his third mistake was not caring until it was far too late and he held his firstborn son lifeless in his hands. While Alexandria hadn't told him all these things, he knew they were true. Being here was slowly bringing things back to him. Not full-blown memories. Just snatches of thoughts he believed were true.

Closing his eyes briefly against an unexpected wave of pain, he silently admitted as fervently as he'd hoped Alexandria's recollection of such agonizing events was biased, Aimee and the king reassured him they were not. There was no absolution from that direction. They not only verified her recounting but added a few choice details he never wanted to hear like how he'd held Alexandria through the agonizing loss of their child and been beside himself when he thought she wouldn't make it.

In the end, it was learning he'd acted in ways so out of character that finally persuaded him to give their union another chance. He'd known deep inside that only a fool would throw that life away without trying to recapture some part of what once was. If they couldn't, he could always leave knowing they'd tried and that was good enough.

Opening his eyes, Thor looked over the moonlit moors knowing sunrise was still a few hours away. While he doubted either of them would fall back asleep, there were more pleasurable ways to pass the time. While he couldn't care less if he was seen, he was pleased the master's solar was shielded from prying eyes by architecture and the cover of darkness.

Knowing this, he didn't hesitate to put action to his thoughts. Slowly pushing her chemise over her hips, Thor wasn't surprised when Alexandria leaned forward welcoming his intimate possession. As much as he wanted to believe otherwise, he was beginning to believe the stories were true. He was content in this place with this woman. Whether he would be in the future remained to be seen.

However, he no longer wished to write his marriage off without sincerely trying. There was something about the woman welcoming his possession and shuddering her silent release beneath him that piqued his interest in several ways. Gripping her hips, Thor concentrated on finding his pleasure before resting his chin on her shoulder as they both fought to regulate their breathing. Pulling free of her body, he smoothed her chemise over her hips before turning her in his arms.

"You haven't changed as much as you think." Alexandria lightly caressed his chest. "We've always been good together, and you've always been more forthcoming at times like this."

"You mean I get loose-lipped," Thor laughed as he led her back to their bed. "after slaking my lust."

"Perhaps." Alexandria removed her chemise before joining him. "Not that you've ever shared more than you please."

Nor would he ever. They both knew that.

"That's good to know." Thor leaned back on his pillows and lifted his arm for her to slide beneath. "I should hate to think I shared all my secrets."

While he had been known to cuddle with Aimee, his other lovers were not afforded such closeness. He rarely stayed after the act was done preferring to return to his bench near the king's chair. A man's man, he wasn't overly comfortable with idle feminine chatter.

"Not all, but a few." Suddenly uncomfortable with the level of intimacy her words suggested, Thor pulled her across his body instead. "And nothing you don't already know you've shared." Leaning in, she kissed him before resting her hand against his cheek. "Thor, I will never force you to give more than you're willing to give. I never have. I never will. To try now would only drive you away."

Nodding, he rested his cheek against her hair and closed his eyes content to have her sprawled across his chest.

CHAPTER THIRTY-ONE

"How are you?" Finding her cousin in the storage room inspecting the herbs for mold was no surprise. Alexandria often sought solace in her work. "We haven't had a chance to talk since the Wolf returned to his lair."

"No, we haven't." Alexandria agreed pointedly ignoring the slight smirk conveying her cousin knew why neither she nor her husband had been seen in the great hall since his arrival. "As we both know why, we don't need to discuss it. If things continue as they have started, I shall be with child despite my best efforts to prevent that from happening. If I didn't know better, I might suspect that is his intent."

"Seeing Siward and the twins has reawakened that part of him." Reina nodded. "Good. He was always an attentive father who adored his family."

"Yes, he was." Alexandria agreed. "And he will be again when the time is right."

"But that isn't now?" Reina wasn't sure she agreed. "Why not?"

Alexandria shrugged. "He's not sure he's going to stay."

Reina digested her words. "Has he said that?"

"More or less." Alexandria nodded. "That he enjoys sharing my bed doesn't mean things are right between us and..."

"Unlike Thor, you remember how things used to be." Reina finished for her. "This situation is more difficult for you than him."

"It is." Alexandria agreed. "Unlike him, I remember, and what exists between us now doesn't compare...I'm not sure I can do this if he can...I'm not sure I want to."

"But he still pleasures you?" Reina watched her rehang dried rosemary on a hook. "And you still pleasure him?"

"What do you think?" Alexandria shook her head at her cousin's ridiculous questions. "We have always communicated well in bed."

"That's a start and more than you had a few months ago." Reina gently reminded her. "It sounds like there is a tenderness to your joining that wasn't there before."

"Perhaps." Alexandria agreed. "More importantly, we have talked and Thor promises to remain faithful to our marriage bed."

For the time being. She was under no illusions his word would remain his bond if their relationship didn't quickly develop a depth it didn't yet have. That was what frightened her most. The possibility that what happened once may not happen again.

While Thor had grown to love her before, that happenstance had less to do with her and more to do with the fact he'd admired her before they wed. Admiration coupled with physical compatibility made her offer more appealing. Had he chosen not to wed her, they both knew he would have walked out the door without a backward glance. None of her men would have stopped him.

Harming the Golden Wolf would have cost everything they fought to protect. However, had he turned her down, they were damned anyway. Drummond would have fallen to the MacLarens before she did and there would have been no one to get her back. They were fortunate Thor chose to stay. That foundation of respect and admiration didn't exist this time around. The only weapons at her disposal were her godfather's threats and her body. Both were poor footings upon which to build a life.

"Again, that is a start," Reina repeated. "You must bide your time and accept what he is willing to give. Don't expect too much too soon as you did the first time around. Thor isn't the same man, and you aren't the same woman. Unlike him, you know what lay between you. While that might be good, it will be bad if you let your emotions destroy what you hope to be."

She remembered uttering similar words a lifetime ago. While Alexandria followed her advice in the end, it wasn't easy. She'd often had to rein her emotions in. If the past was anything to go by, making their relationship work wouldn't be easy for her this time either. Zan would likely fight her advice as she did before.

"I know you're right." Alexandria nodded. "But the heart wants what it wants."

"The heart is a fool." Reina snapped. "If you listen, your heart will cost you everything."

"You are right." Alexandria carefully noted the herbs she needed to restock on her next visit to the burgh. "I will try to endure as long as I can."

"You will try to endure until you win." Reina corrected. "I know you."

"Perhaps." She wasn't up against a man with a hardened heart anymore. Her opposition was something far less tangible and more difficult to overcome. "Perhaps not."

"Then we shall see." Reina grabbed several sprigs of rosemary, artfully arranged them, and tied them into a hanging bundle. "My shilling is on you."

"Thanks." Alexandria laughed. "I wouldn't be so quick to part with my coin if I were you."

"I'm not." Reina laughed. "I'll use Lionel's instead."

"I'm sure you would." Alexandria shook her head. "And he would let you." Lionel denied his wife little and they both knew it. "He'd likely give you his purse before you asked for it."

She was sure he would although she didn't know if that was because he loved her too much or because he felt guilty for not loving her enough. She didn't want to think about it. While she'd believed she was doing what was best for everyone at the time, she now felt she'd done both Reina and Lionel a disservice.

She'd thought Reina was so wonderful that Lionel would come to love her cousin as he'd loved her with time. That he would stop loving her. That didn't happen. While he loved his wife, it wasn't the same. Everyone knew it although they did their best to ignore that truth. With time, she'd wondered if her cousin would have been happier if they'd broken her heart instead.

"He already has." Reina laughed softly. "You know my husband doesn't have a head for numbers. He is a man of war."

"Right." Glancing at her cousin, Zan knew that was a lie. "If that is true, it's because you offered to review the accounts every month. We both know your husband is quite well educated even if you want to deny it."

"Yes, he is." Reina agreed. "But with everything happening here, our extra duties have left little time for other things."

"I'm so sorry." Her cousin was right. Both she and Lionel had been so busy taking care of her that they'd had little time to manage their estate. However, unlike Peter of Clydesdale, their seneschal was an honest man grateful to have the job. His monthly reports and their annual inspection of the coffers and the estate always tallied nearly perfectly. "I never meant to make life harder for either of you."

"Neither did I." Both women looked up to see Thor studying the neatly organized room around him. "Have I been here before?"

Alexandria nodded. "You have, don't you remember coming in here?"

"No." Thor shook his head. "It's an impressive room that should be hard to forget."

Even Oswald's infirmary wasn't filled with such a wide array of jars, ewers, and stoppered vials. The dried bundles of herbs were a more familiar site. Studying the room around him, Thor noted that the neatly organized shelves held not only the expected tinctures, ointments, and salves; but a generous supply of bandages, needles, thread, and other implements he refused to contemplate. From what he could see, everything needed to treat serious injuries was readily available.

"It should be." Alexandria agreed. "But I'm not surprised you don't remember your grand tour. I don't think you ever returned after that first time."

She'd always been amused that a man who could tolerate the overwhelming scents of war wasn't that fond of herbaceous aromas. Then again, it might have nothing to do with smell and everything to do with some of her plants disagreeing with him. She seemed to remember him sneezing a time or two.

"I doubt the smell was the issue." Then again, a phantom reek assaulted his nose giving lie to his statement. "I'm going to find Lionel and check in with my men."

"That sounds like a good idea." Alexandria agreed. "While I'm sure our people have taken good care of them, it's probably not wise to leave a dozen men at loose ends indefinitely."

"Knowing them," Thor didn't try to disguise his amused tone. "You're probably right."

He'd be surprised if one, or more, of his men hadn't gotten slapped for his trouble by now. They weren't bad men and would never willingly harm a woman, but some were full of themselves. It wasn't every day a warrior was personally selected by the Golden Wolf to accompany him to his home. That meant they were part of an elite squad their lord found worthy of his trust. That was quite the honor. They knew it and he knew it, but that didn't mean the sweet young things would find them as appealing as they now believed themselves to be. Therein might lie the rub.

"Then we'll see you in the hall for dinner." Alexandria watched him leave before turning to her cousin. "What do you think about that?"

"The Wolf is home to stay." Reina stared her down. "Now it's up to you to believe it."

"I will try." That was easier said than done. "You have my word."

"Good." Reina didn't expect anything more. "Changing the subject, did you catch Thor's face when he said he didn't think it was the smell?"

"The one that said he'd just caught a whiff of one of his battle-weary warriors after a week in the saddle?" Alexandria laughed. "I sure did and I think he recalled the time he came home early and caught us dying cloth."

"You're probably right." Reina put the last of the herbs away. "He left as fast as he could that day after turning a rather interesting shade of gray."

"And he never came back again." While dying cloth was a stinky business she'd grown used to the smell long ago. "One day I'll tell him what he just recalled. Right now, I'll leave him wondering."

"That's so mean." Reina followed her cousin out of the room. "But I don't think it matters."

"Neither do I." Alexandria locked the door behind them. "Before he is done, Thor will recall bits and pieces of a forgotten life without understanding how they fit into his life or even if they're real memories."

This wasn't her first encounter with this kind of injury. It was, however, her most personal.

"That is why you are so worried." Reina followed her down the stairs. "You think he will be overwhelmed by his memories."

"Since I don't know what he's been told by other people," Alexandria stopped on a stair to look at her cousin. "I think it's possible."

"But you will do everything you can to stop that from happening." Reina followed her towards the kitchen. "Won't you?"

"Of course." Alexandria looked over the organized chaos and decided Bertie had her domain under control. "But there's no guarantee that will work."

"No, there isn't." Reina waved at the cook as they left. "But there are no guarantees in life."

"You are right." Alexandria looked over the great hall. "It appears Everette has everything under control. What do you say to a ride before dinner?"

Nodding, Reina followed her cousin out the front door towards the stables. If anyone needed them, they could find them on the moors. Given her cousin's current mood, she doubted either would return until they needed to change for dinner. Not that she thought that would be a problem. Their servants didn't need supervision. They took great pride in performing their duties and it showed.

CHAPTER THIRTY-TWO

E ntering the nursery, Alexandria stopped in her tracks. The last thing she expected was to see her husband sitting on the floor playing with their children. While Thor had grown more comfortable handling their bairns in public she didn't know he sought them out in private. He didn't remember, but she'd often find him in the nursery enjoying the company of Siward and the twins before his captivity. Knowing that, she shouldn't be surprised he did so now, but she was.

Catching the nursemaids' eyes, Alexandria silently motioned for them to take a break. To her surprise, Thor was too engrossed in Maryse's enthusiastic gestures and babbles to notice the two women curtsey in his direction on their way out. Or to see his wife take Maidlin's seat in her stead.

"My lord," Bending forward, Alexandria laughed softly at the surprise on his face. "That's quite a sassy miss you have there."

"Perhaps." Smiling, Thor brushed his daughter's cheek. "But I prefer to think she's thanking me for her new doll."

"Really?" Alexandria leaned back in her chair. "Is that what you think?"

"It is." Thor quirked a brow at her. "Do you believe differently?"

"I do." Alexandria laughed. "I think she's saying she wanted a dolly with brown hair like Uncle Lionel," Maryse couldn't keep her fingers out of her cousin's glorious sable mane. "Not gilded like her brothers."

"You're serious?" Thor glanced at the wooden doll dressed in the finest silks before glancing back at her. "Then Arnulf will paint her hair brown."

Laughing, Alexandria sat on the floor and took the doll from her daughter. "I doubt she'll be playing with dolls much longer anyway. She's not much younger than me when I started riding my brothers' stick horses waving wooden swords."

"Unlike my sons, my daughter will never wield a weapon or ride into battle." Thor glanced at Siward careening about on his trusty stead. "I will see to that."

The same skilled woodworker creating Maryse's new doll and Sweyn's miniature castle had made Siward's mount. Glancing at the toy, Thor was pleased with the craftsmanship. The beautifully carved and painted horse's head mounted on a sturdy pole was ornamented with elegantly braided red leather reins. That the woodworker followed his instructions and produced such quality pieces had ensured him the patronage of the Sheriff of Lothian.

"You will change your mind the first time Maryse shows up at the training yard bearing one of my swords." That same tactic worked for her. "Though you may not believe that now."

"Perhaps." Thor agreed. "Until then, I'm content to protect her."

Alexandria snorted softly knowing that no daughter of hers would ever rely solely on the men in her life for protection. "And allow me to teach her the ways of a lady."

"Yes." Thor's look said that went without saying. "While I teach our sons the ways of a warrior."

"You do that." Ignoring Sweyn's happy squeals, Alexandria cuddled him mercilessly. "However, remember unconventional mothers often have unconventional daughters. Don't stop our daughter from being who she is for the sake of fitting in."

"I will take your words to heart." Thor steadied Sweyn when his son careened into him. "I think you have ridden long enough."

He set the horse aside as his son dropped to his bottom to assail his brother's castle with a wooden ram.

"I believe the training has already begun." Alexandria shook her head over boys with their military toys.

"It has." Thor rose to his feet. "Our sons will be familiar with the weapons of war long before they hold them in their hands and our daughter will be confident in her duties long before she performs them."

Rising to her feet, Alexandria followed him out the door as Maidlin and Annas walked in. Falling in step beside her husband, she silently noted Thor spoke only of the children they already had. Not of the bairns they would have in the future. Whether intentional or a slip of the tongue, she knew he was torn between his old life and the man he was now. Despite her best intentions, the pieces of their life weren't coming together as easily as she'd hoped.

"That is as it should be." Alexandria smiled at how much that sounded like the old Thor. "However, our children are not you and I. They may surprise both of us."

"They may." Thor stopped at the bottom of the stairs. "While I wanted to see the children before I left, I have a mill to inspect this morning, and Beorn to join at the West fields this afternoon. I'll be gone most of the day, but I will return in time to dress for the evening meal."

"I'll see you then." Thor and the village leader were overseeing the planting of the winter crops. If she didn't miss her guess, her husband would return with a sweat-stained tunic and dirt under his fingernails. He couldn't resist working the fields beside the men even when he didn't plan to. "As of now, we have no guests."

While that could change, Alexandria hoped the evening stayed that way.

"Good." Thor touched her cheek. "I'll return as soon as I am done."

Alexandria nodded as she watched him walk out the door. While she had her reservations, she hoped he always felt that way. The closer they got to Thor leaving to perform his Shire Reeve duties, the more uneasy she became.

While she tried not to look for trouble where there was none the last time she'd felt this way Thor failed to return. She prayed history didn't repeat itself this time. Shaking her thoughts, she headed back upstairs to the sewing room. There were tunics to be made and embroidery to be done, not to mention three young girls who had yet to learn their stitches.

EPILOGUE

Accompanying Thor to the bailey where Caturix patiently waited, Alexandria turned to her husband hoping apprehension didn't show in her eyes. While the past months had restored a fragile semblance of normalcy, she had no illusions that all was well. Nor did she deceive herself that her marriage was what it should be. The best she could say was Thor seemed content. That was enough for now. To ask for anything more was folly.

Watching her husband inspect Caturix's saddle, Alexandria silently acknowledged her misgivings. All were valid. They were finally getting their relationship back on solid footing after spending so many months apart. It hadn't been easy. It still wasn't. Yet this was the first real challenge they'd faced since the Golden Wolf appeared outside her gates unannounced.

In truth, they were doing better than she'd expected. Thor had taken to country life as readily as he had the first time around. She still remembered the day he'd reminded her that he came from farming stock. His father's people tilled the land and raised livestock long before they raided these lands.

Though a lord's son, he'd grown up with his hands in the dirt. True to his word then, he was no different now. As amusing as it seemed, she was just as likely to find him plowing in the fields with the villagers as in the training yard. The only difference was the fresh scars littering his body that weren't there a year ago.

As for their personal lives, she had no real complaints. None justifiable under the circumstances. Thor was an attentive husband and father. While she knew he didn't love her and might never love her again, the Wolf had made every effort to get to know her as she'd tried to learn the man he was now. It wasn't easy for either of them, but they'd made progress. More than she'd believed possible a few months ago.

233

However, she still had grave misgivings about interrupting their momentum. While he wouldn't be gone that long on this leg of his rounds, Thor was leaving a couple of weeks early to meet with the wool merchants in Stirling. Once that was done, he would begin his duties as the Sheriff of Lothian.

How smoothly his rounds went determined the length of his absence. It always had. If all went well, he would finish quickly. If he found discrepancies, they would have to be resolved. That meant more time at the royal keep. While she knew her godfather wouldn't keep his Wolf any longer than necessary, their meetings would add to his time away. The longer they were separated, the greater the likelihood that everything they'd accomplished would come undone.

"I'll return..." Thor stopped midsentence at the look in her eyes.

Alexandria shook her head. "Don't make promises you may not keep."

"What does that mean?" Thor cocked his head studying her intently.

"You'll know when the time is right." While cryptic, the gist was clear.

"You fear I won't come home." The idea had never crossed his mind.

"I do." Her smile was pained.

"Then don't." Thor brushed a lock from her cheek. "I will return as soon as I can."

For his children if nothing else. She knew that. He couldn't imagine his life without Siward or the twins. He would give almost anything to have the child they'd lost. He'd said that over again.

"You don't know that." Alexandria rested her hand on his chest. "I don't know that. How you feel once you're free of this place," She motioned around her. "Of us, will reveal whether the past few months are a new beginning or the beginning of the end."

"You don't mean that." Thor rested his hand on hers. "Who says I'll feel anything other than the desire to come home again?"

While the connection he felt to Drummond felt right, he wasn't as comfortable with other emotions he felt. He knew from experience that such foolishness was a liability to a man like him. However, admitting that didn't mean he felt nothing for his wife or family. Nothing was further from the truth. Reluctant to assign a name to the growing regard he felt, he knew those emotions were different. How he didn't know.

"I do." Alexandria tipped her head to gaze into amber eyes. "While you will never admit it," She smiled softly. "You frequently ponder whether your feelings are real or the result of what you've been told. I'd be a fool to believe otherwise."

"Don't say that." Thor refused to admit she was right

"Why not?" Alexandria closed her eyes briefly before opening them again. "It's true."

While Thor wanted to deny her words, he couldn't. He often wondered whether his emotions were real. Or the product of the tales he'd been told. He didn't know. But he didn't want Alexandria to know he felt that way either. Despite his efforts, she'd known anyway.

"Perhaps." Thor reluctantly agreed. "But that doesn't change the fact I wouldn't go if I had a choice."

He'd said that before, too.

"I know," Alexandria reassured him. "But I also know part of why that's true is because this life is still new and exciting."

"It is." Thor agreed. "But it's also fulfilling in a way court never is."

"Maybe." Alexandria smiled softly. "While I want to believe that, you won't know if that is true as long as doubts linger in your heart."

"You are right." Thor agreed. "I won't."

"Think about what I've said while you're gone," Rising on her toes, she kissed his lips. "And you will know when the time is right." She watched him swing into the saddle before leaning down to give her one last kiss as he'd done so many times before though he didn't know it. "Now you must go."

Nodding, Thor waited for the men stationed a respectable distance away to fall in line around him. Giving Alexandria the faintest touch of a smile he urged Caturix towards the gates slowly opening before him.

While a part of him had no desire to leave, his wife was right. This journey was a necessary evil no matter how long it lasted. If for no other reason than to quiet the questions in his head. The ones that threatened to undermine everything they'd built. While reluctant to admit it, they'd reached the crucial turning point that would decide whether their relationship blossomed with possibility or shriveled on the vine.

Snorting, Thor knew he must have heard that phrase from Alexandria. It wasn't something he would normally say. But it wasn't wrong either. While leaving with every intent of returning to his wife and family, they both knew he might grow to feel differently as the influences of Drummond waned. And muddied thoughts cleared. As much as he wanted to say nothing would change over the coming weeks, he couldn't.

It was better to admit none of them knew what the future held.

Don't miss out!

Visit the website below and you can sign up to receive emails whenever Tori Lennox publishes a new book. There's no charge and no obligation.

https://books2read.com/r/B-A-SKFX-RJCMC

BOOKS 2 READ

Connecting independent readers to independent writers.

Did you love *Back from the Shadowlands*? Then you should read *A Necessary Convenience*[1] by Tori Lennox!

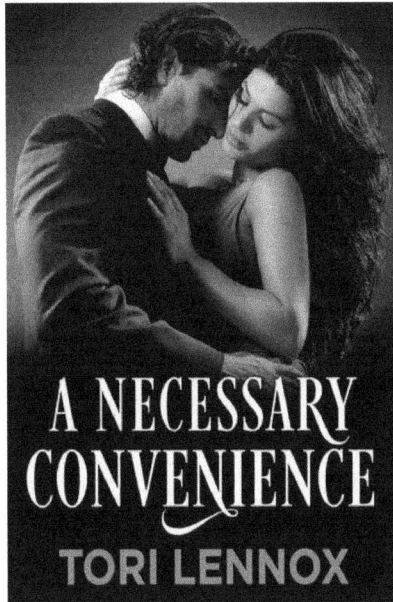

They say the road to hell is paved with good intentions. They're wrong. It's paved with lies, surprises, and necessary conveniences...

Aila Peterson is living the dream. Between her career as a nurse practitioner and raising her five-year-old daughter her life can't get any better. Or so it seems. Until the sudden death of Sofie's birth mother exposes that life is built on betrayal and deception. Not only did Abby lie about Sofie's biological father not wanting her, she never told him she was pregnant in the first place.

Not unless you count the letter Jackson delivered to billionaire businessman Nolan Bishop after her death.

While not his fault he's been MIA all of his daughter's life, Aila doesn't want Sofie's father intimately involved in their lives. He's a womanizing, globe-trotting business mogul. Not exactly prime daddy material. However,

---

1. https://books2read.com/u/38WVMO

2. https://books2read.com/u/38WVMO

she isn't foolish enough to believe she can defeat him in a custody battle. Fortunately, Bishop is a reasonable man, so it likely won't come to that. Not yet anyway. Not until she answers that final question burning between them...

Does she risk losing Sofie or sacrifice her soul to keep her?

Also by Tori Lennox

The Golden Wolf Series Book 2
Back from the Shadowlands

The Golden Wolf Series Book One
The Wolf and the Warrior

The Shards of Promise
Tattered Promises

Standalone
A Necessary Convenience
Toxic Illusions

About the Author

Tori Lennox has always preferred reading to sleeping. With a love for all genres of romance, she enjoys writing both contemporary and historical romances, Originally from South Carolina, Tori now lives in Florida. When she isn't writing, she enjoys cooking, gardening, and walks with her toothless blue and tan dachshund, Mir.